Paul Eastney

MATTER OF FIRE

Design, typesetting and publishing by UK Book Publishing.

www.ukbookpublishing.com

ISBN:978-1-917329-09-5

One

Damlon, state capital of the Kingdom of Rarland

A bren Medloe woke up to find strange, coloured lights floating above his head. Tiny, bright flecks that glinted blue, red, golden. Abren stared up at them, openmouthed. He rubbed his eyes and looked again. They were still there. He lay gaping, mesmerised.

A sudden pounding on the door made him start. Hennis, the knocker up, called out his customary cheerful greeting, 'Get up, ya lazy sod.' The coloured lights vanished as if startled themselves.

Abren looked at the peeling, grey plaster on the ceiling, listening to Hennis's clogs stamping further up the stairs. He swung his legs over the side of his cot and sat staring at the bare floorboards.

There was a weak gleam coming in at the grimy little window. The spring dawn was on its way. He rubbed his eyes again and looked around his cramped living space, but the pale, melancholy beam only picked out languid motes of dust drifting through the air.

Abren frowned in bewilderment, but he had no time to ponder the mystery now. He got up and walked across the room; the floorboards creaking beneath him. He poured some water into his chipped washbowl. With each movement, he felt himself re-emerging into his everyday world. The cold water on his face completed the process. He dried himself with a threadbare towel, the rough fibres catching on his dark stubble.

He pulled on his work clothes, planted his black, cloth cap on his head and picked up his bag of tools from the floor. Hunching his broad shoulders, he went out the door and onto the narrow staircase. Others were emerging from their doorways into the meagre light from the lamps Hennis had lit.

The tenement was crowded. Families, single men and women, all crammed in together. A nest of worker ants. Abren was lucky. From what his father had taught him, he could earn enough to rent a room on his own.

Out on the street, he stopped to get his breakfast from a baker's shop front. A small selection of loaves and cakes along with a bowl of boiled eggs were laid out on a wooden shutter that had been lowered and propped up to form a counter.

Abren was one of the first customers and the thick slice of bread and two eggs he bought were still warm. Not wanting to converse with any of the others milling about he went around a corner and huddled against a wall while he devoured his food.

Coloured bloody lights, he thought. *Damn it, what were they? My eyes must be going funny.*

He tossed away the last bits of crust to the waiting sparrows, stamped the early morning chill out of his feet and set out for the docks.

The high street was already full of people. In the growing early morning light, stallholders were just setting up. Others, like Abren, were on their daily trudge to work.

Some shivering men and women in drab, ragged clothes loitered alone or in small groups. They seemed to have nothing better to do than watch the street merchants put out their wares. He often wondered how they managed to feed themselves.

Small boys in dirty brown coats and young girls in dirty brown dresses chased each other barefooted among the stalls, earning a curse or a kick if they got in a merchant's way.

Abren walked past it all with a determined stride. He had somewhere to go; he had no time for loitering.

A dog barked at his back as it followed him down the street. It had been doing this for the last few days. Irritation brought a grimace to his face. Why him out of all these people?

He tried to ignore the wretched thing as he usually did. But then, on an impulse, he stopped and turned around. He glared at the animal, willing it to shut up, and to his surprise, it did. It not only stopped barking but sat down, wagging its tail as if expecting a treat or a game. It was just a medium sized cur like any number of others around the neighbourhood. This one was a grubby white colour with several random black patches on its face and back.

'What the hell do you want, eh?' Abren knew he should be getting to work but sensed the dog might have an engaging personality. His question was rewarded with a single loud yap.

'He likes you, that's all.'

Abren looked up. It was a young woman grinning at him.

'Well, all right then,' he replied. 'Yours, is he?'

'Yeah. His name's Gitt.'

'Gitt? That's not a very nice name.'

'He's not a very nice dog.' Her hair was a chaos of tight blond curls that bobbed and swung with the slightest movement of her head.

'Seems fine to me.' By this time, Abren was scratching behind Gitt's ear. The dog was clearly enjoying it.

'That's because he likes you. If he don't, well, his bite's worse than his bark then. He's our guard dog. Me and Fran, my sister. We've got the fruit stall.' She gestured back down the street. Abren saw a tall, auburn-haired woman hefting a crate from a cart with a somnolent-looking donkey harnessed to it. The woman shot them a resentful glance.

'Well, better get back.'

'What's your name?' Abren asked her.

She tilted her head a little and smiled again. After a pause, she said, 'Jessel.'

'Abren.'

'Right. See you around then. Come on, Gitt.'

Abren walked on. When he reached the entrance to the docks, he pushed his way through the press of men in front of the gate, a fidgeting, anxious morass of desperation. As usual, they were slow to move aside and let him pass. The men were hoping to be taken on for the day, but he was a regular hand. He had a skill. As much as he now hated his father, this regular morning ritual wrung a reluctant gratitude from him.

'Terral,' he nodded to the warden.

'Abren,' the man returned as he opened up for him.

Damlon's vast docks were like a city of their own. Rarland had prospered through its commerce with other countries across the known world and this was the chief port of entry and export for trade goods.

The sun was beginning its daily struggle with the fog that was already starting to smother the sky. But as he made his way along the busy, cobbled road between the towering warehouses to his place of work, he was only dimly aware of it; likewise, the rich, shifting smells that changed every couple of hundred yards. Spices, tobacco, coffee. Familiarity had dulled his perception of them.

The five other carpenters were already there when he entered the compact, cluttered workshop, including the charge hand.

'You're late, Medloe.'

'I got attacked by a dog,' Abren shot back.

'Oh yeah? And where did it bite you then?' Jemmy Frimms looked him up and down.

'His owner stopped him.'

'Right, well, next time you'll get a fine. Dog or no dog.' Jemmy was a short, moody individual, one day laughing and joking, the next a dark thundercloud, rumbling and spitting out angry bolts of rebuke. 'Get to mending those barrows. The porters are breaking them faster than we can fix them.'

'Someone should tell them to be more careful,' Abren suggested.

'Heh! Might as well tell a dog not to bark.'

An hour later, Abren was threading a new axle through the wheels of a barrow laid out on his workbench, tapping it gently with his mallet. Jemmy had gone out to fit the hoist strut he had been making. A man came in clutching a small sack.

'Nails,' he said.

Abren looked round. He had not seen this man before. His bottle-green coat and brown leather boots looked like they might have been decent once.

'Put them on the bench over there,' he told him, then returned his attention to the axle.

After dumping the sack, the man stood watching him for a moment.

'I could do that. Anyone could do that.'

'It's not as easy as it looks,' Abren said, still concentrating on his task.

'Oh yeah? Well, it looks easy enough to me.'

He continued watching. Abren sensed the hostility oozing out of him.

'What's up with you? Haven't you got anything else to do?'

'You shoved me at the gate. Shoved me in the back like you think you're important or something and I'm just nothing.'

Abren stopped what he was doing and regarded the man. A cold rancour glared back at him from dark, narrow eyes.

'Look, I'm sorry, all right? I was late.'

'What do you get for doing that?'

'What?' Abren was thrown by the abrupt change in the man's line of attack.

'Why should you get paid more than me for doing something anyone can do?'

Abren sighed. He had conversations like this before in The Crown, but not here.

'I learnt a trade. So could you.'

'No, I can't. There aren't any openings around here. So the likes of me have to fight it out at the gate like a herd of animals.'

'What do you want me to say? What do you want me to do?' Abren spread his arms. He realised he was still holding his mallet.

The man opened his mouth to retort. Then he seemed to realise the other men in the room had all stopped to watch the drama. He grunted, then turned on his heels and left. Abren shook his head.

'For hell's sake,' he muttered.

He glanced over at his workmates.

'I thought you were going to hit him with your mallet, Abe,' Serrick said.

'So did he, by the look of him,' Nad said.

They all laughed at that, even Abren, then they all got on with their work.

At midday, they put down their tools and went outside to get something to eat. Abren and Nad sought out one of the food carts that came to feed the hungry dock workers.

Then they sat on some old crates on a nearby quay to eat their meat pies.

'I've never seen that fella before, Abe, have you?' Nad asked, wiping a dribble of gravy from his chin. He was not much older than Abren, but his hair had gone prematurely grey. He was a genial, easy-going sort of man and Abren liked him the most amongst his fellow workers.

'No, I haven't. But there's so many taken on every day he might've been working here for weeks and we'd not seen him.'

'It's funny he got to drop off those nails the day you shoved him, though. I reckon he's got it in for you now. He seemed to have a right grudge, didn't he?'

Abren watched as a crane slowly swung a net full of sacks out over the quayside. Three men waited below to unload it. A group of porters stood ready to race each other. Trundling the goods to a warehouse where importers and merchants would haggle over prices.

'I reckon he had a good job at one time, despite what he said about having no trade,' Abren said. 'But then he lost it. They're the most resentful types.'

Nad took a drink from a flask he had brought. 'Well, he can't do much to you in here. Might want to watch out on your way home, though.'

Abren made a dismissive, guttural sound in response to this piece of advice.

When they returned to the workshop, Abren noticed straight away, even amongst the haphazard jumble of benches, trestles, boxes and pieces of timber. He felt a nervous jangling in his guts and hands.

'Where's my tool bag?'

He looked at the puzzled faces of his workmates.

'Has anyone shifted my tool bag?' he demanded, knowing full well none of the other carpenters would touch his tools without asking his permission.

Blank stares and shaking heads were the only responses he got. He began what he knew would be a futile hunt round the room.

'Bet it was that fella, Abe,' Nad offered.

'Yeah, that's what I was thinking.' Abren cursed. What use was a carpenter without his tools?

He hurried to the door, where he almost collided with Jemmy on his way in.

'Where are you going?'

'Someone's pinched my tools,' Abren blurted as he pushed past.

'I don't know,' Jemmy called after him. 'First, you're late, then you lose your tools.'

Outside, Abren ran a few yards, then came to a stop. Where was he going to look for the man? He could be anywhere if they had given him the job of delivering stuff around the place.

More than likely, he's gone off to sell them. I expect I'll see them for sale on some stall or other tomorrow morning.

'Lost something, Abren?'

Abren turned. It was Boz, a wiry young boy who hung about the docks hoping to earn the odd copper running errands. He was from the orphanage, so the gate wardens let him in each day out of kindness.

'Yeah, I have. Seen anything, Boz?'

'I saw a man I didn't know in a green coat come out of your shop not twenty minutes ago, carrying a big bag. He was trying to look all innocent-like, but he seemed a bit shifty to me, so I followed him.'

'Where did he go?' A tentative hope rippled inside him.

'He dropped the bag down a hole in the alley behind number two.'

'Into the sewers?' Abren's twisting emotions lurched into a naked disgust.

'Yeah. That bag yours then?'

'Yeah. It's got my tools in it.'

'Are you going to go down and get them back, then?'

'Have to. Show me which hole, Boz, will you?'

As they hurried towards the looming bulk of warehouse number two, Boz said, 'I've heard the ghosts of drowned sailors get washed up into those sewers.'

'That's just silly talk,' Abren replied. 'There's nothing down there but rats.'

Nevertheless, he was aware of a growing sense of foreboding.

As they entered the narrow alley, an oppressive gloom gathered about them. Daylight never penetrated into this claustrophobic crevice. The way was littered with all kinds of discarded refuse, broken barrels and crates, heaps of frayed rope, rusting chains.

A perfect place for doing some secretive misdeed. But also where a scrap of a lad might hide and watch.

Boz came to a halt beside a metal grate fitted into the cobblestones. Abren could see it had been removed recently by the dirt spilt around it, and even from up here, the smell made it seem like the sewer's contents had been disturbed as well.

'Down there,' said Boz, pointing and screwing up his bony little face. 'You're going to need a lantern.'

'Yeah, right. I'll fetch one from the night watchman's lodge.'

Boz straightened himself out of his habitual slouch and stood like a guardsman on parade. He extended a hand towards Abren.

'Best of luck down there, mister,' he said in a grave tone. 'And if I don't see you again, it's been nice knowing you.'

Abren grinned despite the situation he was in. He reached out, but instead of taking Boz's proffered hand, he ruffled the lad's greasy, brown hair.

'Get on with you, ya monkey. It'll take more than a few rats and dead sailors to finish me off.'

He did not wait to discern if Boz was in earnest or just mocking him but strode away to get himself something to light his descent into the dock's forbidding sewage system. When he got back to the grate, Boz was gone.

Well, he can't earn anything by hanging around in a back alley, Abren supposed.

He decided to give the boy a copper coin later and maybe buy him a pie if he retrieved his tools. Or even better, a couple of apples from Jessel's stall. Thus fortified with the image of that young lady's smiling face in his mind's eye, he set about his task.

Taking hold of the bars, he found he could lift the grate without too much effort. Lighting his lantern and crouching next to the hole, he could see iron rungs set into the wall beneath him. He could not see the bottom.

The stench was so strong he wondered if the noxious vapours were inflammable and the lantern would explode in his hand. When he got down there, he would cover his nose with his handkerchief, but for now, he needed one hand for the lantern and one to grip the rungs. All he could do was hold his breath for as long as possible.

He had expected the rungs to be slippery, but they weren't. They also seemed to be sturdy.

At least something's going right today.

He had still not got to the bottom when he simply had to draw breath. He tried to take air in through his mouth, even so, his stomach lurched and his eyes blurred. Finally, one foot splashed and then the other. He turned, leaning his back against the wall, and fumbled for his handkerchief. He expected his bag would be right under the hole, but it was not.

'Bastard's swung it away somewhere,' he muttered.

Raising the lantern, he could dimly make out a tunnel leading away in both directions. A world of filthy bricks and foetid water. Wiping his eyes dry, he lowered the lamp again and began shuffling to his right, searching the black liquid muck that came up to his ankles and overflowed into his boots. He was just beginning to think the thief must have tossed the bag in the other direction when he became aware that his was not the only light down there. He looked up.

There were more of them than in his room earlier, but they moved with the same slow, hypnotic swirling. Abren stood transfixed. They were beautiful, alive. He saw more colours this time. Every colour imaginable. He dropped his handkerchief. The stench no longer troubled him. He stretched out his hand, but the lights began to fade. A sudden sadness flickered through him, but then he perceived there was another illumination a little further down the tunnel.

A vertical slash of white trembled and took form. Abren thought he could make out a figure of some kind, human but also not human, hovering above the slime. Man or woman, he could not tell, but it seemed to be smiling. The radiance grew brighter and brighter until Abren could not bear it anymore. He needed to cover his eyes, but he was afraid to. Afraid that if he did, the vision would vanish and it would break his heart.

Two

Amdris, state capital of the Republic of Mellia

Taygret Egring carefully carried the tray across the yard. When she got to the door of the outbuilding, she kicked at it. A young man opened it and stood aside to let her in.

'Your lunch, sir,' she announced.

'Thank you, put it on the table over there, please.'

'Certainly, sir.' Taygret enjoyed playing the maid's role when the servant had the day off. She had even tied up her long, black hair. She deposited the tray as instructed and wrinkled her nose.

'Why is it so smelly in here? It's like rotten eggs.'

'Oh, it's the metal filings dissolving in acid. It's how your uncle and I produce fire gas,' he told her, indicating a large glass vessel filled with a white vapour which was part of the jumble of apparatus on the table beside him.

'Fire gas? That sounds dangerous, Eldam. Are you going to blow us all up?'

'No. It's not dangerous,' he said, his broad pale face breaking into a mocking grin. 'Provided we make sure the gas never gets mixed with air, it's perfectly safe. Before long, we'll be illuminating our streets and houses with it.'

'Indeed?' She thought it an improbable notion but did not say so. 'Will there be anything else, sir?'

'Yes, there is. Come here and give me a kiss.'

'Oh, sir. That would not be at all proper.'

'Let's be improper then.'

She went, chuckling, the charade dropped again.

When they finally pulled apart, she said, 'I'd better get back to the house. Uncle will be wanting his lunch too.'

'I'll see you this evening then,' Eldam said.

As she headed for the door, she noticed a grey stain on the front of her light green dress.

'What's this?' she said, turning. Then she saw similar marks on the front of Eldam's jacket, almost hidden amidst the grey cloth.

'I'm sorry,' he said. 'My fingers get dirty handling the metal filings, and I can't help wiping them on my clothing.'

'Arg!' Taygret exclaimed. 'Now I'll have to change my dress. I'll bring a bowl of water for you to wash your hands in.'

'Thank you,' he said as she left, brushing uselessly at the stain and muttering mild oaths.

'Hello dear, I thought you were going to let me starve.' Gorje Egring smiled and put down his newspaper. 'You've changed your dress.'

'I'm sorry, uncle. Yes, it got soiled while I was crossing the yard. I can't lift my skirt when I'm carrying a tray like this.' Taygret set down her burden of food and drink and passed him a bowl of chicken broth and a plate of sliced bread. Then she sat beside him.

'Ah, I see. That's odd. Linna never seems to have that problem.' His smile had gotten wider.

Taygret cleared her throat as she poured some tea. 'What's in the paper?' she asked. 'How's the war going?'

'Not well, I'm afraid.' His smile had gone, clouding his usually affable features. 'The Pragnars have crossed our western frontier and are laying siege to Vorskran. It also says that Skigland is assembling an army to the north.'

'What will become of our brave little republic? It seems all our neighbours are bent on crushing it.'

'I still think we'll win in the end. The people fought hard to be rid of the king and his brutal laws and crippling taxes. Many are willing to die defending that freedom.'

'Will you have to go and fight?'

'No, I'm too old. But I suspect they will enlist us all to make some contribution. Our lives are going to be disrupted, I'm afraid. There's talk at the university of forming the students into a militia company. If that happens, I won't have anyone to teach.'

'A militia company?' Taygret's stomach tightened, and she put her spoon back in her bowl.

'Don't fret, Eldam won't be conscripted. He's a foreigner, remember? But…'

'But what?'

'Well, there's a growing suspicion of foreigners. The government's afraid of spies.'

'But Eldam's Rarlish and Rarland aren't at war with us, are they?'

'No, but there's a lot of anxiety about. Some of our leaders want to rally the people by declaring Mellia stands alone against the world.'

'Merciful Divine. What's going to happen, uncle?'

'I don't know. We must hope the firebrands in government don't get their way.'

They ate in silence while Taygret worried through some dark scenarios.

Then Gorje said, 'Right, I'm going to see how that boy is getting on in the laboratory. I hope he's making the most of his day free of lectures.'

He wiped his mouth with a linen napkin and got up.

'Be careful.' Taygret thought of the fire gas.

'We're always careful.' He bent and kissed her forehead. 'Thank you for the lunch.'

Just before he got to the dining room door, she said, 'Oh, I told Eldam I'd bring a bowl of water over for him to wash his hands in.'

Gorje laughed. 'Now I know why you had to change your dress, you little minx.'

Taygret felt herself blush. 'You could use it too,' she said.

The next day Gorje and Eldam were at the university. Taygret sat in the parlour mending one of her uncle's shirts, enjoying the quiet simplicity of the work. She heard the front door open and a loud male voice she did not recognise entered the house. She jumped up and hurried into the hall. The first thing she saw was Eldam looking very annoyed. Behind him were two men in scarlet tunics and black bicorne hats. Constables.

'Pack your belongings,' the loud voice said. 'We'll wait here. Be quick about it.'

Eldam gave Taygret a look full of pain and anger.

'What's going on?' she said. 'Have you been arrested?'

'Not exactly,' he replied through his clenched teeth.

'I'm sorry, Miss, we cannot bide here long,' said the second constable, a large, muscular individual with a bristling red beard. 'We have a lot of people to round up. Master Medloe will be accommodated at the town hall until transport can be arranged. You can speak to him there.'

'Transport?' Taygret echoed the distressing word.

'I'm being deported.' Eldam suddenly looked close to tears.

'Hurry along now.' Loud voice pushed him gently in the back. Eldam half turned but then sighed and stomped up the stairs.

Taygret went to go after him, but the bearded constable said, 'Stay with us, Miss, if you please. We can't brook any delay.'

She felt like saying it certainly did not please her but thought better of it. Instead, she asked, 'Does my uncle know about this?'

'Your uncle?' said the loud constable.

'Master Egring. He's a professor at the university.'

'Yes, I should think so. The whole university is in an uproar. There are quite a few foreign students.'

Taygret was incredulous. 'Are you deporting all foreigners?'

'No. Your Master Medloe is fortunate he comes from Rarland. Anyone from hostile countries is being imprisoned.'

After a short while, Eldam came back down carrying two large bags.

'Can I go with him?' Taygret asked.

'No. We have a wagon full already,' said red beard. 'But like I say, you can see him at the town hall once he's been processed.'

'I'll come,' she said to Eldam. She wanted to say something reassuring, but no words came. He seemed equally at a loss, so she threw her arms around him and kissed him for as long as the police allowed.

The black carriage Eldam had to compress himself into looked to Taygret like a prison cell on wheels; the windows were just barred openings. They added his bags to an already large pile on the roof.

As the wagon rolled off down the street, Taygret wondered where she should go first, the town hall and wait to see Eldam or to the university to find her uncle. She went back into the house to change her shoes and put a shawl around her shoulders. The maid was standing at the kitchen door; her face a mask of sorrow.

'Oh, Linna. Did you hear? They're sending Master Eldam away.'

'Yes, Miss. I'm so sorry.'

Taygret realised her own anguish must be obvious. Linna hesitantly raised her arms and Taygret flew into them.

She did not realise her uncle had come in through the open door until Linna stiffened and released her.

'Forgive me, Sir. I…' The maid stammered.

'It's all right, Linna. I know what's happened. Thank you.'

She dropped a brief curtsy and retreated into the kitchen.

For a third time, Taygret sought the solace of another person's embrace.

'What can be done?' she asked.

'I don't think there is anything we can do, I'm afraid,' he said, stroking her hair. 'All foreigners have fallen under suspicion. At least Eldam won't be thrown into prison.'

'But if he were…' Confusion stopped her.

'If he were in a prison in Amdris, you could still see each other every day. But could you really bear seeing him incarcerated like that? Prisons are dreadful places.'

'No. It was just a selfish notion.' She stepped back and pulled a handkerchief from her sleeve.

'And you cannot go with him. The government wouldn't allow it. As I told you yesterday, they will want us all to help the war effort.'

'The police said I could go and see him at the town hall.'

'Yes. I spoke to a commissioner at the university. He told me they won't begin transportation to the coast until tomorrow. We will have time to say farewell.'

'Tomorrow?' Taygret made full use of her handkerchief.

Taygret went to the town hall straight away but had to wait two hours in a dreary, draughty corridor before being admitted into the cavernous basement. She had never seen the inside of a prison, but she was sure this must be very much like one. Dark stone walls enclosed the chamber, and broad, black wooden beams stretched across the ceiling. Small lanterns, hung from sconces, struggled to dispel the gloom.

Taygret sat opposite Eldam, a wide table between them. A constable stood to one side. Eldam had only been in custody for a few hours, but he already looked haggard.

'Where will you go when you get back to Rarland?' she asked him. 'You have never told me about your family.'

'I will try to get into a university to continue my studies. My father works on a country estate, so it wouldn't be practicable to live with him. I have a brother, Abren, who works as a carpenter in the Damlon docks, but he lives in just one room in a poor tenement building.'

'And your mother?'

'She died of the plague ten years ago.'

'Like my parents then.'

Eldam nodded solemnly. 'It took so many.'

'First a plague, then a war. What on earth does The Divine think He's doing?'

She glanced anxiously at the constable, suddenly afraid he might arrest her for blasphemy. But the policeman just stared impassively back at her.

'My uncle is confident that we will win,' she continued. 'Then you can come back. I will help make uniforms and tents for our soldiers.'

She had been determined not to cry, but her facade of assurance was melting. She saw her hurt reflected in Eldam's eyes.

'I've never loved anyone like this before. Please come back,' she managed to say before her voice broke.

'I will. I promise. We'll celebrate Mellia's victory together.'

They both reached their hands across the table.

'No touching.' The constable's bark made them flinch back. 'And your time's up.'

Their precious minutes had slipped away. At the door, Taygret Egring blew Eldam Medloe one last kiss before being steered out of the bleak basement chamber.

A couple of hours later, Taygret was pacing the parlour floor.

'What can I do, uncle? I must have something to do. You said the government would want us all to help.'

'The decree will come soon enough.' Gorje stood looking out of the back window. 'I will welcome it as well. Most of my students are already required to do military training for four hours a day. And with Eldam gone, there is no one to help with my own work.'

Taygret stopped. 'I could help you.'

Her uncle turned and regarded her, a look of mild amusement on his face. She waited for him to dismiss the idea.

'Very well,' he said at last. 'Come with me.'

She expected him to take her to his laboratory in the outbuilding. Instead, he led her upstairs and into his study. She had only been in this room once before when her uncle had something important to tell her. Even Linna was not allowed entrance. She expected to find dust-covered chaos and was surprised to see it was clean and tidy.

Books lined two of the walls, and a large desk squatted by the window with writing materials and neat stacks of paper covering much of its surface. Gorje went round the desk and opened a drawer. He took out a small sheaf of papers and handed them to her.

'These are notes I have made on my work so far,' he said. 'Read through them and make notes of your own on anything you don't understand or any questions that occur to you, and we'll go over them this evening.'

Taygret was so moved her eyes prickled. She bowed her head, afraid that if he got the impression she was succumbing to some womanly emotion, he might change his mind.

'Thank you,' she said. 'I will.'

When she went to bed that night, Taygret had her head full of new words from her uncle's writings and new images from his drawings. Ferrusite filings, vilsic acid, flasks, tubing, rubber balloons and the sinister-sounding fire gas. But as she tried to get to sleep, they were all replaced by just one word and one image—Eldam.

She had always done her best to follow the teachings of The Faith, and so she prayed now for Eldam's safety and for his swift return. The prayers did not comfort her, though, and sleep would not come. Anxious thoughts chased each other around in her head.

A pastor had once told her she could still her troubled mind by savouring her breath. 'Only breathe,' he had said. 'Relish each breath as if you are drawing in The Divine's grace and you will find peace.' She closed her eyes.

It was indeed peaceful, riding on the rhythm of her breathing, and she eventually drifted into the arms of a soothing slumber.

Three

Damlon, state capital of the Kingdom of Rarland

A bren clung onto the iron rungs as though a deep ocean lay below him instead of a few inches of sewage. With the spectral figure gone, he felt himself to be drowning in forlorn darkness. The lantern had gone out the moment it had slipped from his fingers. He might have hung there for an eternity, but gradually the reality of his situation crept into his awareness.

His stunned resolve faltered back into life, and he forced his reluctant hands to release their hold. He groped hesitantly for what he had lost—the lantern and his bag of tools. Eventually he found both, and with his bag slung over his shoulder he slowly climbed back up to the mundane world. Even the weak light of the alleyway made him squint in discomfort, such had been the profound darkness of the pit he had escaped. But he had not escaped the reek of it. His boots and bag were the worst. He stumbled to a pump in the yard outside the smithy.

As he rinsed off his boots, it was like he was watching someone else doing the task, someone in another realm. A realm he had left and needed to get back to, only he lacked the heart to make the transition. His otherworldly experience in the sewer still possessed the greater part of him. Slowly he removed the tools from his bag, one by one, trying to recall their familiarity. Gradually, washing the bag, replacing the tools, dousing his face, he recovered a sense of his normal existence, his workaday self.

'Where the hell have you been all this time?' Jemmy scowled. 'And what's that awful smell?'

'He threw my tools into the sewer.' Abren was determined not to be embarrassed by something that was not his fault.

A couple of the others were grimacing, but Nad said, 'So it was him then?'

'Yeah, Boz saw him.'

'You'll have to go home, Medloe,' Jemmy said. 'I can't have you stinking the place out for the rest of the day.'

'It's mostly my bag and boots. I'll put them outside. I don't want to lose a half day's pay.'

'Be just your luck if he came back and pinched your boots, Abe,' Nad observed.

This wrung a wry smile out of Jemmy's pudgy features.

'Not been your day, has it?' he said to Abren. 'Well, just hang them out the window where you can see them. We'll have to imagine we're working on a farm for the afternoon.'

As he joined the mass of workers making their way home, Abren felt like he needed a drink, so he invited Nad for a quick ale in The Crown.

'No, sorry. Love to, but the missus would have them dragging the dock if I'm not back at the usual time. It's all right for you single fellas. Maybe tomorrow night if I give her fair warning. Besides you're still a bit whiffy,' he added with a grin. 'They might just chuck us out.'

'Ah, well. I'll see you in the morning then, Nad.'

Deprived of the prospect of his friend's bright company, the lure of the tavern lost its appeal, and Abren turned reluctantly towards his lodging house.

The streets were still busy, and he had to halt on a corner when a brewer's wagon got stuck on a post as it tried to make the turn. He was about to offer his help to push the wagon free when he noticed something in the shop window he was standing next to.

He had passed this shop many times before but had never given it much heed. Vaguely aware that it sold books, he had always just hurried by, having no interest in them. This evening, however, something in the window captured his attention.

They had given one book pride of place. It lay open in the centre, its white pages prominent among the sombre covers of the surrounding volumes. Abren drew closer. Peering in at the book, he saw not words but a drawing of some kind. Then an unnerving jolt of recognition shot through him. The figures in the picture were like the one he had seen in the sewer.

He made the plum pudding he had bought at the cookshop last as long as possible, putting off the time when he must extinguish his candles and surrender to the waiting dark. In a way, he knew this feeling. He had loved a girl once. Both longing for and dreading any encounter with her, any sight of her, any look or word from her.

The lights had preceded the figure's appearance. Perhaps that was its way of lessening the shock. A forewarning of sorts. Was it being kind to him? He thought it had smiled at him. Surely it could mean him no harm, and yet... it was unnatural. Or was it unreal? His mind lurched under the implications.

One of his candles guttered out. His strength seemed to go with it. A sudden, smothering weariness overcame him. Whatever might happen between now and the morning, he must try to sleep. He undressed, pinched out the other candle and slid beneath his blanket. Abren turned onto his side, facing the room, not the wall as he usually did. But when he closed his eyes, the weariness left him.

He lay awake during the interminable hours of the night, turning one way then the other. Then sitting on the edge of his cot. There was no moonlight. Nothing to see. Nothing to hear but the scratchings of mice. He had a taut sense of waiting. Waiting for something to happen. Waiting for the night to end.

It seemed he had only just fallen asleep when Hennis's blows resounded through the room. He dressed hurriedly and set out.

I'm going to need some coffee this morning.

Having gulped down the bitter beverage, he ate his breakfast as he strode towards the street market. There was something he needed to do before going to work, and he did not want to be late again.

As he approached the stall, the first thing he noticed was a young boy loitering suspiciously by a pile of oranges. Jessel and Fran were busy unloading their donkey cart, and Gitt seemed to be dozing under the stall. The boy looked like he was about to snatch a fruit and make a run for it. Abren was making ready to shout and give chase, but the dog, without moving or even opening an eye, growled so loudly the lad jumped back in fright. In his haste to be gone, he stumbled over a heap of old clothes laid out on the ground next to the stall.

'Oi! Watch where you're putting your feet, ya little scamp,' screeched the woman sorting out the garments.

Abren watched the boy as he made a dash for a passageway between two boarded-up shops. When he returned his attention to the stall, Jessel was dumping a basket of apples on it.

'He's an excellent guard dog, that mutt of yours,' he said to her.

'Yeah,' she replied. 'He stops the kids pinching the goods and stops the men pinching us. He earns his keep, that one. So have you just come to admire Gitt, or are you going to buy something?'

'Yeah, I'll take a couple of those apples, please, Jessel.'

'Right-o, pick them out then. That'll be a copper for the two.'

During the exchange, Fran came up, and Abren felt annoyingly self-conscious as he said, 'Actually, I was wondering if you would do me a favour.'

'Oh yeah? What kind of favour?' Jessel had cocked an eyebrow, but her expression showed amusement.

'You know the bookshop on Broad Street?'

'Yeah, I know the one.'

'Well, there's a book in the window.'

'Never!' said Jessel.

'This one's open,' Abren continued, trying to ignore Fran's snigger. 'It's got a picture in it. If you get a few minutes, would you go in there and ask them what it's a picture of? The shop's always shut when I pass it.'

If anything, Jessel's look of amusement had broadened.

'You want me to go over to the bookshop and ask what the picture is in one of their books?'

Abren was certain she was about to laugh in his face, so he felt rather sheepish when he said, 'Yeah, that's right.'

Jessel did not laugh, but she obviously found the idea entertaining.

'All right,' she said. 'Didn't take you for the bookish sort, though.'

'I'm just interested in the picture, that's all. I just want to know what it's of.'

'I'll pop over this afternoon. Fran can mind the stall for a bit, can't you, dear?'

'Yeah, of course. Don't worry about me,' replied her sister.

Abren was not sure what he caught in Fran's tone. Sarcasm? Resentment? Jealousy?

'Right then, come by tomorrow, and I'll tell you what they said.' Jessel still had that disconcerting smile on her face. 'Now bugger off. We've got work to do.'

'Yes, Ma'am,' returned Abren, and he strode off with a little smile of his own.

At the dock gates, he watched out for the man who claimed he had shoved him and then stolen his tools, but he saw no sign of him. When he reached the workshop, he was surprised to find the entrance blocked by Serrick, who was fitting a lock to the door.

'Should have been done ages ago,' said Jemmy, who was overseeing the work. 'Tools are valuable. It's a wonder nothing's been taken before.'

Abren was relieved at this tightening up of security. He did not want to be fretting about his tools with everything else on his mind.

Later that day, Serrick joined Abren and Nad for their lunch break. The three of them were eating in silence, watching the busy activities of the quayside, when Boz ran up.

'Heard about the accident?' he gasped.

They all shook their heads. Accidents were not uncommon in the docks.

'Crate fell on a man over by South Quay. Crushed his legs. I heard someone say he was sure to lose one at least. Thing is, Abren, I got a look at his face as they carted him off. He's the one who pinched your tools.'

'Serves him right,' Serrick said. 'Looks like his thieving days are over.'

'Yeah,' Abren agreed, but he found no satisfaction in the news.

He dug the apples out of his pocket.

'Here, these are for you,' he said as he gave them to Boz. 'And this.' He tossed the boy a copper coin. 'For helping me out yesterday.'

'Aww, thanks, Abren. You're a top man. Glad he got his comeuppance, though.' He grinned before racing off again.

As they were going back to work, Nad said, 'I'm on for a drink after if you like, Abe. Mallie said it was all right as long as it's just one and I don't come home sotted.'

The Crown was as busy as usual at that hour. A constant babble of male voices rumbled around the smoky saloon. They were standing at the end of the bar, each with a glass of the tavern's renowned Dockie's Best Ale.

'You seem to get on well with your missus,' Abren said.

'Sounds like you think it ain't normal,' Nad said, grinning. 'We have the occasional row, but yeah, we get on well enough, I suppose. Is that why you're not married, Abe? Think you'll be at each other's throats all the time?'

Abren was looking at some galloping horses illustrated in a picture hung from the tavern's dark wainscotting.

'No, not really. Just haven't found the right woman yet.'

'What about that one on the fruit stall?'

'What?' Abren's attention snapped back to his friend. 'How d'you…'

Nad laughed. 'My missus saw you yesterday, chatting to her, petting her dog. She's a nice girl. Mallie knows her quite well.'

'Yeah, all right, hold your horses, mate. I've only had a couple of little chats with her.'

'Well, anyway, she's not with anyone right now,' Nad confided. 'Thought you might like to know.'

They talked amiably about work and a backstreet show Nad had sneaked off to one Lordsday while his wife had taken the kids to visit her sister. True to his word, after finishing his drink, Nad said he should be getting along, and they both shouldered their way to the street door.

Once again alone in his lodgings, Abren ate the baked potato he had bought outside the tavern. As on the previous evening, he struggled with ambivalent anticipation, but this time it was the prospect of another meeting with Jessel and not the eerie manifestation of the sewer.

He had never regarded himself as handsome, and he was afraid his request about the book had made him seem ridiculous to her. But he could not deny he liked her, and Nad saying she was unattached certainly sharpened his interest. She had seemed willing enough to help him, and he did want to know about the picture.

Despite these turbulent emotions, his lack of sleep the previous night was catching up with him. This time slumber did not prove so elusive, and he dreamt his way through an unending labyrinth of dark tunnels, chasing a laughing ghost with wild blond tresses.

The next morning Abren followed his strategy of the previous day, devouring his bread and egg as he marched along.

Maybe I should get Hennis to knock me up earlier, he thought as he wiped his mouth with his sleeve. *I can't keep doing this.*

Jessel had her nose in a tin mug as he came up. She swallowed the steaming drink and, on seeing him, cleared her throat like she was going to give a lecture at the public library.

'Right, the picture is of angels,' she began.

'Angels?' Abren said.

'Yeah, angels. It's a drawing by a man called Glavin Pender. Apparently, he saw them in a vision or something.'

Abren knew he was trembling. He stared at her, eager to hear more, but she said, 'Are you all right? You look like you're about to pass out.'

'Yeah,' he said, rubbing his forehead.

'What? You're all right, or you're about to pass out?'

'All right. Don't suppose he mentioned where this Pender fella lived? I'd like to go and see him.'

'You can't do that, Abren. He's dead. And in any case, the man in the shop said he was crazy.'

'Crazy?'

'Yeah, crazy. Look, I think you should sit down a minute. There's a stool around here somewhere.'

'No, no, I'll be fine. Angels… drawn by a crazy man.' He gazed at the produce spread out before him. When he glanced up again, he saw Fran was there, and both sisters were looking rather concerned.

'If you're interested in angels,' Jessel said slowly. 'There's some in the graveyard over at Saint Raul's faith house. Maybe you should go and talk to the priest, Father Laniolus.'

'Right. Tomorrow's Lordsday, isn't it?'

'Yeah. If you go about ten, you'll catch him saying farewell to the worshipers at the faith house door. You don't work Lordsdays, do you?'

'No,' he told her. 'You seem to know a lot about this faith house, Jessel.'

'Yeah, well, I used to go sometimes.'

Abren thought she looked a little embarrassed, as if it were something to be ashamed of. A sudden idea struck him.

'Come with me,' he said.

She laughed incredulously, but he pursued the notion, nonetheless.

'You could show me the angels and introduce me to the priest.'

'You're a strange one, Abren,' she said, shaking her head. 'You get me to visit a bookshop, then you ask to go out walking with me in a graveyard.'

'Well?' He was still trembling but for a different reason now. 'Will you?'

'All right then. Meet me at the gate at a quarter to ten, and if you stand me up, I'll pelt you with rotten fruit next time I see you.'

All that day, the buoyant thought that Jessel had agreed to meet him vied with the weighty disquiet of what his vision might mean. He kept reminding himself that the angel, if that was what it was, had seemed wholesome, benevolent. But if it was an illusion, something conjured from within his own unsound mind, then was he facing a descent into some kind of insanity, like poor Pender?

Perhaps it won't happen again. Perhaps it was just some transient peculiarity.

But that night was to dispel any such hope.

The lights woke him. Their bright movement played across his eyelids. He knew before he opened his eyes what he would see. They filled the space above him, swimming slowly through the night air, casting a tender luminance over the poor furnishings of his room.

When the lambent figure shimmered into view, Abren sat up and faced it. It was still dazzling, like the flare from a giant torch, but not as brilliant as in the sewer. He could not breathe, as if breathing would be too crude a thing to do in the presence of such a being. He stared at it for a few moments, and it seemed to gaze back. Was there fondness in its eyes? He was not certain.

'Are you an angel?' he said at last.

The answer came in a high-pitched whisper. 'You may call me that if you wish.'

'Why have you come?'

'I have come to propose an alliance.' The thing's voice gave no more indication of its gender than its appearance.

'An alliance? With me?' Abren pinched his thigh. This was no dream.

'Yes. I have already done something for you. I punished the one who stole from you.'

'You did that? Broke his legs?'

'I caused it to happen, yes. But soon, I will require something of you in return.'

'What?'

'You will know when the time comes. For now, be assured that you will profit from our accord.'

The room darkened as the vision faded.

'Wait, I never asked…' But Abren knew his pleading was of no use. He was left alone in dumb shock. He fell back onto the bed, and an impotent confusion swallowed him.

Four

Amdris, state capital of the Republic of Mellia

Taygret woke up with a start when Linna knocked on her door. The maid came in carrying a pitcher of steaming water.

'Good morning, Miss. Did you sleep well?'

'Yes, well enough, I suppose.' She had been shaken out of her pleasant dreams and into the dismal, waking world. Eldam really was going to be taken away.

Once Linna had filled her wash bowl, she got out of bed and splashed her face. She stared down as droplets fell into her reflection. The heartache ignited by Eldam's deportation was burning fiercer than she had thought possible. She dried her face and began her daily routine of washing and dressing with Linna's help.

No use dwelling on sorrow. I must keep myself busy.

She was glad her uncle had agreed to let her help him. He could only work on his lighting project when he was not teaching at the university, of course, but with the students training to fight, that would occupy less of his time.

As it happened, Gorje Egring had the morning free, so after breakfast, they went to the outbuilding. The equipment laid out on the floor and tables was familiar to her from her occasional visits to the laboratory in her role as the maid. Having spent much of the previous afternoon and evening studying her uncle's writings, she now knew the function of most of it.

Taygret stood beside a large rubber balloon which, her uncle informed her, contained the fire gas. The last thing Eldam had done in the laboratory before being taken away was to produce this gas and Taygret could not help thinking it was rather precious. Uncle Gorje intended to burn it, nonetheless. The balloon was attached to a brass tube with a valve that controlled the rate at which the gas escaped. The tube ran horizontally for several feet across a tabletop before the last few inches turned upwards, a cap with several tiny holes covered its end. A solitary candle burned at that end of the table, giving the room its only light. Gorje had drawn a heavy curtain over the window. Taygret waited among the shadows, watching the candlelight dance upon her uncle's thin, pallid face. Her job was to open the valve slightly while Gorje held a taper lit from the candle over the end of the tube. Once the escaping gas was alight, she was to further open the valve by small degrees so that her uncle could observe the quality and strength of the flame.

When Gorje told her to begin, Taygret's hand trembled slightly as she reached for the valve, but by force of will, she mastered it. At first, the valve seemed stuck. She could not move it. Were her feminine fingers too weak to turn the little lever? She closed her other hand around it and increased the pressure. With a jolt, the valve moved, and she looked up at her uncle, afraid she had opened it too much, but he merely smiled and nodded to her.

When the experiment was over, and Taygret had closed the valve, her uncle smiled at her again.

'Well done,' he said. 'You will make an excellent assistant.'

'Were you happy with the results?'

'Not entirely. As the flow of gas increased, the spread of the flames became too broad. But I will make other types of caps and see how they work.'

In the afternoon, with her uncle away giving a lecture, Taygret helped Linna make preparations for supper. She scraped and diced carrots while the maid chopped celery. They were talking about Eldam. Taygret found it helped soothe her a little. Linna was saying how she liked the way the young man had always treated her as an equal when someone knocked on the front door. Linna put down her knife, but Taygret said she would go. She opened the door to find two men in smart, charcoal suits and white cravats.

The older of the two said, 'Good Afternoon. Is Miss Egring at home?'

'I am Miss Egring,' Taygret replied and was amused to see this disconcerted the man a little. He had obviously expected a servant to answer the door.

'Ah, well. Good Afternoon to you, Miss. I am Master Rassish, Professor of Medicine and Chemistry at the University of Amdris, and this is my colleague, Master Urrnik. May we come in?'

'Yes, of course.' She led them into the parlour. 'Please sit down. Can I offer you some refreshments?'

'No, thank you. Miss Egring, allow me to get directly to the point of our visit. I regret to inform you that your uncle is suspected of harbouring royalist sympathies. The university provost has asked me to search his study for anything that might confirm or disprove these suspicions.'

Taygret stared at the man. A whole maelstrom of questions and objections swirled within her. 'But he cannot possibly be a royalist. Only yesterday he was saying how he looked forward to helping the war effort.'

'My dear Miss Egring, what one says and what one thinks and believes may be different things entirely.' The professor regarded her coldly down his long, bony nose.

Taygret noted how Master Rassish's manner had changed. On the doorstep, he had been courteous and respectful, but now a certain superciliousness had taken their place.

'If you suspect my uncle of treasonous sympathies, is it not a matter for the police? Why have you come, and on whose authority?'

'The provost wishes for the matter to be handled discreetly for now. If I can find anything to exonerate your uncle, then no one outside the university needs to know of these suspicions, and our reputation will remain intact. Now, will you please show us your uncle's study?'

'No. Not until he is here and gives you his approval. You have no right…'

The slap came swift and hard. Pain shot through Taygret's head, and she staggered sideways.

'I will not tolerate insolence from you, girl,' Rassish snarled. 'I have tried to be reasonable, but you have exhausted my patience. I thought Egring overindulged you, and now I see I was right. We will find his study ourselves. Now go into the kitchen and stay there. You will not like the consequences if you vex me any further.'

Taygret couldn't move or focus her eyes. She felt someone grab her arm and drag her along. She looked up, and ahead of her, she could just make out Linna's horrified face.

'Get out the way.' It was not Rassish. It must be Urrnik. Linna backed up, and he pushed Taygret after her. They were in the kitchen.

'Stay here.' He closed the door.

'What's happening? Did they hit you?' Linna said, staring wide-eyed at her.

'It's two men from the university.' Taygret rubbed the side of her head. The pain was subsiding. 'They say uncle is suspected of being a royalist. Ridiculous! They're searching for evidence.'

'What shall we do? I wonder, does the Master know they're here? You could go to the university and tell him, or should I go and fetch the police?'

Taygret tried to get her brain working again. 'No. It's a long walk to the university. They would be gone by the time we got back. They will find nothing to prove uncle is guilty, so the police need not get involved.'

Minutes passed. Linna slowly resumed cooking. Taygret paced about, too agitated to work. Eventually, the door opened, and Master Rassish came in, followed by Urrnik.

'Your uncle has his own laboratory here, does he not? Where is it?' Rassish demanded.

Taygret glared at him. 'Why do you want to go in there?'

Rassish sighed. 'Miss Egring, as I told you, we are looking for anything that sheds light on where your uncle's political allegiance lies.' His manner had changed again. Now it was as if he were explaining something to some dull witted student. 'I hope I can find something that will absolve him. It is not in his interests for you to be obstructive.'

Taygret scowled. 'It's in the outbuilding, across the yard.' She pointed to the kitchen's back door.

'Is it locked?'

'No.'

'Well, it should be.'

'Can I come with you?' She resented having to ask and felt like a child requesting a special favour.

'Of course not. A laboratory is no place for a female.'

Again she had to wait. She wanted to help Linna but was reluctant to do what Master Rassish no doubt believed was fitting work for her. After a few moments, she relented and picked a carrot from the sack.

When the two men returned, Rassish looked at her with a smug grin. 'Thank you, Miss Egring,' he said. 'We will leave you to continue your chores.'

'Did you find anything to clear my uncle of these ludicrous accusations?'

'You will learn about that soon enough. Good day.'

'Is it true you're suspected of being a royalist?' Taygret asked again. Her uncle had not responded the first time.

Evidently, he thought it a trifling detail. She had given her account of the afternoon's events, and he still seethed from the news that Rassish had struck her.

'It's the first I've heard of it. I shall demand an interview with the provost tomorrow morning.'

They sat by the fire, and Gorje glowered at the blithe little flames fluttering in the hearth. Taygret allowed him his deliberations.

'Let me tell you about Master Rassish,' he said at last. 'He is, I'm afraid, resentful of the progress I have made in my research. It is, I must admit, partly my fault. I have been rather secretive about it. That is why I have my own laboratory here instead of making use of the facilities at the university. I have discussed my work with one or two close colleagues but not with him. You can call it professional rivalry, but the fact is I simply don't like the man. Perhaps your confrontation with him today will help you understand why.'

'He's a pig,' Taygret said.

Gorje grimaced. 'I certainly wouldn't argue with that assessment. In any case, if he's saying that I'm suspected of royalist sympathies, it's probably a fiction of his own creation.'

'It's a serious accusation. You might end up in prison. But if he has invented this charge against you, he'd know there'd be no evidence of it here. Do you think it was just a pretext to spy on you, read your notes, examine your equipment?'

'Yes, that's exactly what I think.'

'I'm fairly sure he didn't take anything from your study or the laboratory. Unless he hid it in his jacket.'

'I don't think he would resort to theft. But he is a very competent scientist. He could learn much from looking at my notes and equipment.'

'What are you going to do?'

'Like I say. I will see the provost at the university tomorrow and make a formal complaint regarding Rassish's conduct, especially about his striking you.' He paused and sighed. 'But I'm afraid you must be prepared for him to claim that the incident never occurred. It would be your word against his, or yours and Linna's against his and Urrnik's. Either way, the provost is likely to side with his professor.'

'Yes, Linna and I are only women, after all. But I'm not so concerned about that as long as you're not suspected of treason, and Rassish doesn't end up claiming credit for your work.'

'I think both scenarios are unlikely, my dear,' he said, brightening. 'Now, I got someone in the university workshops to make me another cap for our burner this afternoon. This one has just one slightly larger hole in the middle. What do you say to us trying it out after supper?'

When her uncle told her he was ready, Taygret put both hands on the valve. She was unsure whether it would be as stiff as last time, so while her right hand pushed, she kept her left hand ready to either help twist the valve open or stop it if it opened too freely.

Relying on touch to guide her fingers, she watched as her uncle leant forward and put the lighted taper over the new cap. A flame suddenly burst outward with a startling crack. She heard her uncle cry out in shock and then howl in pain. Flames caught on his coat and shirt.

For a moment, Taygret did not understand what her ears and eyes were telling her. Then she hurriedly closed the valve and ran to the bowl of water. Only when she saw the bowl was empty did the panic seize her. She stood helplessly trembling as her uncle staggered in the clutches of the blaze. His harrowed screaming finally propelled her to the door.

'Linna, Linna. Bring water, quickly,' she yelled at the house.

Pulling off her jacket, she flailed desperately at the blackening figure now writhing on the floor. The flames only seemed to leap more avariciously across her uncle's blazing torso. By the time Linna threw the water, Taygret knew it was too late. The maid pulled her away before she could give him one last smouldering embrace.

Taygret's body had chosen a corner of her bedchamber to huddle in, and it sat there now, on the floor, arms around legs, face pressed into knees. Her mind had hardly registered the movements that had brought her there. It was too absorbed in torment.

If only I had been quicker.

Linna had gone for the coroner, and Gorje Egring's remains had been taken away. There had been police and questions, but it had all sunk into the quagmire of despair.

'Shall I help you undress, Miss? It's getting late.'

Taygret had not heard the maid come in. She could not answer. She felt a light touch on her arm and raised her head. Through the blur of tears, she saw Linna crouching beside her. She let the maid draw her up and slowly remove her clothing; she was too numb to do anything for herself. When she stood in her shift, Linna drew back the blankets on her bed.

'Try and get some sleep, Miss.'

Taygret hesitated before going over and sitting on the bed. She took off her shoes and stockings.

'Lay with me,' she said, looking up into the maid's dark, confused eyes. Then she stood and began untying Linna's apron.

Five

Eldam

There were five other deportees in Eldam's coach. Each of them had been students at Amdris University and were among the first to be expelled from Mellia under the new dictate of the revolutionary government. They passed the time exchanging details of what awaited them back in Rarland and how they might rebuild their lives. Eldam did not know any of them very well, they had been at different colleges. They were all in a similar predicament now however, and one of them, a garrulous, restless fellow named Beron Quist, Eldam felt a particular affinity for.

'I tell you, Medloe, I shall miss her far more than my studies. My father always said I was a lazy, romantic fool, and he's quite right. But she is the most adorable, lovely creature you could ever wish to meet. Her smile simply takes my breath away. She let me kiss her once, you know. Such bliss! But now, Lord knows when I will ever see her again.'

Eldam listened to him effuse in a similar fashion for a while. He found it gave him a sort of chastening pleasure, exulting the pain of his own separation.

Eldam was glad that they were in an ordinary coach rather than a prison wagon. But the fact that there were four such coaches in convoy accompanied by eight mounted soldiers told the people they passed they were no ordinary travellers. From villages and fields, everyone seemed to stop and stare at them as they clattered by, some just bewildered, some with more hostile looks on their faces.

It was a full day's journey to the port of Frenbar, where they would be put on a ship to make the short voyage across to Rarland. Eldam had to admire the efficiency of the Mellians. Within forty-eight hours of his being apprehended, they will have thrown him out of their country.

It was dark by the time they got to Frenbar. There seemed to be some sort of festival going on. Colourful lanterns hung in the trees lining the streets and people thronged beneath them, laughing and shouting. Vendors weaved among the crowds calling their wares—oysters, oranges, roast almonds. They passed through a square where a band of musicians played a lively tune. Couples jigged, and onlookers sang along. Taverns had put out tables and chairs. Waiters and waitresses hurried to bring large jugs and tankards to clamouring drinkers. If the fighting in the west of their country worried these folk, they were trying their best to forget about it.

They halted outside a large inn. Despite the festivities, their arrival had not gone unnoticed, and a group of people stood watching curiously as the passengers descended from the coaches. It was the soldiers who had drawn attention to them. They were under guard, and Eldam guessed that meant in the eyes of the locals, they were either dignitaries or troublemakers.

'Filthy foreigners,' someone shouted, but no one took up the call, and the travellers entered the inn under the bemused gaze of Frenbar's citizens.

The spacious saloon was already crowded, but the revellers made way as the soldiers conducted the deportees towards some stairs at the back of the room. More perplexed stares watched them as conversations were interrupted.

They stopped at the foot of the stairs, and a stout little man with a wide moustache pushed his way towards them.

'Tonight of all nights,' he said to one of the soldiers. 'I could have rented these rooms for a good price during the Scomber Festival.'

'Spare me your complaints, innkeep. You will be adequately compensated,' the soldier countered. By the epaulettes he wore, Eldam took him for the commander of their escort, although he looked no older than Eldam himself.

The landlord was obviously far from mollified. 'Why don't you accommodate them at the prison?' He had to raise his voice as the inn's patrons had lost interest in the newcomers and resumed their chatter.

'The prison will be full of drunken rowdies.' The soldier was clearly trying to sound reasonable despite also being obliged to almost shout. 'Besides, these people are not felons.'

With an oath, the innkeeper reluctantly conceded the argument. 'Gizzie,' he called angrily at a serving girl. 'Show these… guests to the rooms I've allocated them and get Domash to lock their bags in the closet.'

Eldam stretched out gratefully on the bed, but his roommate did not seem in the least bit fatigued by the journey. Beron looked excitedly out of the window.

'A festival,' he said. 'Mellians certainly know how to celebrate.'

'No doubt,' Eldam replied. 'But all that means for us is a disturbed night's sleep.'

The sounds of laughing, shouting, music and singing had been joined by the crash and crackle of pyrotechnics.

'Well, I say we go and join them. It would be a fitting way to spend our last night in Mellia.' Beron was craning his neck, trying to get a better view.

'You can forget that, Quist. They've locked our door, and the soldiers have posted a sentry. Besides, our ship sails early tomorrow. There must be something in this room I can stuff in my ears.'

'They haven't locked this window.' Beron pushed it open, and the noise from outside increased. 'We can get out,' he said gleefully. 'The stables are right below us. We can get down onto the roof and then onto a coach they've left in the yard.'

Rather reluctantly, Eldam got up and went to join his new friend.

'I suppose it's possible,' he conceded. 'But our guards won't be thrilled if they find us carousing in the streets.'

'They won't see us if we mingle with the crowds. And in any case, they are already going to deport us in the morning. What else can they do to us?'

Beron hoisted himself up onto the window ledge and squeezed his slender frame through until he was sitting with his legs dangling outside. Then he dropped the few feet onto the roof below.

'Come on,' he said. 'I love this country, and I want to make a proper farewell.'

Eldam sighed. *Well, I suppose he's right. We haven't got much to lose,* he thought as he followed Beron's example.

As they were carefully crossing the stable roof to a point where they could get down onto the top of the coach, Eldam noticed a woman watching them from a window on the opposite side of the yard. Beron saw her too and waved, but she backed away into the shadows behind her.

When they were finally on the ground, Beron turned to Eldam. 'Have you got any money, Medloe?' he asked. 'I've just realised I left my purse in the room.'

'I have some,' Eldam told him, more amused than annoyed.

'Jolly good. I'll pay you back when we return.'

The yard was illuminated by a lantern hung over a door to the inn on their right and by another next to a door to the woman's tenement to the left. The gates across the entrance to the yard were closed, but as they approached, Eldam saw they were merely bolted. Before they got to the gates, however, two men came out of the tenement door.

'So, the dirty, foreign snoops are trying to escape, are they?' one said.

The men closed on the students, quickly cutting off the way to the gate. The one who had spoken was shorter than his companion, but both were burly and carried long, thin knives. Eldam smelt fish from their clothes, and they were clearly the worse for drink.

'We're not snoops,' Beron said, spreading his arms. 'We're Rarlish students who are unfortunately being kicked out of your wonderful country.'

'Rarlish students.' The short man grimaced his distaste of the words. 'Loyal subjects of His Majesty, King Murcial.' His tone showed he had no less contempt for Rarland's reigning monarch. 'Going home to stir up hatred towards us, I'll wager. We know Murcial only wants an excuse to join the war against us so he can send his warships over here, seize our fishing grounds and blockade our harbours. I fancy you're going to give him his excuse.'

'Not at all, my friend. We…'

Beron was not able to finish as the men attacked.

The man who came at Eldam, the taller of the two, waved his knife in front of the student's nose. He was not fully in control of his limbs. Eldam managed to block his arm and move inside his reach, trying to barge him over. The fisherman swayed back, but his strength kept him upright. He grabbed Eldam's shoulder with his free hand and began bearing him down.

Then Eldam remembered something his father had said when teaching him and Abren how to defend themselves when they were boys. He tilted his head back and slammed it into the man's face. There was a soft crack and a screeching cry. The man dropped his knife and covered his face with his hands, lurching away. The other man grabbed his companion's arm and pulled him back towards the door. Eldam watched as they disappeared inside the tenement. Then he heard the moaning.

Eldam had studied anatomy and physiology and learned the symptoms of many diseases, but nothing had prepared him for this. Beron was lying on his back, his hand over his belly. Blood was oozing liberally between his fingers.

'Oh Lord,' Eldam muttered as he crouched beside his friend. He untied his neckcloth and pushed Beron's hands aside. But when he tore open Beron's shirt, the sheer volume of blood told him it was not just a stab wound but a deep slash. He pressed the neckcloth down hard.

'Help! Help me.' Eldam's shout echoed off the walls of the yard. 'You're all right, Quist. You're going to be all right.'

Beron shook his head and clutched at Eldam's arm. 'My shoe,' he gasped. 'Take off my left shoe.'

'Don't be a fool, man. Lay still.'

'No. For Lord's sake, please. In my shoe… a letter. Find it.'

Eldam frowned, but his friend was so insistent, spitting out his message between groans of pain. He put Beron's hands onto the neckcloth, already soaked red and pulled off the shoe. Sure enough, he found a piece of paper, folded and sealed.

'Take it to the Foreign Department in Damlon.' Beron's voice was losing its strength but was no less urgent. 'It's of vital importance. Keep it hidden. Trust no one.'

'Yes, yes I will, I promise.' Then he raised his voice again. 'Help! Help us.'

Beron closed his eyes, fading. But then he rallied, his eyes jerked open again.

'Mattil...' he blurted. 'Mattil Yennsing... Willit House, Candle Street, Amdris. Tell her... tell her, I send her all my love... from heaven.'

And with the effort to make this one last plea, he was spent.

Finally, the soldiers came. Too late. Eldam could not respond to their questions, but he was dimly aware that they followed some sort of trail into the tenement as someone led him back to the inn. They took him into a small room with a desk. A woman gave him a glass. When he drank, he discovered it was brandy. As he revived, he thought of the letter. He fumbled in his coat pockets. To his relief, he found it. He did not recall putting it there.

The Foreign Department... of vital importance.

Good Lord, Quist. Why on earth were you carrying a letter to a government department? What had you gotten mixed up in?

Six

Abren

Somehow Abren was at the faith house gate early. He was glad; he did not want to make Jessel wait for him. Getting up this morning, washing, dressing, eating, he had got through like a numbed automaton, not wanting to dwell upon his second meeting with the angel.

The clock on the tower rising above the building's sloping roof told him he had fifteen minutes before Jessel arrived, assuming she was on time. He heard singing from behind the high windows of the faith house.

He leant on the red stone gateposts, and the recollections started to edge their way into his mind. It was so vivid. The angel had spoken to him. Told him it had avenged the theft of his tools. Crippled the man. But angels were good, weren't they? Would a real angel do that? But if it wasn't an angel, what was it? And what did it want from him?

He shut his eyes. It was as if he was between two worlds. The weird, disturbing realm of unearthly visitations and the bright excitement of a new friendship with a lovely woman. He tried to focus his thoughts on her and hoped she would think to wear a hat. He had noticed dark clouds advancing across the sky as he walked there. It would hide her beautiful hair, but...

'I'm impressed. You can sleep standing up.'

He opened his eyes, and there she was, smiling as she always seemed to and with a navy blue bonnet framing her pink face.

'Err… I was just thinking.'

'About angels, I suppose.'

'No… Well, yes.' He was tempted to say he had been thinking of her and that she was an angel, but he suspected she would just pour scorn on such a soft-headed notion.

'You're early,' he said, hoping to change the subject.

'Yeah. It looks like it's going to rain. So I thought we might have a quick look at the graves and then shelter in the doorway if we have to until the devotions are over. Come on. I think there are a couple of angels around here.'

She led the way down one side of the faith house. Most of the gravestones were simple, grey slabs. Some were plain, bearing just an epitaph. Others had what Abren took to be some likeness of the deceased carved on them. But then ahead he saw there was some of a more elaborate construction. The first Jessel stopped in front of had a small kneeling figure, head bent as if in grief. It looked like a child with little feathered wings sticking out behind him. Abren stared at it, shaking his head.

'No? Well, how about this one then?' Jessel walked on to a much more imposing monument. On a square pedestal stood a young woman with long, flowing hair. Wings folded behind her, she gazed reverently upwards, hands clasped together.

'She's a bit more like those in the drawing isn't she?' Jessel observed.

'Yeah,' Abren said as he stood rubbing his chin and frowning at the statue. He was trying to remember if his vision had wings.

'Why are you so interested in angels, Abren?'

He had expected her to ask him that question, but he had no answer prepared for her, so he just remained staring at the stone figure, his jaw muscles tightening.

The first large drops fell as she said, 'You see them, don't you? You see angels.'

The rain gathered strength, and the graveyard darkened. He looked at her, and after a long moment, he replied, 'I've seen one.'

They stood oblivious to the downpour, silently staring at each other. Abren could not read the look on her face, though he very much wanted to. He waited anxiously for her to react to his revelation.

Finally, she said, 'We'd better get inside,' and with the spell broken, they ran to the main door of the faith house.

The first members of the congregation were just emerging, and the priest was at his post, ready to offer his valedictions. Carriages had drawn up at the gate, and servants were hurrying with umbrellas to escort their employers through the deluge.

Jessel and Abren pressed themselves against the wall in the faith house entrance to allow the worshipers past. These wealthier members of the congregation cast disdainful glances at them, bedraggled as they were.

Those that came after, mechanics, shopkeepers, domestics, in their Lordsday best clothes, merely looked at them with grim amusement. Several recognised Jessel and exchanged a friendly greeting with her before darting off into the drenched world outside.

With the last of his flock departed, Father Laniolus turned his attention to the two pitiful creatures dripping puddles onto the floor of his faith house vestibule. He was younger than Abren had expected, with a direct, earnest countenance.

'We haven't seen you here in a while, Jessel,' he said, smiling. 'You are welcome to shelter here until the rain passes if you wish.'

'Father, my friend here would very much like to speak with you.' Jessel said.

'Oh, indeed?'

'Please, Father, I was hoping you might help me,' Abren said.

'If I can, of course. I must visit some of my congregation who cannot attend devotions now, but if you were to call at my residence at, say, three o'clock this afternoon, we can talk then.' He gestured to the building opposite the faith house door.

'Thank you. I will.'

'Very well then. I'll see you at three. How may I call you?'

'Abren. Abren Medloe.'

'Lord be with you, Abren. Jessel.'

He retreated into the main body of the faith house, leaving them gazing out at the rain. Abren was desperately trying to think of something to say. She had guessed, and he had not denied it. She knew, but what did she think?

Before he could find any words, she said, 'Looks like it's easing up a bit. I'd best get back. Me and Fran are going to visit our aunt today.' And without another word, she trotted off, out the gate and down the street.

Abren stood and watched her go. He folded his arms across his chest and let out a long sigh.

That's that, then. She thinks I'm mad. She'll want nothing to do with me now.

She had called him her friend, but even as he recollected it, he knew it did not really mean anything.

The next few hours were bleak indeed. He walked; he did not care where. The rain gradually stopped. He found himself by the river and stood at the top of some wooden steps watching the traffic on the water. Three scrawny boys were roving the bank just below him. One carried a tattered basket, and the other two were delving into the mud with sticks, searching for any saleable refuse left by the retreating tide.

The scene took Abren back to his own childhood in the country manor, where his father managed the estate for a rich family. He still felt a sour rancour at the contrast between the privileged life those people led and the hardship that now surrounded him. Why was it that a few fortunate folk lived in luxury while so many struggled through a wretched existence?

The estate had been a wonderful place for a young lad to grow up, though, with its fields and woods and lakes. He had learned to ride and catch fish. But his time there had ended in bitterness. As he gazed out over the wide, busy river, he no longer saw the cogs and wherry boats plying up and down and across the waterway or the urchins digging in the muck.

It was a hot midsummer's day, and flies were troubling his horse. They were on a track beside a brook that led down towards the estates farm buildings, beyond which were the stables. Abren stroked the colt's neck as the steed swung his head to and fro and stamped his hooves.

'Easy boy, easy now, Jester. We'll be back soon.'

'Having problems with your mount, Medloe?'

Abren looked up at the sound of Peta's drawl. The young man must have emerged from behind the cowshed and was now standing by the side of the track. He was carrying a long-barreled hunting rifle and one of his spaniels prowled at his feet. Abren felt his jaw clench; he did not want to appear an inept rider, especially in front of Sir Nortach's eldest son.

'It's the damned flies.' Abren hated how he always seemed to copy Peta's plummy accent when they spoke.

Then, to Abren's consternation, Jester plunged his head forward and began to buck his hind legs. Aben pulled hard on the reins trying to get the horse's head up. Peta laughing derisively.

'I can't wait to tell Launy about your pitiful horsemanship,' he called out. 'She won't want to go riding with you again.'

As if drawn by the young man's voice, Jester lunged towards him and reared. The dog barked and Peta screamed.

'It was an accident. Jester must have been bitten or stung or something. There were a lot of flies.'

Abren's father stood with his arms crossed, shaking his large head as his son tried to explain. 'Peta was nearly killed. He's still in a coma. You know how to control a horse. You let it happen. You thought to rid yourself of your rival. Well, you can forget about Launy now. You are to leave here in the morning. I never want to see you again.'

'But, Dah...'

'I am not your dah. Not anymore. Sir Nortach has been good to our family, even paying for Eldam's schooling. Now I can barely look the man in the eye. You let your jealous rage get the better of you. Peta is heir to this estate. The Lord only knows what will become of him now.'

'Toss us a copper, Mister.'

Abren stared stupidly at the boys for a moment, then rootled in his coat pocket. He threw the three coppers he found and watched them scramble. Achingly hollow inside, he turned for home. He would need to change out of his wet clothes before paying a visit to the priest.

The priest's residence was in some ways similar to the faith house on the outside, with the same red brick walls and white casing around its tall windows. As he approached, Abren could not resist a glance over at the faith house door where he and Jessel had stood together not so very long ago.

A middle-aged maid answered his knock and showed him into a sitting room just off the entrance hall. It had pale yellow and green patterned wallpaper and pictures of the six saints hung at intervals. Raul, in his sapphire robes and pointing skywards, had pride of place above the mantel. Two armchairs stood by the fireplace where a small mound of coal burned. He felt rather rough and out of place, but when Father Laniolus joined him, he greeted him cordially enough.

'Please sit down, Abren. Enill will bring us tea shortly.'

Abren sat in an armchair and fingered the edge of his jacket.

'You have the look of a working man,' the priest observed.

'Yes, Father, I work in the docks as a carpenter.'

'Ah, you have a trade, very good. Many of my congregation work in the docks.'

Abren merely nodded. None of the men he worked with attended the devotions as far as he knew.

'So, what was it you wanted to speak to me about?'

'Well, I…' He wished he had thought this out beforehand. 'Do you know anyone who has seen an angel?' It came out in a rush.

Laniolus looked a little taken aback. 'There are accounts of angels appearing to people in the scriptures, of course. But no, I haven't heard of it happening to anyone in the here and now, as it were. Why do you ask?'

He could not put it off any longer. He looked into the fire. 'Because I've seen one. Twice, in fact. I think it's an angel, but it might not be.'

'Can you describe this angel?' There was a change in the priest's voice. Abren continued to gaze into the flames.

'It was bright, dazzling. It seemed friendly. I don't think it had any wings, though.'

'Did it have a halo? A glow around its head?'

'No, not especially. It glowed all over… It spoke to me.'

'Oh?'

'It told me it wanted to form an alliance with me, that it hurt a man who robbed me. Said it wanted me to do something, but it wouldn't say what.'

Do I sound like I'm raving?

'It hurt someone?'

'Yeah. A man stole my tools at work. The next day a crate fell on him and crushed his legs. The angel said it had caused it. Do you think it might want me to do something bad?'

'An angel is a messenger from The Lord, Abren. It would not harm anyone or ask anyone to harm another.'

'No. It can't be an angel then, can it?'

'Forgive me but... had you been drinking when this happened?'

'No, no. I wasn't drunk, Father. I swear I wasn't. The first time was at work. I'd lose my job if I were drunk at work. But if it's not an angel, what can it be?'

'I am uncertain. You said it wanted you to do something.'

'Yeah. It didn't say what, though. What if it's evil? What if it wants me to hurt someone?' Abren realised several days of pent-up worry and bewilderment were unleashing themselves into the room.

'Hmm, I must consider this... I'll just go and see what has happened to the tea.'

After the priest had left the room, Abren got up himself. He went to the window. The sky was a dull grey, but the rain had not returned. Carriages and carts were passing up and down the road, people strolling by on the footpath. A sense of separation from this normality came over him as if he were somehow set apart from the everyday events of the world. Voicing aloud his experiences to another had left him feeling strangely adrift, belonging nowhere.

Father Laniolus came back in after a while, followed by the maid carrying a tray.

'Here we are. Let's have some tea, and we can continue our chat.'

Something in the way the priest spoke these niceties intensified Abren's unease. He reseated himself.

'Do you like honey in your tea?'

'No, thank you.'

He took the cup offered to him.

'Now tell me more about your angel. Let's call it that for the time being.'

Abren gazed down into the black liquid, he did not feel like drinking. He recounted everything he could remember: the coloured lights, the first wordless encounter in the sewer, the conversation in his room. When he had finished, he repeated his question from earlier.

'What do you think it can be, Father?'

The priest cleared his throat. 'Well…'

There was a knock at the door. The maid entered. Abren felt a stab of concern for her, she looked so anxious as she clutched at her apron with a tight fist.

'There is… someone to see you, Father,' she stammered.

The peace officer did not wait for an invitation before coming into the room. He ducked his tall, black hat under the lintel and stood regarding Abren with an imperious stare.

The priest was on his feet. 'I'm sorry, Abren. I will help you all I can, I promise. But I think for your own safety… for the time being…' He moved aside as the peace officer advanced to where Abren sat, dumbfounded.

'Right then,' said the officer. 'Let's you and me take a little walk, shall we? We can have a nice chat about what's been going on down at the station. Father Laniolus will join us in good time, I'm sure.'

Abren would have cause later to wonder if what he did next was the wisest course of action. He carefully placed the cup on a small table. Then with the instinct of a cornered sewer rat, he launched himself out of the chair, swinging an elbow as he did so. The peace officer doubled over, gasping and wheezing, and Abren bolted for the door. The maid recoiled with a squeak of fright, leaving him with a clear run to the front entrance.

Once outside, he ran off down the road taking the first turning into a side street and then another. There he slowed to a brisk walk so that no one would suspect the distant clacking of the peace officer's rattle had anything to do with him.

Seven

Taygret

Taygret clung to her maid's warmth until she fell asleep. When she awoke, Linna was gone. She got out of bed and drew back the curtains.

Bright sunshine fell on the slate roof of the outbuilding and the pink paving stones of the yard. The tulips she had planted in the little plot in the corner were beginning to unfold their purple heads. It looked so peaceful, as if no great tragedy could ever happen there. She stood gazing down as a bleak aching grew inside her.

After several minutes Linna returned, and Taygret began preparing for the first day without her uncle's love. In the kitchen, she ate a little porridge and took a few swallows of coffee. There was a broom propped against the wall by the back door. Taygret stared at it while she ate.

When she had finished, she got up, seized the broom and crossed the yard. The equipment looked sturdy, but Taygret found the glass jars and flasks smashed easily enough once she had swept them off the table. She picked up a shard of broken glass, ignoring the pain as it cut into her. She stabbed at the rubber balloon until it popped, releasing the hated gas into the room.

Then she wrenched the brass tube from the tabletop and threw it clumsily at a shelf full of bottles. They toppled and fell with a loud crash, splintering and spilling their contents across the stone floor. All except one. Taygret stooped, retrieved it and drew back her arm to hurl it at the wall, but then Linna was there calling to her, and the rage left her, and she sank to her knees, cradling the bottle in her bleeding fingers, sobbing.

Quietly and calmly, Linna led Taygret back to the kitchen and sat her down again by the table. Then the maid carefully cleaned and bound Taygret's wounded hands. When she had finished the two young women regarded each other for a few moments, silently exchanging their grief and compassion. At last, Taygret rose and went up to her uncle's study. As she entered the room her mind went back to a day nearly three years ago.

'I need to show you something important,' Gorje had told her. 'In case anything ever happens to me.'

She took a stool from under the desk and carried it over to one of the bookcases. Behind a particular set of books on a high shelf was a small ornate box, and in the box was a key. She retrieved it and opened the iron-bound chest in one corner of the room. She took the bag of money to the desk and divided the silver and gold coins into two plies, a larger and a smaller. The larger she put back into the bag, the smaller she put into a purse.

Her hands were stinging, and the binding made it difficult to grip, but she worked the cork from a bottle of ink and dipped a pen. She wrote two brief letters, waited for the ink to dry, then folded them. She did not trust her hands enough to make seals.

She went down to the parlour and called Linna.

'I cannot stay here,' she told her maid. 'Single women cannot inherit property. I'm so sorry, but you will have to find employment elsewhere.' She felt her emotions were going to get the better of her, but she pressed on. 'This is a letter of recommendation. It's glowing, of course. You have been…' Her voice broke.

'Oh, Miss.'

Taygret saw Linna had tears in her own eyes. She made herself continue.

'And this is some money to see you through.' She handed over the purse. 'And this is a letter saying that I have freely given the money to you, so no one can accuse you of stealing it.'

Taygret held Linna in her arms, waiting for the waves of grief to subside. Eldam, her uncle and now Linna.

'Where will you go?' the maid asked when they had released each other.

'I honestly don't know. Master Egring will have left everything to my other uncle, Lagmore. He will no doubt want to sell the house. I definitely don't want to go and live with him. He is the complete opposite of his brother. He would make me his slave. I'll probably go to another town and find work, perhaps looking after some nice people's children. I hope you find something soon.'

'Don't worry about me, Miss. There are always openings for domestic servants with good references. My sister can put me up until I find somewhere.' She hefted the purse. 'And it seems like you've been very generous. Thank you. I'll be fine. Shall I stay with you tonight?'

'No, it's all right. I think I want to be alone for a while.'

Linna went to pack her belongings and Taygret knew she should do the same but could not find it in her to face the task just yet. She wandered through the house and stood silently in each room as if to absorb the memories they held so she could take them all with her. When Linna was ready to depart, Taygret gave the maid one more tender embrace.

'Good luck, Linna. I shall miss you. You have been like a good friend to me. For this last parting, please, call me Taygret.'

Linna gave her a sad smile. 'Farewell, Taygret. I hope you can make a happy life for yourself wherever you go.'

With Linna gone the house seemed completely empty, devoid of life. Taygret had wanted to be alone but now she found no succour in the lonely evening and as the coming night darkened the vacant spaces around her, she drifted like a lost soul up to her room. She sat gazing at her bed; it had no appeal for her. She closed her eyes, but attempting to breathe tranquillity into her anguished mind was out of the question.

When she sensed the change in the air, she opened her eyes again. She was astonished to see that a swarm of weird, gleaming insects had gotten into her room. Glow flies, perhaps. They were massing at the foot of the bed. How did they get in?

She stood up, wondering how she would get them out again but then realised she did not want to. They were so pretty. Then something very odd happened. The insects disappeared all by themselves. What replaced them was even more peculiar.

It was midmorning on the next day, and Taygret stood in the dining room. For the last few hours, she had been very industrious, reducing her life into two portmanteaux that now awaited her at a nearby coaching inn.

She had thought hard about how to transport her uncle's money. There were just too many coins to carry herself. Whilst sorting out her belongings, however, she had found several reticules, a couple of which she had made herself. Most of the coins were now distributed in four of them, two tucked away in each portmanteau. The rest were in two pockets tied round her waist under her skirt. She hoped if any would-be thief searched her bags and found one cache, he would not look further and she would only lose a portion of her wealth.

Now she just wanted to get away from this place where happy memories had been plunged into heartache. She was trying to decide if there was anything else she needed to do before leaving her home for good but for the umpteenth time, other thoughts intruded on her deliberations.

What was that thing? Was it a dream? Had she dozed off in the chair? Or had her torment thrown some perverse folly into her awareness? But it had been so bright and lovely. And it had spoken to her. She could recall what it had said.

'Do not be afraid, dear Taygret. I mean you no harm. I want us to be friends. You have suffered so much misfortune lately. Perhaps we can help one another. I have something to show you.'

She had been so stunned by the appearance that she had not managed to respond. As it faded away, she glimpsed another figure. At first, she thought it was Eldam but then saw it was not. Like him but not him.

Taygret did not know what she should do about the vision or even if it was real. She was gazing vacantly at the blue plates and bowls propped up in their glass cabinet when there was a knock on the street door. The idea that it might be her uncle Lagmore coming to take her to his house made her freeze. The second knock was louder. Should she hide? Pretend she was out? But she had not locked the door after returning from the coaching inn. She walked out into the hall. Summoning her determination to fight for her independence, she pulled the door open. It was not Lagmore.

'My condolences, Miss Egring. Your uncle is a great loss to us all,' Master Rassish said once he had followed her into the parlour. He looked at her bandaged hands. 'You're hurt.'

'It's nothing. Minor cuts only.'

'Hmm. The provost has asked me to recover your uncle's notes. They will be an invaluable asset to the university. We will ensure his legacy lives on.'

'You know where they are.' She could not look the man in the face.

'Yes. Thank you.'

When he had gone up the stairs she sat down, wondering if he would want to go into the outbuilding. It gave her some small pleasure to think of what he would find there. She decided to visit it herself one last time. It would offend Rassish even further if he were to discover her there amongst the wreckage.

A laboratory is no place for a female.

As she stomped across the yard, she felt the fury crackle again inside her.

When she returned to the house, Rassish was still in her Uncle Gorje's study. She went slowly up the stairs.

'I've nearly finished here.' He had made a pile of papers on the desk and was putting them into a satchel.

'You killed him, didn't you?' Taygret said.

'What?' Rassish looked up, his eyes wide and startled.

'You mixed air into the gas, didn't you? It wouldn't have exploded otherwise.'

'Foolish girl. You don't know what you're talking about. Your uncle was careless, and it caused a tragic accident.' He was talking quick and loud. *Nervous,* she thought. 'You are grieving, I know, and doubtless very upset, but you should not make scurrilous accusations. It would land you in a lot of trouble.'

'You're a slimy, murdering toad.' She wanted to make him shout at her, and she succeeded.

'You impertinent bitch.' Master Rassish put particular emphasis on the last word as he raised his hand.

And it was at that moment the contents of the cup she had been carefully carrying hit him in the face so that the acid burned the inside of his mouth as well as his eyes, nose and cheeks. His scream died in his throat, and he staggered back, gagging and gasping. He put his hands up to his searing flesh but as they too were scorched, he flailed his arms frantically in front of him.

She dropped the cup and pushed him to the floor, where he writhed helplessly.

Just like Uncle had done, she thought with grim satisfaction.

She closed the study door behind her, then she went down the stairs. She did not bother to lock the street door as she left the house.

Eight

Abren

Abren's mind was in a whirl. Where was he to go? He had told the priest where he worked but not where he lived. The peace officers were sure to look for him at the docks, eventually. They could find out where he lived from the Dock House but not on Lordsday. He thought it would be safe for him to go back to his lodgings for the night, but he would need to be out early in the morning, taking what belongings he could with him. But where then?

As he turned his steps towards home, he tried to understand what had happened. The priest had obviously concluded that he was mad, perhaps dangerously so. He had told him too much. He should have said it was a friend who was seeing the angel or whatever it is. What would the peace officers do if they caught him? Lock him up in a madhouse? He could not believe this was happening to him. Was he really going insane?

When he reached his lodgings, he half expected peace officers to be waiting for him, but everything appeared normal. He met old Graylie Pyke carrying a bucket on his way out to fetch water from the pump along the street. He had to push past several boisterous children playing on the stairs. A couple were shouting at each other in the room below his.

Once he had closed his door to the world, he felt some sense of security. He relit his fire, opened a bottle of ale and unwrapped a sausage he had saved for his Lordsday supper. Then he sat down to think. Who might he turn to at a time like this? Nad was his best friend, but he wasn't sure where he lived. He could not risk going to the docks tomorrow to ask him for help. And how would he explain his need to hide? Good friend as he was, how would Nad react if he told him the truth?

Apart from the priest, he had confided in only one other person, albeit in the briefest way possible. She had gone off before he had been able to explain further. Did that really mean she wanted nothing more to do with him? He felt a keen longing to see her again and find out. He knew where he would find her first thing in the morning.

As the afternoon darkened into evening, his fears seemed to creep in upon him like sinister shadows. What if the peace officers found his lodgings somehow and came for him in the night? Could he escape out the window and over the rooftops? He hoped he did not need to attempt that in the dark. What if they were right, and he really ought to be put away? Shoving that thought aside, he determined to stay vigilant as long as possible, to keep watch over his liberty and sanity.

Through long, unlit hours, he sat up listening and watching for any earthly or unearthly intruders. What portion of the night he spent alert, he could not tell, but when the wake-up call came, he was asleep in his chair.

In some ways, it was like any other Raulsday morning, the first day of the working week. Abren strode along in the early murk with his most precious things in his bag, his tools, on top of which he had piled a change of clothes.

Relieved there had been no nocturnal visitations, having left his lodgings for good and knowing he could not return to work, a curious feeling of liberation came over him which contested with a future filled with uncertainty.

He kept a wary eye out for peace officers, but his primary concern was how Jessel would react when she saw him again. He had tried to go over in his mind what he would say to her, but he had abandoned any hope of preparing a persuasive monologue. Nad had called her a nice girl. Abren hoped she would be nice to him this morning.

When he saw her, the familiar sensations of fear and longing slowed his steps. She appeared to be arguing with her sister. She stood, arms folded, while Fran railed about something, waving her own arms in frantic angry gestures. In the half-light of the dawn, they were like shadow puppets acting out an intense drama. Gitt, caught up in the agitation, was barking at them both.

He heard Jessel say, 'It's up to her, Fran. It's her decision, not yours.' At this, Fran stormed off down the street with a growl of frustration. Jessel leaned forward and yelled at the dog, 'Just shut up, will you?' Straightening up, she noticed Abren, who had come to a halt in front of the stall.

'And what do you want?' she snapped.

'Nothing. It doesn't matter.' He turned and trudged away, hefting his bag higher on his shoulder as he went. He realised he was heading towards the docks out of habit and stopped to consider which way to go now.

'Wait… Abren, wait.' Her lusty stallholder's voice carried to him with ease. When he looked back, she was gesturing to him to return.

'I'm sorry,' she said as he approached the stall once more. 'Fran and me were just having a row about our aunt.'

'She seemed pretty annoyed.'

'Yeah, she's a fiery one, she is. She'll just go stomping around the block and calm down after a while. She'll punish me for disagreeing with her by making me set out the stall on my own.'

'I'll help you.' Abren felt a shiver of excitement.

'What? Don't you have to get to work?'

'Not anymore.'

'Why? What's happened?'

'I'll tell you as we go.'

Abren stowed his bag under the stall alongside Gitt and set about lugging the crates and baskets off the sisters' cart and laying them out for display. He thought he would be reasonably safe doing this work, the peace officers were unlikely to look for him here, and he enjoyed having Jessel telling him what to do. He gradually told her what had happened at Father Laniolus's house. When he included a brief description of the angel, she merely looked a little puzzled, but she stopped and gaped at him open-mouthed when he got to the part where he escaped arrest.

'You bashed a peacey! Good Lord, Abren, they'll lock you up for sure if they catch you.'

'Yeah, I know.'

'Where are you going to go?' She glanced nervously down the street.

'Well… I was hoping you would help me.'

Her gaze shot back to him. 'How?'

'Err… I thought maybe…'

'So, taken on a new hand, have we?' Fran stood, fists on hips, glaring at him.

'Oh, there you are. Got over your little tantrum, have you?' Jessel said to her. 'Abren was kind enough to help me while you were cooling off.'

'Fine. Well, I'm back now, so he can go about his own business.'

'Actually, he needs our help as well.' Jessel had her arms crossed again. 'The peace officers are after him because he hit one of them. We need to put him up for a day or two till he can think what's best to do.'

Abren wondered at this woman's powers of perception. She knew exactly what he was going to ask her. He felt a surge of gratitude.

'What? I mean, I don't mind helping someone who's bashed a peacey, but what about Morriline?'

'She needn't know. She'll still be in her bed. If Abren sneaks in now and stays quiet, she won't find out.'

'Damn it, Jessel. If he gets us slung out…'

'He won't. We'll be careful. Now you can finish up here, dearest. I'll be back in no time.'

They left Fran scowling and shaking her head.

'Who's Morriline?' Abren asked as they hurried past other stallholders putting out their goods.

'Our landlady. She doesn't allow us male visitors unless they're family. She's very religious. It was her who got me going to the faith house in the first place.'

Jessel led Abren a little way back along the high street, and then they turned off into a side road before entering a narrow alley. Darkness enveloped them. She was surefooted, knowing the way, but he tripped and stumbled over debris hidden in the gloom. The alley opened into a tiny courtyard. Jessel unlocked a door, and shushing him a warning to be quiet, entered the house.

The dim, unfamiliar place perturbed him at first, but when Jessel clutched his hand and led him on, he lost his apprehension completely. They came to a staircase and went up. Abren tried very hard to concentrate on where he put his feet despite the delightful sensation of her hand in his. On the landing, she quietly unlocked another door, and they went into the sisters' apartment.

A window admitted a dull light, and Abren looked around at the alien female world. The room had colour and cosiness that made his seem drab and austere. They had a rug and chairs with cushions. A mirror hung over the fireplace, and even a few flowers stood in a yellow vase on the table. Everything looked well used and worn, but all was clean and tidy.

'Well, here we are,' Jessel whispered. 'Not much, but it could be worse, I suppose.'

'It's really nice,' he replied and meant it.

There was a door to their right, which led into another room, and he just glimpsed an iron bedstead with a patchwork coverlet before Jessel closed it.

'That's our bedroom. You're not allowed in there.'

Abren felt his face redden.

'You can sleep out here with Gitt. He snores, I'm afraid.' She smiled. 'I think we have a couple of spare blankets we can give you. There's some bread and cheese in the press, and fruit, of course. Water in that jug on the sideboard. Oh, and err…' She disappeared into the bedroom. When she came back, shutting the door again, she had a large, white chamberpot in her hands.

'I'll empty it this evening,' she said, grinning. 'There's a privy out the back, but I think Morriline stays in a lot during the day, so best not to risk it.'

'Thanks, Jessel, I really appreciate this. I won't be putting you out for long.'

'We'll talk about it tonight. I'd best be getting back now, and please, no noise. Fran was right. If Morri finds you here, she might well throw us out.'

When Jessel had gone, Abren took a little of the food in the cupboard, just enough to keep his hunger at bay for a while. There were some coins in his pocket. He got paid only two days ago and, although he hadn't managed to avoid the rent man on Lordsday morning, it was still the flush part of the week, so he should be able to pay his way for a few days at least.

Sitting down, he sought to fill the hours before the sisters' return by trying to map out a future for himself in the coming days and weeks. He had to lie low, maybe even leave the city or at least this part of it. How rigorously would the peace officers pursue him? He had knocked the wind out of one of them, and they probably considered him a dangerous lunatic. Every peacey on the beat might have his description by now and be keeping an eye out for him. But he also needed to earn some money. He did not want to become a beggar.

Thoughts chased each other through his mind, but no appealing idea came to him. As his ruminations died away, he began casting his eyes about the unfamiliar room. Then he noticed something he recognised, the bonnet Jessel had worn the previous day hanging on the door. He suddenly felt an urge to touch it, hold it, feel her presence. Getting up, he began sneaking across the room.

'Jessel is that you?... Fran?' A woman's voice called up from below.

He froze. The landlady had clearly heard something, but he had not been aware of making any noise. He cursed himself for a fool and held his breath, hoping the woman would think she had been mistaken. But to his horror, he heard footsteps on the stairs. Would she come in to check the apartment? He was sure Jessel had not locked the door. If Morriline tried it and found it unlocked... There was a gentle rap.

'Hello? Anyone at home?'

There was nowhere to hide in here. He had to break Jessel's injunction. Creeping hastily to the bedroom door, he pulled on it just as the outer door swung open. He turned, an abject apology ready on his lips.

'Oh, Morriline. I kept wondering if I'd locked that door.' Jessel's voice. 'I just popped back to check it.'

'Oh, there you are. I'm sorry, I wouldn't have come up, but I thought I heard something.'

Abren could not see the landlady. She was hidden behind the open door to the landing. She had obviously stopped and turned to face Jessel. He edged backwards into the bedroom, then to one side to conceal himself in case the women came in.

'I'm sure it's nothing, but I'll just have a quick look round.'

'Be careful, dear. There might be a housebreaker.' Morriline was rather belatedly whispering.

Jessel came into the bedroom, crouched down and looked under the bed, opened the wardrobe, glared at Abren, and then went back out.

'No one here,' she announced cheerily.

'Oh dear, I must be hearing things. Sorry for troubling you.'

'Think nothing of it. Thank you for being so vigilant.'

Abren heard the outer door close then Jessel say in a low voice, 'You can come out now.'

'Jessel, I'm so sorry…'

'You made a noise and went into our bedroom. I'm glad I didn't tell you not to do anything else.' She pointed to a small parcel on the table. 'I brought you a pasty, but maybe I should give it to Gitt instead.'

'I really didn't think I was making a sound. I thought with the rug…'

She let out a sigh of exasperation. 'Take your boots off next time.'

'I'm really sorry, Jessel,' he repeated. 'You've been so kind to me. I'll leave right away. As soon as it's safe.'

'No. You'll probably blunder into a peacey around the first corner. One more chance. Take your boots off and don't, I mean it, for Lord's sake, don't tell Fran what happened.'

'I promise,' he said and dared to offer her a little smile. To his immense relief, she smiled back. He wanted to throw his arms around her.

'Right, I'm going. See you this evening.' She went out and locked the door, leaving the parcel on the table.

Nine

Eldam

'So, you and Master Quist climbed out of the window of your room and got down to the stable yard,' the chief of Frenbar's police said again. He did not have a hair on his head and, along with his prominent jaw and fierce gaze, Eldam found it quite disconcerting.

'Yes. The festivities were too much of a temptation, I'm afraid. It being our last night in Mellia, or so we thought.' The ship had sailed, taking the other deportees back to Rarland, but Eldam was still in the port town, assisting the police with their investigation into Beron's murder.

'And you are certain that the two men we have under arrest are the ones who attacked you?' This was all repetition. Eldam sensed the police chief was probing for any doubts Eldam may have. He was determined not to convey any.

'Yes. The light from the lanterns showed their faces clearly enough. They were obviously drunk and took no care to conceal their identities.'

'Very well.' To Eldam's astonishment, the policeman was actually smiling at him. 'Thank you for your assistance, Master Medloe. I will require you to make a written statement, but then you will be free to go. The army corporal who escorted you here insisted you board the next ship across the bay, so I cannot detain you any longer. National security is more important than felony, you understand. We will write to Master Quist's family and arrange for his remains to be transported to them in due course. It has been a pleasure to meet you, and I hope you can return to Mellia once this war reaches a satisfactory conclusion.' He offered Eldam his hand, and still a little bewildered by the man's sudden cordiality, he took it.

The festival still had the town in its dissolute grasp, but after he had finished penning his account of the previous evening's disastrous events, the two soldiers left to watch him led Eldam back to the inn. Before returning to Amdris with the rest of his men, the corporal had warned Eldam that if he tried to leave the inn without permission again, his guards would find a corner of a prison cell for him. He had lost all appetite for the carnival in any case and sat down in his room to write something else, this time the most difficult letter imaginable. He took a long time over its composition.

Poor Mattil. It might so easily have been Quist writing a similar letter to Taygret.

The police chief informed Eldam that the next ship crossing Kimmikk Bay was due to sail in two days' time. In the afternoon following his interview, he was playing checkers in his room at the inn with one of his guards. The soldiers had introduced themselves; this one was called Jak. He was a quiet sort of fellow but amiable enough. Eldam was confident he was about to win another game when they heard the cannon fire.

'What in the world is that?' Eldam exclaimed.

Jak had gone pale, and without a word, he got up and went out into the hallway. When Eldam reached the door, he saw the soldier was looking out of the window at the end of the hall.

'It's coming from the port,' Jak said. 'Good Grace, they're attacking the port.'

'Who are?' Eldam could feel the inn shaking, or was it just his legs?

'Skiglanders most like. Oh, where's our ships when we need them?'

Eldam joined the soldier at the window. Beyond the town's rooftops, he could see clouds of grey smoke billowing into the sky. Jak turned and headed down the stairs. Eldam went after him. When he arrived at the spacious saloon, he was surprised to find the innkeeper and his staff still serving customers. All seemed unconcerned about the bombardment. He recognised a passing waitress.

'Gizzie, what's going on?'

She flicked her big, amber eyes at the ceiling. 'Oh, it's only the Skigs having another go at the harbour. They come along every month or so, sink a few fishing boats, do a bit of damage to the warehouses, then sail off again before our ships arrive—too late as usual.'

She went off to deliver the three plates of food she was carrying, and the cannon fire stopped. Jak came up, and Eldam saw from the relief on his face that he had received a similar report from the landlord.

'Let's finish our game,' said the soldier.

As the next morning wore on, Eldam suspected his departure was going to be delayed again because of the raid on the port. Sure enough, at around midday, word arrived that he would be obliged to enjoy Mellian hospitality for several more days. While the state recompensed the inn for the room he occupied, he had to pay for his meals, and his funds were running low. He resolved to sell some of his belongings, but the soldiers were under orders to keep him at the inn, and they were not prepared to disobey them even though Eldam's sojourn had been prolonged unexpectedly.

'I'll go for you,' Jak offered.

Eldam had come to like the young soldier, but he was still wary and frowned in uncertainty.

'Look, you've got to stay here. I'll get a better price, anyway. People like soldiers more than foreigners.'

Eldam saw he had no alternative. He began sifting through his clothing. On his bed he made two piles, one to keep, one to sell. When he had finished, he saw the former dwarfed the latter.

I must be more ruthless. Just one spare set. I can buy more once I'm settled in Rarland.

He transferred a couple more shirts, pantaloons and some undergarments. He only had two pairs of shoes as it was but, after some painful vacillation, he decided to part with the older pair. Reluctantly, he also put another jacket in the 'to sell' pile.

He began filling one of his bags which he was including in the sale, saddened that he was having to leave so much behind. The thought made him stop dead. Cherished things he was leaving behind. He quickly retrieved the jacket and searched frantically through the pockets, sighing audibly as his fingers closed around the tiny object. He pulled it out and stared at the miniature. The little face peered back at him, a mischievous look in her dark brown eyes. Taygret, the most cherished thing of all.

When Jak returned, Eldam was disappointed with the amount he brought but chose not to accuse the soldier of cheating him. At least now he should be able to afford the coach fare to Damlon from Tarrinsmouth, where his ship would eventually dock.

He planned to find his brother, Abren, in the Rarlish capital. He had an address for him, and he hoped his brother would not mind if he turned up on his doorstep without warning. If necessary, he was prepared to sleep on Abren's floor. Then he would need to write to their father and ask him to divert his allowance.

There was also the secret letter. He had not followed Beron's example by putting it in his shoe. That, he thought, was likely down to his late friend's penchant for melodramatics. He trusted it instead to the inside pocket of his coat. Having thus hidden it away from he knew not what threat, it seemed to exude a subtle, unnerving influence over him, like some enchantment from a children's fairytale. Eldam began to feel he was being watched.

Keep it hidden. Trust no one.

The sooner he got to Rarland's Foreign Department, the better.

As he waited for the port to reopen, Eldam filled much of his time going over his study notes. Especially those he had made during his work with Master Egring. It was a ground-breaking project, and it frustrated him he could no longer be at the heart of it. They had almost got to a point where they could test how the fire gas burned under controlled conditions. Perhaps he could recreate the experiments in Rarland, but the equipment Taygret's uncle had assembled was quite specialist. By the time Eldam had the use of another laboratory, if he could ever manage such a thing, Master Egring would probably have made significant advances. Assuming Amdris was not overrun by foreign troops.

Ten

Taygret

Taygret gazed out the coach window at the vast, seemingly endless expanse of flat fields. The sky was filled with low grey clouds that drizzled onto the dejected terrain. Her mood mirrored the depressing panorama. The elation she had felt at having wreaked vengeance on Master Rassish had gone. It had enabled her to make bright, trivial conversation with her three fellow travellers. But their interest in one another had faded, and now the bleak reality of her situation pressed down upon her like the lowering weather.

She looked at her bandaged hands. If Rassish died, then she was a murderer like him, and even if he survived, he would be hideously disfigured. Either way, the police would look for her sooner or later. She hoped that with the country facing an invasion and the authorities in Amdris preoccupied with rounding up foreigners, they would not have the resources to carry out a rigorous hunt.

She thought of Eldam. He seemed further away than ever. She could not write to him, she did not know where he was, and now he could not write to her either. So much loss in so short a time.

Such was the dark absorption that had overcome her she did not notice they had entered a town, and she was surprised when the jolting movements of the carriage came to a halt. She had decided to travel south, where it was warmer and away from the fighting in the northwest. When she bought her ticket to Orvikk, the coachman had told her they would not arrive until evening, so this must be a staging post.

She sighed, and a deep weariness came over her. She let the other passengers get out before hauling herself up from the seat and stumbling down the steps to the inn's courtyard. A firm hand caught her arm and steadied her. Taygret turned to find a large grinning face close to her own. She was about to thank the man, but then she felt his hand slip around her waist. She caught alcoholic fumes as he murmured,

'Allow me to assist you, Missy,' close to her ear.

Pulling away, she swung to smack hard on his unshaven cheek. Now considerably more alert, she lifted her skirt clear of the muddy yard and stomped towards the inn's open doorway. She did not glance back even when the sounds behind her clearly indicated the man she struck had lost his balance.

As she entered the smoky saloon, another man addressed her. With barely suppressed humour in his voice, he said, 'You must be very strong, Mistress. You've knocked poor Master Pontill clean off his feet.'

From the grubby apron he wore, Taygret guessed he was the innkeeper.

'Does that drunken, lecherous oaf work for you?' she demanded.

'Oh, Master Pontill is not in my employ, Mistress. He is our local magistrate.'

A ripple of apprehension ran through her. 'A magistrate?'

'Yes, and he is not a man to cross lightly. Most people here fear and hate him.' The landlord glanced out the window. 'It looks like he has gone to put on clean clothes, but you would be well advised not to be here when he returns. He is a very proud and vindictive man, and you made him look a fool.'

Taygret shrugged her shoulders. 'I'll just continue my journey to Orvikk,' she replied.

'I'm afraid it is not as easy as that. Pontill knows you were travelling on that coach. If he does not catch you here, he will have it stopped.'

'Then what am I to do?' Taygret asked, raising her arms in frustration.

He continued to gaze silently out of the window, watching as fresh horses were being harnessed to the waiting carriage. He was a tall man with short, sandy hair, and he stood with his head inclined to one side. It was a long moment, but when he finally turned back, Taygret saw a controlled anxiety in his eyes, and she knew he had chosen the courageous path.

'I will help you,' he said quietly. 'Come with me.'

He led her towards the back of the inn, down a short, narrow passage and into a small scullery where a young woman stood vigorously scrubbing a large pot on a wooden table. A jumble of similar vessels lay on the floor beside her, awaiting her attention. The innkeeper put a hand on her shoulder and bent his head towards her as he spoke.

'Kelie, I'd like to talk with you, please.' His voice still had the quiet, almost secretive, quality to it.

'Oh, yes, of course, Master Jaurey,' she replied, straightening her white cap.

She took off her apron and followed as the landlord led her and Taygret out into the corridor. When the three of them were standing in an alley at the rear of the inn, Master Jaurey turned to his employee.

'Kelie, this young lady needs our help. She has offended Master Pontill, and I fear for her safety.'

'What did she do?' asked Kelie, her green eyes wide with awe.

'Never mind that now,' he said. 'Take her to your house. She can stay there until we decide what to do next.'

As Kelie nodded her consent, the innkeeper spoke to Taygret. 'Go with Kelie. I will have your bags brought around. When Pontill returns, I will tell him you have gone to a relative's house in the town, but you didn't say where.'

'But I...' Taygret began.

'Go now. Pontill will be back, I assure you, and he must not find you here.'

The urgency with which he spoke made her start, and she found herself hurrying with Kelie along the alley, across a back street and down a lane of dirty puddles. The rain had stopped, but the sky warned her it might not be for long.

'Our house is not far,' Kelie said breathlessly as she glanced over her shoulder. 'It's not very big. There's just Mama and me.'

'Thank you,' Taygret replied. She really was grateful to these people so willing to help a complete stranger.

They came to a small cottage, one of a few straggling along beside the lane. Taygret noticed they were near the limits of the town. Farm buildings stood just a little further down on the opposite side.

Kelie pushed open the door and went in.

'Mama! Mama, it's me. I've brought someone,' she called out. Then turning to see Taygret hesitating on the threshold, she said, 'Come in, come in. This is where I live.'

'Thank you,' said Taygret again, feeling a little awkward as she stepped through the doorway.

It was quite dim inside, but it seemed to Taygret that there was only one room. A damp, musty smell hung in the air and something else, a sort of delicate vibrancy that seemed vaguely familiar.

'Take off your coat, Mistress. Would you like something to eat? We have some ham and some bread. We even have tea. I do quite well working at the inn.' Kelie was talking quickly and excitedly. This was obviously a big event for her. She was moving off to one end of the room, but she stopped and wheeled around.

'Oh! This is Mama,' she said, gesturing towards a large figure in a faded maroon dress slumped in an armchair. Then raising her voice, she said, 'Mama, this is a lady from the inn. I'm sorry, Mistress, I don't know your name.'

'Please, just call me Taygret.'

'Taygret, Mama, this is Taygret,' Kelie announced to the seated woman. Then lowering her voice once more, she whispered, 'Mama is blind.'

'Blind but not deaf,' muttered the old woman. It was apparent this was not the first time she had made this observation to her daughter, and yet there was no trace of irritation in her voice.

'Sorry, Mama,' said Kelie loudly as she turned and went off to prepare the food.

'Good day, Mistress,' said Taygret, taking a couple of steps forward, her feeling of awkwardness rising still further. Her mind had not yet caught up with this sudden twist her journey had taken.

'Good day,' replied the old woman, smiling. 'Please sit down. Just move anything that's in your way.'

Taygret lifted a pile of worn-looking clothes from the chair opposite Kelie's mother and looked around at a loss for where to put them. She eventually deposited them on the corner of a large table that stood between the chairs and the area where Kelie was working. Taygret sat down and, not knowing what to say, observed the woman in front of her. Her wide face was contoured by heavy wrinkles and framed by long, lank, grey hair. She held her chubby hands calmly in her lap. Her eyes were closed. Beyond her, Taygret saw an enormous bed.

Kelie returned carrying two plates with chunks of bread and slices of ham.

'So tell us what happened with Master Pontill,' she asked eagerly, handing a plate to her guest.

'Thank you. Well, as I got down from the coach, he… err… well, he got too close and touched me as a stranger shouldn't, and it was obvious he had been drinking.'

'Ooh. So what did you do?' Kelie had given the other plate to her mother and was now perched on a stool.

'Well, I slapped him, of course.'

On hearing this piece of news, Kelie gasped and stared at Taygret open-mouthed.

A little taken aback by Kelie's reaction, Taygret looked sheepishly at the floor and said, 'I think he must have fallen over... into the mud.'

At this, Kelie burst into a torrent of loud, joyous laughter.

Relieved by this response, Taygret herself chuckled. 'I was tired and irritable, and I didn't want to put up with any nonsense.'

'Oh, my Divine,' said Kelie through her mirth. 'I wish I'd seen it.'

Kelie's mother, a little smile on her face, said, 'So Master Jaurey at the inn sent you to hide here.'

'Yes. He seemed to think this Pontill would come back to look for me,' Taygret answered. She paused and grinned, then said, 'Once he has changed his pantaloons.'

Renewed gales of laughter broke from Kelie, and she clapped her hands in glee. Her mother's smile widened for a moment but then quickly faded.

'You must understand, my dear, that we in Peridere live in some awe of this man,' the old woman said. 'He is very powerful in this town. I think it likely he would want to have you arrested for striking him like that, no matter how much he deserved it.'

These words brought an instant sobriety into the room.

'Oh, sweet Divine, what shall we do?' said Kelie.

Before anyone could answer this question, however, a sharp rap on the door made the two younger women jump.

'Oh, my Divine, who is that?' Kelie whispered in horror as if she was afraid her careless laughter had brought Pontill and the police to the cottage.

'You had better go and find out,' her mother said mildly.

Kelie got to her feet, hesitated and glanced apprehensively at the other two women before walking slowly to the door. But instead of opening it, she stood hesitating once more. Another louder knock, and Kelie flinched and gasped.

'Who… who's there?' she called.

'Jaurey,' came the reply. 'I've brought Mistress's bags.'

'Oh, thank The Divine,' sighed Kelie as she hastily pulled the door open.

Master Jaurey came in and deposited Taygret's bags on the floor.

'Thank you very much.' she said, smiling at him.

'My pleasure, Mistress.' Then, turning to the older woman, he said, 'Mistress Hettrig, good day to you. I hope you will pardon this intrusion. I'm sure the young lady here has explained the circumstances.'

'Yes, she has, and I am perfectly happy to offer her what small hospitality I can. Has Master Pontill returned to the inn yet?'

'Yes,' Jaurey replied in a heavy tone. Taygret and Kelie exchanged nervous glances.

To Taygret, he continued, 'As I said, I told him you had gone to seek relations in the town, but you did not mention where they lived.'

'Was he angry?' Kelie asked.

'Yes he was, very angry. But he seemed to accept my explanation, so I think you are safe for now, Mistress, as long as you are not seen around the town.'

'If Peridere is not your true destination, then it would surely be best if you continued your journey as soon as possible,' observed Mistress Hettrig.

'There's not another public coach to Orvikk for three days, and I'm not convinced it would be safe for the young lady to take it even so,' replied Jaurey. 'But it's no great distance. I'll speak with Fredrik, my ostler, and see if it's possible to get you there sooner, perhaps avoiding the main road out of town.'

'I'm truly very grateful,' Taygret said to him. 'You seem to be taking a big risk on my account.'

'I'm more than happy to assist you, Mistress. Pontill has done me the disservice of choosing to drink at my inn. Now everyone assumes I am his man, and I have lost some of my old customers. Now, Kelie, you had best be getting back to work. There is still some clearing up to do.'

'Oh, my Divine,' cried the young woman. 'Nollit will kill me.' And without another word, she disappeared through the door.

Jaurey also took his leave in order to seek his ostler. Taygret and Mistress Hettrig belatedly began eating and for a while concentrated on the food Kelie had provided.

The older woman broke the silence.

'Do you have relations in Orvikk, Taygret?'

'No. I had to leave my home in Amdris when my uncle… died. So now I've decided to go to another town and look for work.'

'I'm very sorry to hear about your uncle. Are you all alone in the world then?'

'I have another uncle, but I don't like him. I would never live with him.'

'I see. What kind of work will you look for?'

'Well, my uncle, the one who died, arranged for me to have some tutors when I was younger.' She began to cry. 'He was very kind to me.'

She could say no more. She buried her face in her hands and let the sobs come and shake her. When the ferocity had sufficiently abated, she looked up to find Mistress Hettrig holding out a handkerchief towards her. The old woman seemed as tranquil as before.

'Thank you,' Taygret said as she accepted the handkerchief, the intensity of her emotion shifting to one of embarrassment. 'I am so sorry. You must think me a foolish young girl.'

'Not at all.' There was a marked emphasis on these words that brought more tears flowing from Taygret's eyes, but this time she kept her head up, gazing at the woman before her.

'Was your uncle's death rather sudden?' Mistress Hettrig continued. 'That is always particularly distressing for the family.'

'Yes, it was very sudden.'

There was a pause. Taygret realised she was holding her breath.

Then Mistress Hettrig said, 'Forgive me for saying this. I am a nosy old woman, and I will, of course, understand perfectly if you do not wish to say more, but it seems to me you think it was no accident.'

Taygret was shaking from both anger and fear, but there was something very curious about this blind, plump, aged woman. She had known her for such a brief period because of a freakish chance meeting, but Taygret felt doors of trust were opening within her. She had never come across anyone remotely like Mistress Hettrig before. It was as if she had found something of a kindred spirit and this unexpected, yet keen sense made her feel safe enough to say,

'I believe a rival murdered him. I knew I wouldn't be able to prove it, so I took matters into my own hands.'

Mistress Hettrig raised her eyebrows but otherwise seemed unperturbed. 'In what way?'

Taygret took a deep breath. 'I threw acid in his face.'

The older woman pursed her lips. 'You are clearly not a woman to be trifled with.'

'Just saying it like that... I'm shocked that I did such a thing.'

'But you don't regret it, I think.'

Taygret shook her head. 'You are very astute, Mistress.'

Her confession had lifted some of the weight from her heart, but she knew the old woman was right.

'So you have fled and plan to start another life in another town. But is there no young man in Amdris seeking your hand?'

'No, not at present.'

'Really? I would have thought half the men in the city would wait upon a girl as pretty as you.'

Before she could prevent it, the word 'but' escaped from Taygret's lips.

'Yes, I cannot see it in your face, but I can hear it in Master Jaurey's voice.' Taygret's puzzlement clearly amused the older woman.

Taygret blushed. 'There is someone, but he is Rarlish, and they have sent him back to Rarland. He said he would return after the war, but who knows when that will be, and how would he ever find me now?'

'Ah, I see,' Mistress Hettrig replied. 'And what is this young man's name?'

'Eldam, Eldam Medloe.' It raised her mood a little further just to say it.

'You obviously love him a great deal. Do you know where in Rarland he will have gone?'

Now there were more tears for Taygret to cope with. 'No, not exactly. He said he had a brother living in Damlon, but I don't have an address I can write to. It's an impossible situation.'

'Hmm.' Mistress Hettrig was clearly intrigued by this statement. 'If you think it is impossible, then it will be. But if you were to believe otherwise...'

Taygret slumped back into her chair and let the words sink into her. She breathed in the singular atmosphere of the room. She closed her eyes and savoured it. Then she understood why it seemed familiar. It was like when the peculiar thing appeared in her room last night. She opened her eyes and sat up, but before she could ask Mistress Hettrig about it, she heard footsteps outside. A loud knock shook the door.

'Come in, Master Jaurey,' the old woman called out in response.

As the innkeeper crossed the threshold, he had a smile on his lips.

'I'm pleased to say that I have arranged for Fredrik to take you to Orvikk by the back roads, Mistress,' he said. 'You'll be quite safe, I assure you, my man knows the country well, and you can trust him completely.'

'I am very grateful,' Taygret said.

'Yes, thank you for your efforts, Master Jaurey.' There was a curious, almost playful tone in Mistress Hettrig's voice as she continued, 'But you see there has been a change of plan. Our young friend now wishes to go to Rarland. Can you kindly arrange that?'

'Oh, indeed?' he said, scratching his chin. 'That'll require a little more consideration. The inn will get busy again soon. I suggest we sleep on it tonight and see if we can find a way of getting the young lady to Rarland in the morning.' Turning to Taygret, he said, 'I think it will be safe enough for you to stay in one of our rooms. I'll take your bags. Just come in through the back door when you're ready but don't go into the taproom. You'll find Kelie in the scullery or the kitchen. She will show you to the room.'

Taygret got up, put her plate on the table and went over to him. She stretched up and kissed him on the cheek. 'Thank you. Truly.'

Master Jaurey smiled. 'Like I say. I am perfectly happy to be of service, Mistress.'

'Taygret. I'm called Taygret.'

'Taygret. Very well then. I'll see you later.'

Alone once more with Mistress Hettrig, Taygret sat and summoned the courage to broach what she thought might be another dangerous topic.

'I had a very curious experience last night. I saw something in my bedchamber. I don't think I was asleep. But it was so peculiar. There was a ghostly figure, and it spoke to me. Said it wanted to be friends with me.'

'Indeed?' Mistress Hettrig did not seem in the least bit surprised. 'Tell me more about this figure.'

'It was dazzling. I couldn't tell if it was a woman or a man, but it was... beautiful.' She was crying again but carried on. 'It was not long after my uncle was killed. Perhaps it was trying to comfort me. I'm sorry, but there's something about this room... about you, that makes me think you might be able to help me make some sense of it.'

The old woman was silent initially, and Taygret felt that perhaps she should have kept it a secret. But then Mistress Hettrig said,

'Yes, I can help you with that. In fact, I can tell you exactly what it was. It was a mardene, a visitor from the spirit realm. They only choose to befriend one person at a time as far as I am aware and apparently it wishes to make you its companion in this world.'

'A mardene? I've never heard of them,' Taygret said.

'Very few people have. They are named after a mystic back in the time of the old Kimmikk Empire, Elonir Mardene. She was the first to write about them. You should know that The Faith considers belief in mardenes to be heresy. They have repressed knowledge of them very effectively. They will have anyone professing such beliefs placed under arrest. Some who have refused to recant have never been released.'

'Good Grace,' Taygret exclaimed. 'That's awful.'

'Yes, it is. Needless to say, you should tell no one you do not trust what you saw.'

'It said we might help one another. Why would it choose me to help it?'

'That I cannot tell you. It will no doubt explain further when it visits you again.'

A chill ran down Taygret's back. 'Have you…?'

'Yes.' The old woman smiled. 'As you discerned, a mardene is an occasional visitor of mine. I call him Wraith; it seems to amuse him. They have no gender, but I like to think of him as masculine. I cannot see him of course, but I can sense the brilliance you described.'

'Has he helped you in any way?'

'In small ways. If Kelie is not here, he sometimes helps me move freely about the cottage or out into the little garden we have at the back. But mostly we just talk. I was brought up in a convent, so we have some engaging conversations on religious matters. I have not told Kelie about him, incidentally. She can be a little… unguarded when talking to people.'

'The mardene showed me something. A brief glimpse of a man. I think it may have been Eldam's brother. I have never met him, but he looked a lot like Eldam.'

'Indeed? That is curious. Perhaps a mardene has also chosen this man, whoever he is.'

Eleven

Abren

When the sisters came back, Fran had hold of one end of a piece of rope, and Gitt had the other end in his mouth. They were both pulling furiously. She managed to drag him through the door and then crouched down. 'Now, keep quiet,' she said, tapping him on the snout with her finger.

Abren thought he ought to renew his acquaintance with the dog if he was going to spend the night with him, so he got up and held out his hand. Gitt dropped the rope and came to him, sniffing and panting. While he rubbed Gitt's head, Fran flopped into the chair he had vacated. He expected Jessel to take the other, but she went into the bedroom and emerged with a third chair for him. Abren had lit the fire to welcome them home, and Gitt went to sprawl in front of it, alongside Abren's boots.

'Good day?' he asked once they were all settled, keeping his voice down.

'Not bad. Pretty busy this afternoon,' Jessel replied.

'You seem to have a good business going.'

'We do all right. We've charmed some farmers and importers into dropping some of their produce to us on their way to the big market in town.' Jessel's face was flushed from her day's toil, but she seemed relaxed, as though him being there was nothing unusual.

'It means our goods are fresher than what most other stalls have,' Fran added. 'And it helps that we are so near the docks.'

Abren could see the sisters were proud of what they had going.

'You set all this up by yourselves?' he asked.

'Mah and dah got it started,' Jessel said. After a pause, she added, 'Before the plague took them.'

'I'm so sorry.' Abren realised his question had changed the mood in the room. After a few moments, he asked, 'Where do you keep your stall and stuff overnight?'

'We've got a lock-up on Gild's Hill. It's even got a stable for Tinker our donkey.'

'I'll get us something to eat,' said Fran, getting up.

Jessel rose as well. 'I'd better empty that pot.'

But her sister waved her back. 'No. I'll do it. You stay and entertain our guest.'

Abren thought that perhaps he liked Fran after all.

'You must be hungry,' Jessel said to him as she sat down again.

'A bit. That pasty helped, though.' He was very aware he was now alone with her.

'There's a range in the scullery downstairs. We share it with Morriline.' She shifted a little in her chair, then said, 'A peacey came round. Gave your name and a description. Said they're looking for you and asked if we'd seen you.'

'Oh.' The pleasant enjoyment of her company was quickly evaporating.

'The description wasn't very good. I said we see half a dozen men like that every day.'

'Someone else might have seen us coming here, though. I should leave tonight.'

'No one around here is going to help the peaceys unless there's a reward. Even then, I doubt it. They think we're all crooks. No one likes them. But you need somewhere to go. Have you thought of anywhere?'

'No. I think it will need to be out of town. I could easily get work here with all the building going on, but they'd probably find me, eventually.'

'Out of town' had a desolate ring for him. This town had Jessel in it.

'Haven't you got family somewhere?'

'My father wouldn't have me back. He thinks I tried to kill someone when it was an accident.'

'Really? How did that happen?'

'I lost control of a horse I was riding, that's all. I didn't mean to hurt anyone. Anyway, dah didn't believe me. He's convinced I tried to kill the man because... we were enemies.'

'Well, there must be places other than Damlon where they're building. Where you can get work.'

Abren did not want to think about other places. These were precious moments. Fran could return soon, but he found himself studying the pattern on the rug. This would not do.

'Jessel... I, err...'

'You've got sweet on me. Yes, I know. And now you have to leave, and you're afraid you won't see me again.'

He cleared his throat. 'Seems you can read my mind.'

'It's not difficult, actually.' She gave him a wan smile and leaned forward in her chair. 'Look, I like you too. If things were different, I think we would get along quite nicely together. But I don't want to see you in jail. Best if you go away somewhere. It needn't be too far, just 'til they forget about you. It's not like you've committed a murder. Then come back. I'll still be here.'

'But someone else might come along.'

'They might, but… Well, I'm quite choosy, really. Don't let it go to your head, but you're the first fella I've not told to get lost in a long while. You're a good man. I can see that. I wouldn't have agreed to meet you at the graveyard else.'

'I was afraid you thought me crazy when I told you about seeing the angel.'

'I'll admit that sounded a bit weird, but you don't seem like a crazy man to me.'

'I will come back, Jessel, I promise, but how will I know if it's safe?'

She considered for a few moments. 'Me and Fran'll keep our eyes and ears open. We visit our aunt out in Bornell most Lordsdays. It's only about an hour's walk from here. There's a faith house there, Saint Harnin's. Since you seem to like such places, I'll take a little stroll around the graveyard, after lunch, say at two o'clock. If I happen to meet you there, I'll tell you what's what. How does that sound?'

Abren considered the eel stew Fran produced the best thing he had ever tasted. A fresh lightness lifted him from inside. The optimistic feeling he had this morning had won out against the doubts he faced, at least for the present. If he knew Jessel would wait for him, then he had a future worth facing.

Despite having only a rug between him and the floor, and Gitt growling away in his sleep, Abren slept soundly that night.

The sisters had to be up very early to take a delivery from one of their bewitched farmers. They did not need anyone to wake them, Fran had informed him, because Jessel always knew when it was time for them to rise. Abren had merely smiled when he heard this. From what he knew of Jessel so far, it did not surprise him. He had determined to get up when they did and begin his journey out of town while it was still dark.

Fran and Gitt led the way downstairs. Jessel was about to follow when Abren touched her arm. She turned, and they stood regarding each other for a few moments. He wanted to savour and remember her face. He was holding his breath. Then she said,

'Look, if you're going to kiss me, get on with it. I really need to get going.'

As he trudged along, he held onto the memory of that kiss. It had been awkward and altogether too brief, but Jessel had favoured him with a smile and a peck in return. It, and the other memories he had of her, must sustain him in the days and weeks ahead until he might see her again.

His idea was to take the back streets and reach a canal that led out of the city. He reckoned it was the safest way to go, avoiding the main roads and turnpikes. He was grateful for a clear sky and a little light from a moon still more than half full. The morning chill kept his pace brisk. Few folk were yet astir in these smaller streets. It was too early even for dock workers. Abren was glad. He did not want to come across anyone who knew him. But he was aware the peace officers patrolled even at this hour. He kept his cap pulled low.

He came to Radial Road, one of the major routes into Damlon from the farmlands to the west. Lanterns hung from some of the buildings, sending feeble glows out into the street. A few wagons were already grinding their way in towards the central markets. Each had a man sitting at the front controlling the labouring heavy horses and a boy with a stick perched at the back to ward off any would-be pilferers. He wondered if any of them were going to rendezvous with Jessel and Fran. He felt a pang of jealousy.

He hurried across the road and took to the side streets once more. When he got to the canal, he had to go over a narrow footbridge to get onto the towpath, which would lead him in a straight line away from the metropolis. The odious smell creeping out of the water reminded him of his escapade in the sewer beneath the docks.

As he walked, the buildings dwindled, and after a while, open countryside surrounded him. He knew the waterway would eventually lead to a river at a village called Haston or Hoston, something like that. Beyond that was a mystery to him.

A rural hush gathered around him, a quietness that was never quite achieved in the city, even at night. But before long, he sensed the stillness was not complete. It was as if a presence hung about him. Not close, but unsettling nonetheless. He glanced behind, but he knew the path would be empty. Was it the angel? Could he discern it now in the silence of the country? Was it stalking him, displeased at his flight? It had told him it would require something of him. Did that mean it needed him to stay in Damlon to carry this out? But the angel had caused this. If it had never appeared, he would not have gone to speak to the priest.

He stopped, willing it to manifest. He wanted to confront it. It had told him it wanted an alliance, but where had it been when he needed help? He had only escaped arrest by hitting out and making a run for it. He thought of calling out a challenge but baulked at disturbing the quiet. Abren hurried on. Perhaps it was madness that pursued him after all.

Entering the village, he passed a few poor cottages. Several people were emerging from their doors and making their way towards what looked like a large mill. Men with their hands deep in the pockets of their coats, women with their shawls wrapped tight around them. They met workmates in the lane and huddled together as they walked, chatting amiably.

The mill stood near the junction of the canal and the river. Another footbridge led over the river to the opposite bank. Abren crossed it, then halted. He put his bag down and stood watching the mill's waterwheel slowly turning as the morning's light grew beyond it.

He wondered what his own workmates' reactions would be when they heard of his disappearance. The peace officers would have been to the docks by now and probably to his workshop. Everyone would know he was missing. Nad would be shocked to find out the peaceys wanted his friend. He would not believe the allegations. Jemmy would probably say he had always thought there was something shifty about him. It did not matter now; he was unlikely to see them ever again.

He shook himself out of his reverie and looked around. The land on this side of the river was flat and misty. He had to decide which direction to go. He hoisted his bag onto his other shoulder, took a long breath and turned upstream.

A while later, he had to make way for a man leading a horse. The horse was pulling a barge; a tarpaulin covered its mound of cargo. He considered asking what towns lay ahead and the prospects for employment, but a notion that he should preserve his anonymity, for now, stopped him. A stranger asking directions might leave a trail the peace officers could follow. So he merely exchanged a terse greeting with the man and continued on into the unknown landscape.

Twelve

Eldam

Eldam finally sailed out of Frenbar's battered harbour six days after his arrival in the town. He wondered why no other convoys of Rarlish citizens had come during that time. Was there another route the Mellians were using to avoid the vulnerable port? Or was it just that it was easier to round up students at a university and combing Amdris for individual foreigners took longer?

But these were trivial questions. The letter in his coat was weighing far more heavily on his mind. If it was as significant as Beren believed and needed to be kept secret then someone must want to intercept it, take it from him and perhaps not be too worried about how they got it. How would he react if someone confronted him and demanded he hand the letter over?

As he prowled restlessly about the deck of the ship, he fought the temptation to keep checking if it was still on him or if any of the crew were taking a particular interest in him.

At least, the early morning crossing proved smooth and uneventful. He was just beginning to relax a little when the ship entered the busy docks at Tarrinsmouth. The customs officials, having already encountered other homecoming students, let him pass after giving the contents of his bag a cursory inspection. Fortunately, they did not make him empty his pockets. But as he made his way along the quayside, his cautious, fretful nature reasserted itself. He glanced uneasily around, trying to spot if anyone was following him.

You fool. No one is going to have trailed you all the way here.

But there was a part of himself that remained unconvinced.

Amidst the noise of the dock, he heard a man cry, 'Coach to Damlon.'

'How much?' Eldam asked as he came up to the man.

'Ten silver.'

Eldam winced. That was more than he had expected. He did not want to spend all his remaining money on the fare.

'I can only afford eight,' he said.

'Right. I'll take you to Magshead for that. That's most of the way.'

Eldam had never heard of the place. He suspected it was nowhere near Damlon, yet he had no option but to agree. He thought Jak had probably fleeced him, and he now regretted changing his money with the ship's mate, who had claimed to give him a better rate than the bank in Tarrinsmouth. It felt like he might as well have 'naïve' tattooed on his forehead.

Magshead proved to be no more than a hamlet without so much as a tavern. Eldam watched bitterly as the coach left him behind. He asked an old man sitting outside a cottage how far it was to Damlon. The man took his pipe out of his mouth and pointed with it in the direction the coach had gone.

'Five miles to the suburbs, two more to the centre.'

Eldam was relieved. The coachman had not lied. He thanked the man, picked up his one remaining bag and strode out of the village. But as he walked along, it dawned on him that by the time he got to the centre of the city now, the government offices would almost certainly be closed. He would have to wait until tomorrow to rid himself of the burdensome letter.

It was indeed late afternoon by the time Eldam had passed the elegant villas fringing the city and entered a poorer district. These houses had no gardens, their front doors opening directly onto the road. Groups of ragged children stood watching him or played amidst heaps of rubbish.

He intended to seek out the tenement where Abren lived, but when he saw a thicket of masts towering above the houses at the end of a narrow street, he changed his mind. He was so near the docks, and at this hour, his brother should still be at work. When he reached the entrance, the tall iron gates stood open, but a warden emerged from a small lodge on the left and asked him his business.

'I've come to see my brother, Abren Medloe. He works here as a carpenter. Can you direct me to their workshop?'

The man nodded, a concerned expression on his long, thin face. 'Yeah. I thought you were going to say that. You look just like him. But he's not been in all week. I don't know why.'

'Not come to work for a week?'

'No. A couple of peace officers came asking after him. He's not been seen at his lodgings either, apparently.'

Eldam stared at the man, and a cold anxiety gripped him. 'Peace officers?'

'Yeah. They said he's gone missing and they're looking for him. That's all I can tell you. They might know more at the carpentry shop, though. The peaceys went there too.'

'All right. How do I get there?'

'Go down the main road here and take the second turning on the right, then first left. You'll see a sign saying "Carpenters and Joiners" just down there.'

As he hurried along the broad thoroughfare, Eldam passed carts and wagons of different sizes going in both directions, clattering along over the cobbles. Some were laden with goods, some were empty, some with one horse, others with two. A surprising number of people, nearly all men, were walking about, making the place as busy as a city centre.

So Abren's missing, and the peace officers are searching for him. What in Heaven's name has happened to you, brother?

He took the turns the gateman had described. Bulky, brick buildings with small windows rose up on either side of him. The workshop, huddled between two of these structures, was small in comparison. Inside he found half a dozen or so men hard at work. The one nearest the door looked up, irritation at the intrusion written on his chubby face, but when he saw Eldam, his expression changed to one of surprise.

'I'm Abren Medloe's brother,' Eldam said. 'I'm looking for him.'

'Well, he's not here,' said the man.

'I appreciate that. The fella at the gate told me he's not been in for several days. But I hoped you might know something that would help me find him.'

The man put down the saw he had been using, scratched his forehead and glanced at the other carpenters, all of whom had stopped working.

'The thing is, your brother never showed up for work on Raulsday morning. Peace officers came and said they wanted to find him. They said he'd just gone missing, but I don't know... I got the feeling there was more to it than that.'

Eldam's fears went up another notch. 'What do you mean?'

'Well, they asked if he'd been acting strange lately. I said no, he hadn't. He had his tools pinched, but he'd got them back almost straight away. The peaceys wouldn't say anything else, though. You could try going to the peace station and asking them about him. They might tell you more, seeing as you're his brother.'

Another of the carpenters stepped forward, a young-looking man with grey hair.

'Or... there's a market stall over on the high street. Sells fruit and such. Abe was friendly with a woman who works on it. Girl called Jessel. She may be able to help you.'

'Right, thanks. How do I get to the high street?'

'Oh, just follow the road straight ahead from the main gate, and it'll lead you right onto it.'

'Learn anything else about Abren then?' The gate warden asked when Eldam passed by.

'Not really, but I'll keep looking for him.' He hurried off before the man could question him any further.

He did not relish the idea of being interrogated by peace officers about his brother either, so he took the other carpenter's advice and found the market stall quickly enough. The two young women were busy serving people. Looking at the fruit, he realised he had not eaten since his hurried breakfast before boarding the ship in Frenbar. He put down his bag and began examining some pears for ripeness. After he had pressed his thumb into three or four, he glanced up to see one of the women staring at him, her arms folded. He remembered that although what he was doing was accepted practice in Mellia, people in Rarland frowned upon it. Embarrassed, he was going to tell the woman this but then thought better of it.

'Sorry,' he said. 'Are you Jessel?'

'Yeah,' she replied. 'And I think I know who you are.'

'We are very much alike.'

'He never told me he had a brother.' She ran a hand over her blond curls.

'Well, I've been abroad in Mellia for the last couple of years. I've just been to the docks hoping to find him, but they told me Abren's gone missing and that you might know more about it.'

The other woman was there now.

'Fran, this is Abren's brother,' Jessel said.

'Yeah, I can see that.'

'They also told me the peace officers were looking for him,' Eldam persisted.

Jessel pursed her lips and glanced at the one called Fran, who nodded to her.

'Come with me a minute,' Jessel said.

'Don't be long. We gotta start packing up soon,' Fran told her.

'Give me a couple of those pears before we go,' Eldam said, reaching into his coat. 'I'm starving.'

When Eldam left Jessel after their hurried conversation, he had much to worry about. Not only was his brother wanted by the peace officers, but he had also hit one whilst resisting arrest and gone into hiding; she did not know where. The woman had been vague concerning why they tried to apprehend him in the first place, said Abren had best explain it himself. She seemed fond of him, though. Was she his sweetheart? Eldam had not liked to ask. If she was, then circumstances had forced Abren and her apart just like Taygret and himself.

Taygret, will I really ever see you again?

With a deep sigh, he continued his journey. Not being able to locate his brother, his priority now was to find somewhere to spend the night. When he delivered the letter tomorrow, he decided he would ask for some financial compensation or at least a loan so he could rent a room somewhere, write to his father and think about what to do next.

His feet were reminding him that the shoes he wore were not intended for lengthy walks. Perhaps he should have kept the older pair after all.

He came to a little monument and sat gratefully on the low stone plinth. It supported a statue of someone, but Eldam was not interested in who it was. He pulled out a pear and bit into it. Juice ran down his chin as he relished the taste of the soft, sweet fruit.

A boy driving a hoop along with a stick caught his eye. Intent on his toy, the boy crossed the road in front of a horse, and the rider shouted at him. The lad ignored the tirade and continued skipping onto the far side of the street. But there, Eldam saw, to his dismay, stood a man in a long, grey overcoat staring straight at him. He felt as much as he saw the man's eyes upon him, fixing him from under the broad rim of his black hat.

Panicked thoughts raced through Eldam's mind. Was it some government agent somehow aware of the letter he carried? If so, which government? He knew nothing about the letter's content, only that Beron had implored him to keep it secret.

Maybe I could cope if confronted by one man, like I did with that fisherman in Frenbar. But what if he's got an accomplice or two? Where there's one, others might lurk nearby, like cockroaches.

Or was it a peace officer in disguise, mistaking him for Abren?

He finished the pear and, getting up as casually as he could, headed off toward the city centre. He was limping now from the rubbing his feet had taken, and his bag was beginning to feel very heavy.

Stumbling on, he did not dare to look back but desperately searched the way ahead for some sort of refuge.

Almost immediately, he saw a building with several barrels dumped outside it. He hoped this meant the place was an inn or a tavern. As he got nearer, he could see just how rundown the place was. In fact, it was so shabby that, if it were not for the barrels, he might have believed it was not open for business at all. Dirt covered the walls and windows. A rotted wooden sign that had apparently fallen from its bracket overhead lay propped beside the door. On it, Eldam could just make out a dog depicted with some sort of bird in its mouth.

Eldam tried the door, but it was locked. The barking that replied to his knock was deep and loud, telling him the dog inside was large and fierce. He had an inordinate fear of dogs. When he was a young boy growing up on the country estate, he had innocently tried to play with a staghound and got bitten for his trouble. He had never quite gotten over it.

Why must everyone in Rarland own a damn dog?

'Clear off. Can't you see we're closed?' It was a shrill female voice shouting above the noise of the dog, but not from behind the door. The voice came from overhead. Eldam staggered back a few paces and looked up. A woman had appeared at a window on the upper floor. She was rubbing one eye in her round, flushed face.

'Please, I need to rest… and eat,' he called up to her.

The woman looked as if Eldam had disturbed her from a nap. Her long brown hair fell in dishevelled waves to her broad shoulders. But after surveying him for a couple of moments, she said, 'Hang on then,' and disappeared inside.

While he waited, he risked a glance toward the man in the grey overcoat. He did not appear to have moved, but

Eldam still sensed he was watching him from under his oversized hat.

This letter had better be worth all this bother, Quist, he thought sourly.

As unwelcoming as it was, the tavern at that moment seemed a blessed haven. Although walking the last few miles into the city had taken a toll on his feet, it meant he should be able to afford a meal at a place like this. But then, would he have enough left for a bed in one of the city's notorious dosshouses? He did not want to sleep rough and be prey to anyone intent on molesting him.

He hastened back to the door and, hunching close, he could hear from inside the sounds of a dog being dragged reluctantly away, followed by the clinking of keys.

'Where have you walked from then?' the woman asked as Eldam limped past her.

'Magshead,' he replied, looking around. The large room was every bit as squalid as the outside. A variety of rickety-looking chairs and stools were scattered amongst a few equally decrepit tables of different sizes. Dusty, brown plates and jugs stood on a couple of high shelves. The stone floor had obviously not been swept for some time and Eldam saw several small bones lying under one of the tables. He hesitated, trying to pick a spot which was inconspicuous but afforded a good view of the door.

'Peaceys after you, are they?'

'No... No, of course not.' Startled by the question, Eldam chose a seat more hastily than he would have liked.

'Rum, gin or ale?' She stood uncomfortably close.

'Er... do you not have coffee?'

'Not yet, we don't.'

'Ale then, please.'

To Eldam's relief, she retreated into the darkness that enshrouded the back of the tavern. The place stank of alcohol and grime, and its mistress seemed a condensed version of the whole in this respect.

He tried to compose himself and assess his situation, but fatigue was creeping over him. His head was swimming, and his feet were aching. He wanted to take off his shoes, but he felt vulnerable enough as it was. The woman had relocked the door so his sinister observer could not get to him for now. He had a seat from which he could see whoever came in once the place reopened, but he was too near the door. Anyone entering would immediately see him.

He was looking around for a better spot when the door at the back of the room swung open. But instead of the woman coming with his ale, it was a man in a brown waistcoat, the large white tails of his shirt hung from beneath it almost to his knees. His hair was long, grey and greasy and stuck out at bizarre angles for want of combing.

Unfortunately, the man's entrance released the dog, which was indeed large, from its remote confinement, and it bounded up to where Eldam was sitting. Contrary to his expectations, however, it did not attack him or even bark but began sniffing energetically around his legs. Eldam broke out into a cold sweat as he tried his best to ignore the animal.

'Welcome to the Dog and Duck Tavern, my friend,' pronounced the man grandly. 'There's the dog, now where's the duck, you wonder.'

'The dog ate it.' said the woman coming up behind with a tankard in her hand. Both she and the man burst into a raucous cackle.

Eldam grimaced. 'Oh, I see,' he muttered.

'My name's Denry Hatshal, at your service, and this here's my wife, Mollis. Now what can we be getting for you today? We don't open proper for another hour, but we can make an exception for a weary traveller like y'self. We've got some nice salt beef cooked up fresh this morning or cold ham or a good strong cheese.'

'No duck though,' put in Mollis, but Eldam's obvious lack of humour quickly stifled any further mirth on the part of his hosts.

'The salt beef sounds fine... Thank you,' Eldam stammered, feeling disconcertingly at the mercy of these two rather peculiar people. He was relieved when the Hatshals withdrew, dragging their over-familiar dog with them.

Eldam returned his gaze to the tavern's front door. He should be safe for the next hour, at least. He hoped that when he left after finishing his meal, he would find the figure in the large overcoat had gone, assuming the man did not come in to accost him when Denry and Mollis opened their odious premises to the public again.

And he still had to find a place to sleep.

Thirteen

Taygret

In a one-room cottage on the outskirts of Peridere, several conspirators gathered for a conference.

'Fredrik has agreed to accompany you,' Master Jaurey told Taygret. 'He knows why you want to get to Rarland, and I can spare him for a few days. I've hired two good horses from a local farmer with the money you gave me.'

'That's wonderful, thank you. I nearly didn't pack my riding breeches. I'm glad I did now.'

'I've got a couple of old saddle bags you can have in exchange for your portmanteaux if you're willing, but they won't hold as much.'

'Never mind. I'll give Kelie any clothes I can't take, if she'll have them.'

'I'm sure she'll be delighted,' Mistress Hettrig said, smiling.

'I recommend you travel to Gennlar,' Jaurey continued. 'It's a sizable port about fifty miles east of here. I think if you have any chance of getting across to Rarland, you will need to find smugglers willing to take you. People who won't scruple over the law prohibiting Mellians fleeing the country.'

'Smugglers? How would I get on board their ship? Will I need to be rowed out from some lonely cove in the middle of the night?'

'No. I think not. They usually hide their contraband amongst legitimate cargo loaded from a dock, I believe. The nighttime visit to a lonely cove would be on the other side. But they'd probably drop you off at a Rarlish port along with their lawful goods afterwards.'

'I suggest you and Fredrik pose as a married couple holidaying on the coast,' Mistress Hettrig said. 'Then you can make discreet enquiries about crossing the bay. Perhaps you should choose another first name as well as Fredrik's last name.'

'What is his last name?' Taygret asked. She realised that the old woman knew that attempting to emigrate was not the only crime she might be accused of.

'Draillis,' Jaurey informed her.

'All right. Then from now on, I'll be Linna Draillis.'

They set out late in the morning on the day after Taygret's arrival in Peridere. At first, Fredrik avoided the lanes to ensure they did not run into Master Pontill or anyone else who might be on the lookout for the harridan who had slapped him. They traversed fields and rode through woods under a dull, metal-coloured sky that threatened more rain.

Despite all that had happened to her and the bitter grief lurking just below the surface of her mind, Taygret felt exhilarated. She was going to Eldam. She did not have to wait in crippling uncertainty for him to return to her. Even her hands felt better after Kelie had re-bandaged them.

They mostly rode in single file with Fredrik leading the way, but when they reached a wider track, Taygret drew alongside the ostler so they could talk a little.

'I really appreciate you doing this,' she said, thinking she could not express her gratitude often enough.

He looked across at her and grinned. 'It's not every day I get to go on an adventure like this.'

He's not bad looking, she thought. He had high cheekbones and kindly, hazel eyes. His hair was the same dark colour as hers and nearly as long, but he kept it tied back in a ponytail.

'In Amdris, they were beginning to call up young men to fight against the foreign armies in the north,' she said. 'I hope you never have to go.'

'Yes, I heard about that. They haven't come recruiting in Peridere yet. But I might just volunteer, anyway. I wouldn't like to see foreigners come and restore the monarchy. I think we should have the right to decide who is in charge here.'

'Oh, yes, of course. I agree.' She had assumed young men would not want to go to war, but then she recalled what her uncle had said about people being willing to die defending their homeland.

'It's such a new thing, isn't it?' she went on. 'A country without a king. I suppose it's no wonder other kings are afraid they might get kicked out as well.'

'Yes, that's the way of it, I believe.' He smiled again. 'Long live the republic.'

Taygret nodded. 'Long live the republic.' Then she frowned and said, 'But now I'm trying to leave. You don't think I'm a traitor, do you?'

'No. If I loved a Rarlish woman who'd been sent back, that would change things for me too. I'm sure I'd want to go there and find her.'

I will get there, she told herself. *I will.*

When the rain eventually came, they stopped for the night in an isolated barn. As they led their horses in through the large doors, Taygret saw a stack of hay against the back wall but Fredrik also noticed a small pile of wood in one corner.

'This is lucky,' he said. 'We can feed the horses and have something soft to sleep on. This wood is dry and will make a nice little fire but we'll have to watch out the sparks don't land on the hay.'

'I don't know how to light a fire, our maid always did it. So I'll be the ostler for tonight,' Taygret said.

As she saw to their mounts, Fredrik got a little blaze going, and they huddled by it munching on some roasted chicken legs the inn had provided as emergency rations.

'I'm impressed you know how to look after horses,' Fredrik said. 'Didn't you have a groom in Amdris?'

'We kept our horses at some nearby stables and there were boys there who tended them, but uncle insisted I learn how to do it. He told me that if I rode a horse, I should know how to care for her.'

'It sounds like your uncle was a wise man.'

'Yes, he was.'

They ate in silence for a while and Taygret gazed at the pile of dull yellow stalks as the light from their fire flickered over them.

'There's not very much hay in here really, is there? Why is that?' she asked.

'The farmer will have used most of it up during the winter to feed all his own animals.'

She thought of how little she knew about life in the country. A whole different world where people toiled to provide the food she and Linna had bought at the market and took home to eat.

She yawned. 'I'm sorry. I'm just a lazy city girl and all this travelling and thinking about labouring on a farm has made me feel quite tired.'

Fredrik chortled. 'So would your ladyship care to retire for the night?'

'Yes, please,' she said, smiling.

Fredrik stamped out the fire and they made up two small heaps of hay at a respectable distance apart before settling down fully clothed. Taygret was soon asleep.

When she awoke, it was still dark. She lay for some time with the coarse texture of straw against her face; the chill creeping remorselessly into her bones. Rain pattered on the tin roof, and the wind whispered along the eaves.

When the pattering stopped, she abandoned any hope of more sleep. Getting up, she wandered, shivering, into a nearby field, breathing in deep lungfuls of the cold air, her boots kicking through the long, wet grass. She was glad she was wearing breeches and not a skirt, it would have got soaked. The thought reminded her of when she had to change her dress after a secret kiss with Eldam in the laboratory. She had tried to fool her uncle about it but he had caught her out. The bittersweet memory brought a little smile to her lips. How her life had changed since then.

The wind blew her hair around her head, and the clouds slid away. After a while, she stopped and gazed up into the great star-strewn mystery revealed above her. The moon appeared and gave the land its soft silvery light. With her arms wrapped protectively about her, she stood motionless, peering into the unending sky.

'I shall find my way to you somehow, Eldam, I promise,' Taygret whispered to the stars as if they could pass her message on until it reached him.

Then suddenly, the tender light of the heavens was eclipsed by an altogether brighter glow.

'I certainly hope that you shall, brave lady.'

Taygret spun around.

'Mardene,' she gasped, squinting in the glare.

'It is a pretty enough name. I do not dislike it.'

'But… what is it you want with me?'

'As I said previously, I want us to be friends. You heard how one of our kind has befriended that old woman. I would do likewise with you if you wish.'

'Why me, though?'

'You have a certain receptivity. A gift, if you like. It is very rare among humans. And it seems to me you are in need of friendship.'

'That's kind of you.' She hesitated, then said, 'That man, the one you showed me before. Was it Eldam's brother?'

'Indeed, it was. He can also commune with our kind, but he may need our help. Do not be concerned about this for now, however. You must first complete your journey. I will assist you when I can.'

'You can do that?'

'Yes. I can sometimes influence people, even those who are not gifted. That innkeeper was not disposed to help you initially.'

'Oh… Well… Thank you.'

'You are most welcome. Farewell for now, dear Taygret. We will speak again before long.'

'Farewell,' she murmured as the light evaporated.

She stood, alone again in the vastness of the night, overawed, bewildered, her body shaking.

My Divine, she thought. *I'm a heretic.*

She began walking slowly through the half-lit world. The visitation had left her feeling pleasantly enheartened. She felt as though the raw edge of her grief had been soothed a little, and as she looked about her, it was as if the world, too, had changed for the better. She saw shadowy bushes and trees, the old ramshackle barn where Fredrik still slept, mounds of black mud, a useless, rusting old plough, but to her, all of it seemed delightful, beautiful even.

For how long she just wandered and gazed, she paid no heed, but when the pre-dawn light invaded the land, the spell started to fade, slipping gently away. But the feeling of buoyant optimism still lingered.

'Taygret?'

She started at the sudden, anxious word. For what seemed an age, she had been in a place where there were no words, and Fredrik's bemused intrusion shocked her. She realised she must appear rather odd, she certainly felt very odd and for a few moments, it was as though she hung in a shadow realm between nighttime and dawn, between the magical and the mundane.

'Are you well?' Fredrik asked, coming up to her.

'Yes, yes, I'm fine. I just couldn't sleep. It's so cold.'

Fredrik took off his coat and put it around her.

'Remember, you must call me Linna now,' she said.

'Oh, yes. I'm sorry. I'll relight the fire.'

As she watched him working with the hay and tinderbox, she felt the chill receding already, warmed by love and gratitude towards all those who had helped her, were still helping her.

As Taygret allowed her horse to carry her along the road towards Gennlar, she listened to the different sounds the hooves made as they trod—mud, stones, twigs, earth, leaves. She recalled the times she had been out riding with her uncle and some of the other pleasant memories she had of him.

'Farewell, uncle,' she whispered. 'Thank you for everything you did for me.'

She was roused from her ruminations when she and Fredrik came up behind a cart stacked high with a pile of potatoes. The sight conjured an image of some cooked and streaming on a plate. It made her feel rather hungry for a hot meal.

When they came alongside the front of the cart, she said to the man holding the reins, 'Good day to you, sir. How far is it to Gennlar?'

He smiled at her. 'Why, you're nearly there. You'll see it when you reach the top of the next rise.'

'Thank you. Do you know a pleasant inn there?'

'There's several. The Blue Bay is a good, cheap place to stay, so I've heard. Have you come far?'

'From Amdris.'

'Amdris? I've never been there, but I've heard it's a great city.'

'Well, yes, it certainly is that.'

'Tell you what, whenever I'm in town, I stay with my brother-in-law,' the farmer informed her. 'He has a large house. I'm sure he'd be happy to accommodate you and your husband for the night. I would very much like to hear about Amdris. Niklay would be interested too, I know.'

Taygret glanced at Fredrik, who merely shrugged and nodded.

'Very well, thank you. We accept your kind offer, if you think your brother-in-law would not object.'

'Oh, no. There's only him and a servant since my sister died, and he's always glad of some company. He enjoys meeting new people. But I should warn you, Niklay is an artist. You may find him a little… eccentric.'

'Ha! My life has been more than a little unusual lately, so we'll likely get on perfectly well.'

The farmer told them his name was Cass Malling, and once he had sold his potatoes, he showed Taygret and Fredrik where to stable their horses. Then he led them down a narrow street just off the market square. After a short walk, they came to an old timber-framed building three storeys high. Each level jutting out a little beyond the one below.

'Good Grace,' gasped Fredrik. 'Is that your brother-in-law's house? He must be a very successful painter.'

'Niklay inherited the house. He makes a modest income from his landscapes. You can judge their merit for yourselves.' The tone of Cass's comments left Taygret in little doubt as to his own opinion.

The farmer rapped vigorously on the door, and after a brief interval, it was opened by a short, rosy-cheeked woman who ushered them into the presence of Niklay, the artist of Gennlar. When he rose to greet them, Taygret saw he was not tall but cut a rather gaunt figure. He was perhaps about forty years old and immaculately dressed in matching powder blue tailcoat, pantaloons and waistcoat.

'Cass! Welcome, welcome. And you've brought company too. How splendid.'

The interior of the house was every bit as grand as its exterior. Large, wing-backed chairs and small, elegantly carved tables sat upon a richly coloured carpet, beneath an intricately moulded, white ceiling. Taygret felt distinctly travel-worn in these somewhat luxurious surroundings. But their host seemed to be most attentive to their needs.

'Would you care for some refreshment, or would you like to wash off the dust first?' he said.

They chose the latter priority, and the servant settled them into a comfortable room on the first floor. Taygret carefully took the bandages off her hands. She was pleased to see they were healing well but that the cuts would probably leave her with some scars.

When they were ready to rejoin the others, a delicious smell of roast pork pervaded the house. The brothers-in-law plied Taygret with questions while they waited for their meal. Niklay was keen to hear her describe the art galleries and museums in Amdris, while Cass asked about the livestock markets and auctions. Fredrik had never been to Mellia's capital city either, but the two local men were so intrigued by what Taygret had to tell them they did not notice he was largely silent.

By the time the food was ready, she was able to shift the conversation onto other topics. The artist and his lifestyle genuinely intrigued her. There seemed little evidence of the eccentricity Cass had warned may characterise his brother-in-law's behaviour, apart from insisting they use first names under his roof.

'Cass told us you paint landscapes,' she said.

'Well, seascapes mostly. The coastline here is very picturesque in places. I have a local patron who is fond of my work.'

'That's fortunate.'

'Yes. But I would really like to paint portraits. It would attract wealthier clients.'

'What's preventing you?' Fredrik asked.

'Well, put quite simply, I would need to practise. It has been many years since I painted a person. I'm looking for someone to sit for me.' He paused and gave Taygret a curious, searching look. 'May I make a suggestion?'

She raised an eyebrow. 'You want to paint me?'

'Well, since you are here for a little holiday and have yet to find lodgings, I could offer you the hospitality of my home in return for you being my subject. You would only need to sit for a couple of hours a day.'

'Well, I suppose that would be an acceptable arrangement,' she said. 'What say you, husband?'

Fredrik nodded. 'Yes. I'll visit a tavern or two while you do that, my dear,' he said with a grin. 'Sample the local wine. Perhaps meet some sailors and talk about their life at sea. I'd be most intrigued to hear their tales.'

When they retired to their room for the night, Fredrik picked up one of the pillows.

'No,' Taygret said. 'We'll share the bed. I'll not have you sleeping on the floor.'

'But, I…'

She smiled at his embarrassment. 'I've thought about this. Master Jaurey told me you were trustworthy and I've seen nothing to make me believe otherwise.' She took the pillow from him and replaced it.

'Thank you,' he said, 'If you're quite sure…'

'Yes. Now blow out the candle so we can get undressed.'

Fourteen

Abren

As Abren walked, it seemed the waterways sought to confuse him. At first, there was just the river, then there was a canal running alongside the river, and then they joined again only to part further on. He doggedly followed the towpath. He had to cross the canal/river on a couple of occasions, but he kept faith that it would eventually lead him to a town where an experienced carpenter with his own tools could find work.

The sun ascended, and the spring air warmed. He realised he had largely forgotten about nature. He stopped and sat on the bank, watching a green dragonfly. It darted and hovered over the blue water that gleamed beneath a clear sky, free of the city's fumes. This side of the canal was maintained as a limb of industry, the towpath kept clear of growth to facilitate the hauling of trade goods. The water itself drifted languidly along, unaware of the grand enterprise it had been co-opted into. Trees clustered on the far side, life spreading over their branches.

He ate a peach from the store of food the sisters had packed for him. He wondered how far he should go. Far enough to be out of the reach of the Damlon peace officers but near enough to keep his rendezvous with Jessel. He was not exactly sure where Bornell was. She had given him a vague idea, and he had assured her he would find it. She was the one golden thread in the dark fabric that life had woven for him in the last few days. He was tempted to imagine where that thread might lead, but he resisted it; his life had been thrown into too much turbulence. She had given him hope. He would cleave to it in its unembellished form.

He continued on. The canal and river maintained their peculiar flirtation. Sometimes close, sometimes far apart, sometimes conjoined for a short stretch. He passed other barges from time to time, and he judged it to be nearing midday when he thought it would be safe to ask a bargeman what lay ahead.

'Well, there's Hoddon not far from here,' he replied, pointing across the canal. 'But that's but a small place if it's work you're after. Then there's Faren, that's a bit bigger. Or there's Marfryd. That'd be your best bet. It's a market town.'

Abren had fallen in step with the man as he walked along beside his white-faced horse, even though he was going back the way Abren had come.

'How far are these places, friend?' He regarded this man as a friend, being so helpful to him on his dour, solitary trek.

The man drew a large, red handkerchief out of his jacket and wiped his forehead, pushing his brown leather cap to the back of his head.

'Faren's about a two-hour walk from here along the canal, and Marfryd's another hour further on. Although if it's Marfryd you decide on, you could save yourself an hour by cutting across the heath on the other side of Hoddon.'

'Thank you kindly.' Abren stopped and watched the barge slide slowly past him.

'Most welcome, and good luck to you,' the bargeman called over his shoulder.

Abren returned the friendly wave from another man standing on the stern of the vessel and continued his journey somewhat heartened. He did not fancy his chances crossing the heath, so he continued to put his trust in the towpath.

A town Abren supposed was the one named Faren by the bargeman eventually came into view on the opposite bank of the river. He wanted to press on to Marfryd, but he was aware of a grating thirst and decided to seek a pump in the town. He had declined Jessel's offer of a flagon of cider, reckoning the weight of his tools was enough to carry any distance. But after going over a bridge in search of drinking water, the first building he came upon changed his mind. The sign proclaimed it to be the Faren Tavern. He could not recollect drinking ale at this hour before, but seeing the place was open, he was tempted and went in.

After a morning beneath a wide, bright sky, the interior immediately engulfed him in darkness. Everything appeared to be made of black wood; the furniture, the counter, even the walls were lined with it. As his eyes recovered their precision, Abren made out two men standing at the bar. They eyed him warily as he advanced towards them. The landlord came into view, but his gaze was no more friendly than those of his patrons.

'Afternoon,' Abren saluted them. The barkeep at least managed a nod of acknowledgement. 'What's your best ale?'

'Draught Porter,' replied the landlord and began drawing it before Abren could say anything in favour or against the beverage. He put down his bag and watched as the liquid filled the glass. It was the same colour as the ubiquitous wood, but the dryness in his throat made him slide his tongue across his lips.

'Four copper,' said the tavern keeper.

Abren paid and drank a long draught of the refreshing brew. If the three men had been conversing before his entrance, they did not resume it. So when he replaced his glass on the counter, he said, 'I'm looking for work.'

The eyebrows on the barkeep's thin face rose slightly, but they were the only aspect of his expression that responded to this announcement.

'What can you do?' he asked.

'I'm a carpenter,' Abren told him.

That brought rather more animation to his features, and he glanced at the other two customers before asking, 'Can you mend chairs and tables and the like?'

'Certainly.'

'Well, that's a fine thing and no mistake.' He appeared to be attempting a grin. 'You see, we had some… entertainment in here last night.'

One of the other men snorted. 'You could call it that, Ross, to be sure.'

'Three men came in already drunk half an hour before closing,' the landlord explained. 'One of them starts having a go at one of our regulars, Dan Garred. Something about a woman, I think. Anyway, first it was pushing and shoving, then punches. His mates joined in, then Dan's, and before the peaceys arrived, two tables and five chairs got broke.'

'Not something you expect to see on a Raulsday night,' commented the customer who had spoken earlier.

'Anyone badly hurt?' Abren asked.

'Nah, they were too far gone to hurt each other, only the furniture. Anyway, I'm thinking you're not local so if you need somewhere to stay while you're looking around for a job, you can have our spare room for nothing if you like in return for mending the tables and chairs. You can eat with us and all, and if you do a good job, I'll throw in a couple of silvers as well. How's that sound?'

'I'll do a good job. Show me the broken furniture, and I'll tell you how long it will take. Board and lodging would be very welcome, thank you. I'd prefer it if we agree a price on top of that in advance if you're happy with my work, of course.'

Ross regarded him, his brow furrowed. In the interval, the man who had not yet spoken entered the conversation.

'Got an idea,' he said in a slow, reedy voice, 'that old Dotty needs a sideboard mending.'

'I reckon you'd get a fair bit of work in the town if you're good,' put in the other customer. 'The only decent carpenters are over in Marfryd.'

'Wait on,' said Ross. 'He's got to fix my tables and chairs first.'

As he lay in bed that night, Abren tried to come to terms with the changes that had overturned his life in such a brief space of time. He had inspected the wrecked furniture and made a list of the materials he would need to get it back into working order. Ross had given him an advance to cover the cost upon Abren agreeing to his tools being kept in a locked cupboard to which only the landlord had a key. Ross told him he would need to go to Marfryd to find a timber merchant, although glue and varnish were available locally.

He had sat with the family for their afternoon meal which they took whilst the tavern was closed. Ross, his wife Martia, ten-year-old Tam and Judi, who was eight. Martia was very welcoming and convivial, calling Abren heaven-sent. Judi was shy and fidgeted a lot, earning rebukes from both her parents, whilst Tam offered only scowls from beneath his shock of curly chestnut hair. Abren had smiled pleasantly at them all.

He had told them he had grown weary of the dirt and noise of Damlon and, having a good trade, thought he would try his fortune elsewhere. Martia had declared this very sensible. She had apologised for the smallness of his room, but its whitewashed walls were at least free of the dark panelling that ensnared the ground floor. Abren guessed it was intended to accommodate a servant, containing as it did only a little bed and a lockbox, but he did not care. In his straitened circumstances, it would do him fine.

Now in solitude once more, he assessed his situation. If the customer was right about work being available in the town, he might get by here for a while. Once he had restored the tavern's furniture, perhaps Ross would rent him the room for a longer period. When would he risk a rendezvous with Jessel? Not this Lordsday perhaps. It would only be a week since the events at the priest's residence. He would have to wait at least another seven days. Such rotten luck. Just as he had found a woman he really liked and who said she liked him, he had to run away and could not see her.

He could not see her. He had looked all over the graveyard, and she was not there, but something was stirring amongst the headstones. Shadowy shapes flitted on the edge of his vision, vanishing when he turned to see what they were.

He retreated towards the faith house, perhaps he would find her inside. Pushing open the huge wooden doors, he staggered for a few paces, then stopped, adjusting to the murky interior. He heard murmuring, and a metallic clinking, and then a thin wail sent a startled shudder through his belly.

He began to make out people, half naked and impossibly thin, and chains. Hands suddenly seized his arms, pulling, dragging. He heard another alarming howl. This time it was his own.

He awoke, gasping and sweating. The nightmare was over, but the waking horror had just begun. In the confines of the narrow room, the angel's brilliance was even more intense. If there had been coloured lights, he had missed them. The presence was almost looming over him. Its beauty still called up an instinctive admiration but other emotions overwhelmed it now. Would he never be free of this menace?

He sat up, squinting. The figure drew back a little, and its luminance lost some of its strength. Abren stood, and they faced one another, one glowing pure white, the other in a drab, pale nightshirt. Abren wanted to scream at it, but others slept nearby. Even so, his voice spat resentment.

'I'm here because of you. I was forced to run because…'

The awareness that the angel knew this already stopped his tirade.

'You are where I want you to be,' it said.

Abren clenched his fists. 'You told me I would profit from an alliance with you. But I'm wanted by the peace officers, and I've lost my home and my job.' *And Jessel?* But he kept that thought unspoken.

'It is well that you learn to be elusive. Here you have work and lodgings. You are out of harm's way for now. I have guided you a little.'

'Guided me? How?' He was closer to it than on previous occasions, but its features remained difficult to fathom.

'In small ways. The thirst.'

'Why should I learn to be elusive? What do you want from me?'

'Patience, Abren. It was a nice lie you gave the people here, but are you not truly pleased to be out of those filthy streets for a while? I know you miss the girl, but you should be able to return soon enough. It is important that you do. All will be well before long. Trust in me. I will look after you.'

The darkness that prevailed once the angel had gone was profound and, for Abren, deeply disquieting. If it had sought to reassure him by its appearance, it had failed. It had claimed to guide him, to have given him the thirst that brought him here. If that were true, it seemed more like the manipulations of a mischievous puppeteer.

It also knew of his feelings for Jessel. The idea that even the most intimate regions of his life were perpetually haunted by a spectre whose motives were dubious at best made him shiver with rage and apprehension, but both were blighted by a sense of helplessness.

It is well that you learn to be elusive.

Did the angel intend for him to commit some act that meant he would always need to be in hiding? How would all be well if that were the case? Despite its declaration that it would look after him, Abren lay for hours with the stifling conviction that he was in fact cursed.

The next morning, Ross borrowed a small cart and a donkey from Jon Daws, a regular at his tavern. Jon had little use for them, having given up milk delivering. The donkey looked due for retirement itself, but Abren gratefully accepted the loan and set out for Marfryd to buy the few pieces of timber he needed to replace those too splintered to be reused.

Following the tavern keeper's directions, his way took him back across the river before turning west towards the market town. A light breeze brought drizzling rain, but Abren paid it little heed beyond pulling up the collar of his coat.

He had no more thoughts to give to the enigma of the angel, having spent them all during the long, lonely night. He was no nearer to fathoming the spectre's intentions or what he might do about them.

As he watched the back of the forlorn-looking donkey pulling him along, his mind gravitated to Jessel. He began to argue with his own resolve against meeting her this coming Lordsday. Today was Pietonsday. Another four days already seemed like a long time to wait. He tried to recall what he had told her about his visions. When he recounted to her the events at the priest's house, he had mentioned the angel wanted him to do something. He remembered her frowning, but that reaction was mild compared to her shock when he said he had elbowed the peacey out of his way. She had not seemed particularly disconcerted when he claimed to have talked to an angelic being, and she said she did not think he was crazy.

As the timber merchant honed the wood to his specifications, Abren's restlessness took him out into the street. The town was lively despite the rain. He sauntered aimlessly along, glancing disinterestedly into shop windows. So disinterested in fact that he almost missed it. He had gone on several paces before his brain grasped what his eyes had seen. Turning abruptly, he bumped into a lady with an umbrella who glared in reproach despite his apology.

When he got back to the window, he saw it was an advertisement of some kind. The picture showed a woman with a scarf over her head. She squinted a penetrating gaze at him, but Abren's attention fixed on the figures depicted behind her. They were not unlike the ones pictured in the book. Angels? He read the wording.

They may be gone, but they are never lost.
Genuine messages from the spirit world.
Consultations with
Madame Esprit
Red Door
Upper Field Road
Marfryd

It was an ordinary-looking terraced house the shopkeeper directed him to. The front door opened directly onto the street. To the left of the door, a brass plaque told Abren he was at the right address:

Madame Esprit
Clairvoyant

He stood staring at the round knocker, momentarily frozen in nervous hesitation. Then, with a deep in-breath of resolution, he rapped firmly on the door. Almost at once, a smartly dressed middle-aged man opened it.

'Have you come to see Madame?' he asked.

'Yes, I…'

'Good, good. Do come in.'

He stood aside and then showed Abren into a sitting room at the front of the house. It was unnervingly like the one in Father Laniolus's house, if rather smaller. Abren reminded himself to be more careful this time about revealing his experiences.

The gentleman bade him to sit and informed him Madame would join him shortly. While he waited, he searched the pictures on the walls for any depiction of angels. He was disappointed. Madame Esprit chose to adorn her room only with portraits and landscapes.

When she entered, Abren stood up. She was somewhat older than the poster artist would have him believe. Without the scarf, her hair, pulled back into a tight bun, was revealed to be quite grey. The wrinkles around her mouth and eyes were more pronounced, her cheeks more gaunt, but her gaze was no less piercing. In fact, Abren sensed there was a vitality about her that belied her years.

'Good morning,' she greeted him with a pleasant smile. 'Please…' she waved him back into the chair. Once seated opposite him, she asked, 'Have you come for a consultation?'

'Yes, I…'

'Good. It will be one silver for the initial half an hour session. Do you wish to proceed?'

Abren blinked at the business-like manner in which she conducted herself. Also, at the cost, he had only got a little over three silvers a day in the docks.

'Err… yes, all right,' he found himself saying.

If this woman helps me unravel the mystery of the angel, it would be worth it, I suppose.

'Payment in advance, if you please.'

'Of course.' He put his hand in his pocket then stopped. 'What if I'm not satisfied with it?'

He wasn't sure what 'it' was, but he thought he should have some sort of guarantee.

'You will be, I assure you.' Her smile was encouraging, but it was the aura of vibrant energy surrounding her that won him over.

Having parted with his precious silver, Abren regarded the woman expectantly. For a few moments, she silently looked back at him with the searching expression he had seen in the shop window.

'Now, what exactly can I help you with?'

'Well I, err… met a young lady recently…' His brain was in a fever of confusion, embarrassment and anxiety as to how he was to get her to talk about the figures in her advertisement.

'Ah, and you wish to know if she is to be the love of your life, your soul companion, so to speak?'

'Yes… Yes, I suppose so.'

She chortled amiably. 'No need to be ashamed. It is a perfectly natural thing to wonder.'

She leaned back in her chair and closed her eyes. A stillness seemed to grip the air, and Abren felt a chill creep into the back of his neck. He had a sudden apprehension that the angel was going to appear, but after a few minutes, Madame Esprit opened her eyes again and sat up.

'Your young lady may not be as enamoured of you as you are of her, but she may be won round. She is certainly fond of you and misses you a little. You are parted at present, are you not?'

Abren stared at her in disbelief. 'How…? Yes, we are.'

'Being apart for a short time is not necessarily a bad thing. You are a naturally kind and sensitive person, as is she. I think there is every chance your courtship will flourish. Just be patient. Allow her affection for you to develop in its own time. Little acts of thoughtfulness will help things along, I'm sure.'

Here she paused, and the reassuring smile returned to her face.

'Thank you,' Abren muttered, frowning.

'Now I think there is another question you have for me.'

His frown darkened. He could not meet her eyes. But at least he was now confident she would not call a peace officer.

'On your advertisement, in the shop window… are they angels?'

Fifteen

Eldam

A few customers were coming into The Dog and Duck Tavern now. The hour had flown by. To Eldam most of them looked disreputable and one or two gave Eldam a curious look, but no one approached him. There was no sign yet of the man in the grey coat. The salt beef had been tough and the ale strong. An insistent tiredness crept up on him, and he began to sink into a pleasant stupor when a rough hand clutched rudely at his arm.

'Better not doze off, matey. Not here.'

Eldam started, scraping his chair backwards and banging his knee on the underside of the table.

'Easy, my friend, easy. I'm not after you. '

Eldam stared wide-eyed at the swarthy, deeply lined face thrust so close to his own. The man was short, barely needing to stoop.

'What?' Eldam exclaimed in confused alarm.

The man seated himself opposite the flustered student. After a rather theatrically furtive glance around the room, he leaned forward and spoke again.

'They're after you, aren't they, the Mellians,' he whispered. 'I saw that man watching you. I was watching him, see?'

'What? Who? Who are you?'

'I'm a friend, believe me. A friend in need. Lon's my name. I can help you. But we've got to be careful. They're all over the place.'

'What? What do you mean help me? How can I trust you?' Eldam knew dimly that the last question was tantamount to an admission that he did indeed fear he was being pursued, but clear thinking, so vital to his studies, had eluded him for a while now.

By way of an answer to this give-away question, Lon scanned the tavern's saloon once more before pulling up the heavy cuff of his ragged brown jacket and allowing Eldam a brief view of a crude design tattooed on the inside of his left forearm. A boar's head, emblem of Rarland's royal dynasty, sporting an oversized crown.

'See that? That's our mark,' he said, pulling his sleeve quickly down again. 'We've formed a secret society to help defend this country from her enemies. I don't know why they're after you, and I don't expect you to tell me, but I can take you to a safe place where they'll never find you.'

Eldam said nothing. He stared into the small, earnest eyes of his mysterious assailant. The man looked foreign, but he sounded like any other Damlon low-life. He had the smell of the alehouse on his breath and of the slums from his clothing. He might be in the pay of the Mellians, working the taverns to turn up anyone they were hunting concealed amongst the mass of Damlon's poor. The tattoo could mean nothing, just a trick to convince the scared and desperate.

But Eldam was scared. He was sure he was being trailed by someone, probably a Mellian agent, somehow aware of the letter he carried. Knowing he could not get into the Foreign Department until tomorrow, the offer of a safe house tempted him. Better than sleeping in some public dormitory or outside where anyone might come upon him in the night.

'Tell you what,' Lon said. 'To prove to you I'm on your side, I'll pay your bill. How's that?'

And before Eldam could object, he called Mollis Hatshal over to their table and pulled a purse from the depths of his baggy coat.

'No… but I… wait, please.'

They ignored him as the little man settled up with the landlady.

'There now,' Lon said when Mollis had gone. 'You coming with me or not?'

Outside, great, dark clouds loomed over the buildings. To Eldam's consternation, he was being led back towards the monument where he had seen the man in the grey overcoat, but thankfully the menacing figure had gone. Eldam walked painfully beside his would-be rescuer. The rest at the tavern seemed to have increased the soreness in his feet.

They took several turns, and Eldam found himself disoriented. Then a sudden wind blew into his face as Lon entered a dirty alleyway. The wind brought swift, strong rain. Eldam hesitated as he peered into the shadowy space between the two rows of grubby dwellings. A tight wariness gripped his guts.

'Come on,' Lon said, looking back. 'Almost there.'

Eldam took a deep breath and followed him into the gloom.

A damp, musty smell hung about the little sitting room he found himself in. A curtain had already been drawn across the only window, and several candles flickered in the draughts. Three other people sat around him on low wooden chairs. The fire grate was empty, and the faded, beige wallpaper had black, mouldering patches high up under the cracked plaster ceiling. And of course there was a nasty, mottled mongrel lying on the threadbare rug that had snarled menacingly at him as soon as he had entered the house. There had been introductions, and Lon had given his comrades a brief account of Eldam's plight.

'We're all true patriotic souls here, you see,' said Yagbert, a tall, thin man who claimed leadership of the shady group. 'That's why the Melons hate us so much.'

'They want to bring their filthy revolution over here,' added Polly, her large, intense, blue eyes shining out in the candlelight.

'They're trying to stir up trouble and get us to do away with our blessed royals like they did with theirs,' Yagbert said.

'I'm patriotic, I assure you.' Eldam felt he needed to assert this. Something had prompted the idea that these people might somehow know he had recently come from Mellia and that they suspected his loyalties. 'I was studying at the university in Amdris when they started deporting foreigners.'

'Yeah, you're like us. I knew as soon as I saw that fella was watching you,' Lon said. 'That's why we want to help you. You can trust us, I swear. Show him your marks.'

Yagbert and Polly pulled up the left sleeves of their shirts to reveal the same boar tattoo Eldam had seen in the tavern.

'We're a secret society,' Yagbert told him. 'The Rarland Defence League. Rardles, for short. We know there are Mellian agents all over Damlon. We try and keep track of them. Make sure they don't cause too much mischief. And we help people they're after, like yourself. The government doesn't seem to do anything, so we've taken it upon ourselves. Like true patriots should.'

'I've stuck my dagger into a few Mellian bums,' Lon said, proudly. 'Just to let them know they're not welcome here.'

'I see.' Eldam did not know whether to feel perturbed or reassured at this piece of information. 'Is there just the three of you?'

'No, there are others,' Yagbert said. 'It's just the three of us who live here, but this is our headquarters, where we have our meetings… with the others.'

Eldam thought he sounded a little defensive, and he found the notion of a clandestine society operating beyond the auspices of the government rather sinister. But he did think he was being followed, and alone he had felt very vulnerable.

'I need to get to the Foreign Department tomorrow, but I'm not sure of the way. I have a letter to deliver there.' Eldam decided to trust them to that extent.

'Ah, that must be why you were being watched. I'll not inquire into your business, though,' Yagbert said, clearly impressed by the implied gravity of the mission. 'All right then, a couple of us will go with you and keep an eye out for anyone taking too close an interest in you.'

'Can't we take a carriage?' Eldam thought of his suffering feet.

'People are known to have been abducted from carriages,' the leader of the Rardles informed him.

They gave him a room upstairs at the back of the house. It was sparsely furnished but clean enough, though the mattress was hard. Eldam unpacked the few clothes Jak had not sold in Frenbar. He wished he had not included his only other pair of shoes in the sale. A change of footwear would be a welcome relief.

He left his precious student notes in the bag. He knew Gorje Egring would continue working on the lighting project, and Eldam was determined to stay in contact with him as well as Taygret. Perhaps he could still make some small contribution to the great work once he had settled somewhere and resumed his studies.

The next morning Eldam walked uncomfortably into the heart of Rarland's capital city with Polly beside him and Lon a few paces behind. The further they went, the more incongruous he thought they looked. Polly wore a coarse woollen cloak and apron, and Lon the shabby brown coat that was rather too big for him. To Eldam, they stood out even in the smaller streets where well-dressed clerks and advocates scurried back and forth. Neither was he reassured by the way his companions continuously scrutinised their surroundings. He appreciated the need to be wary, but to him, it seemed the epitome of suspicious behaviour.

Eventually, they came out into a broad square lined with tall buildings. In the centre was a small park closed off by iron railings.

'I'm pretty sure the government offices are around here somewhere,' Polly said. 'I'll just ask someone which is the Foreign Department.'

She picked a lavishly dressed dandy to pose her question. The man looked at her aghast before recovering himself sufficiently to indicate a grand edifice halfway along the far side of the square that peered self-importantly out over the park's little trees. Lon tried a gate in the railings but found it locked, so they started to walk around.

As they neared the first corner, Eldam glanced back and saw the dandy in conversation with another man, pointing in their direction. Eldam suppressed the urge to hurry as the second man began to follow them. Lon noticed it too and, to Eldam's horror, pulled a cudgel from inside his coat.

'No,' Eldam implored. 'I have legitimate business here, and the Mellians would surely not attack us in so open a place.'

'He's right,' Polly hissed. 'Put that away.'

Lon scowled and stowed the club back into his coat but kept his hand on it.

They made their way slowly down the side of the square. Eldam gritted his teeth and fixed his gaze on their destination. So far, their pursuer had not challenged them.

When they arrived in front of the building, more iron railings confronted them, but the large gates were open. Two sentries stood to either side. They looked dauntingly grand in their red tunics, gold buttons and epaulettes, but it was the bayonets on their muskets that caught Eldam's attention. Two-foot long spikes which the guardsmen could no doubt use with deadly efficiency. Polly and Lon stopped, but Eldam held fast to his conviction of 'legitimate business'.

'Wait here,' he told his companions and walked as purposefully as he could manage through the gate. To his surprise, the sentries remained impassive, and he continued up the broad steps to the large doors, a boar's head crest looming above them. There was a notice instructing visitors to ring for attention, so Eldam pulled on the chain hanging beside the doors.

As he waited, he glanced back at Polly and Lon. The man who had followed them around the square was standing opposite them. He and Lon seemed to be eyeing each other belligerently. Eldam hoped that no confrontation developed between them before he completed his task.

A young man in an elegant black suit opened the door.

'I have a letter for the Director of the Foreign Department,' Eldam announced.

'I will see that he gets it.' The concierge regarded him with some distaste.

Eldam hesitated, then pulled out the letter and handed it to him. The man read the addressee, nodded and reached into a pocket of his pantaloons. No doubt, Eldam thought, to give him a small tip. But then he turned the letter over, and when he saw the seal, his eyebrows shot up.

'Come in, sir, if you please.'

The hallway into which he was admitted was much as Eldam expected, with a black and white tiled floor, grand staircase, a profusion of candles in gold sconces and portraits of important-looking men hung amidst crimson wallcovering.

'Kindly take a seat and wait a moment. What name should I give?'

'Medloe, Eldam Medloe.'

Eldam hobbled over to a gilded sofa and sank onto it, sighing with relief. As the concierge hurried up the stairs, he could not resist taking off his shoes.

Oh, for a bowl of cold water.

After a few minutes, the young man returned. 'The director's secretary will be down shortly,' he said, managing a smile. 'Would you care for some coffee?'

'No, thank you,' Eldam replied. 'I have a couple of friends waiting for me outside. Should I tell them to go?'

The man glanced at Eldam's stockinged feet. 'I'll inform them you may be some time and let them decide what to do. I'll also dismiss the watchman so he will not trouble your friends.'

'Much obliged,' Eldam said.

The concierge strode off towards the front entrance, and Eldam pulled his left foot up onto his right knee and began massaging it.

While he awaited the secretary, several men came and went, but all seemed to have some particular business in the building, and none lingered in the hallway. The man who eventually descended the stairs and greeted Eldam wore a cream-coloured suit, his eyes almost lost in his flabby face.

'Good morning, Mister Medloe.' he said. 'Mister Gleagan wishes to speak with you personally if you would be so kind as to step this way.'

'Thank you.' Eldam put his shoes back on and went with the secretary up the stairs. He reached for the support of the handrail.

'Are you hurt, sir?' the secretary asked him.

'I have walked rather a long way, and these shoes are ill-fitting.'

'Not to worry. It's not far.'

The Director of the Foreign Department was a lean gentleman with short-cropped, russet hair above an angular face. He rose as Eldam was ushered in and bade the student take a chair in front of his enormous desk.

'Thank you for bringing this letter to me, Mister Medloe,' Gleagan said. 'May I ask who gave it to you?'

Eldam briefly outlined the events that had unfolded in Frenbar.

'I see,' said the statesman when Eldam finished. 'So you have no idea as to the letter's contents?'

'None, except that Quist believed it was very important.'

'Well, I think you are due some explanation as you have performed this service at some inconvenience to yourself. The letter is from the Mellian Ministry of Warfare. They request the aid of our navy to defend their coastline against attacks from Skiglander warships. I will take the matter to His Majesty's Inner Council, but, as I'm sure you are aware, Rarland rarely involves herself in conflicts between states on the western peninsular. We prefer to remain aloof from such matters. While they impoverish themselves in wars of succession and revolutions and so forth, we use our resources to better the lives of our people. The new steam railway, for example.'

He went on to describe in some detail a trip he had taken on this wonder, during which Eldam tried to think of a good reason why Rarland should support Mellia other than that the woman he loved lived there. After some minutes, the garrulous politician was interrupted by a knock on the door. A short man with an enormous nose entered.

'Ah, Portius, do come in,' Gleagan said, getting up. 'This is Mister Medloe. Mister Medloe, this is Portius Lytham, Director of the Interior Department.'

Eldam also got to his feet and shook the newcomer's hand. He could hardly credit the situation. He, a humble student, was in the presence of two of the most powerful people in the kingdom.

After they were all seated, Lytham said, 'I'll get straight to the point, Mister Medloe. You have a brother, do you not? Abren Medloe?'

An icy chill ran down Eldam's back. 'I do,' he replied.

'Yes, well, the fact is we are very interested in this brother of yours.'

Sixteen

Taygret

Taygret had sat for a portrait once before. Her uncle had paid a rather dishevelled old man, who stank of tobacco, to paint a miniature of her. That had been in their drawing room at home in Amdris. She had given it to Eldam and the thought that the little picture now belonged to him made her feel happy.

She was sitting in the spacious, second-floor room that served as Niklay's studio. Several tall windows ensured the room was well lit. It was the day after her arrival in Gennlar. As she watched the artist peeping out from behind the canvas, which he did frequently, she could not help smiling a little. His face was such a mask of grave concentration that Taygret found it rather amusing. She thought at any moment he would rebuke her for her lack of composure.

This room, unlike the rest of the house, was cluttered and untidy. Several pictures rested against the walls or on easels. Lively depictions of breaking waves, rocks and cliffs, more tranquil scenes of stony beaches and rippling water. Most were at various stages of completion. On a table in the centre of the room were glass jars containing colourful powders, small dishes and a large jug, brushes of assorted sizes stuck out from clay pots.

After about an hour, the servant brought them a tray of tea. Niklay put down the stick of charcoal he had been using and said, 'Let's take a break.'

'Can I look?' Taygret asked eagerly.

'No, no. This is just the initial sketching. I will tell you when it is ready for you to see.'

Although she was disappointed, she had no choice but to comply.

As they sat in one corner of the room and sipped the tea, the artist shared with her a rather curious idea.

'You know, I have sometimes thought that if I could find a subject so beautiful that it would please people to adorn their walls with her likeness, then I would paint her over and over and perhaps sell a good many of the paintings.'

'Am I supposed to understand that you think you've found such a subject?' Taygret was well used to flattery from men, but she was not sure she liked the notion of her face hanging from walls all over the town if that was what he was suggesting.

'I know I have. And don't worry I am not about to ask you to sit for more than one painting. I would simply make copies of the original.'

'You seem to have confidence in your abilities despite admitting you need practice.'

'Of course. I believe all of us have particular talents, and we should perfect them as much as we are able.'

It seemed a common enough sentiment, but somehow, it piqued Taygret's interest. She decided to explore the topic a little.

'Are you a religious man, Niklay?'

'Well, I did try to paint The Divine once,' he said with a wry smile.

Taygret chuckled. 'And did He sit still long enough for you to make a good likeness?'

'No, not really. He kept moving from being an old man to a much younger fellow. I thought He should be young and virile, but the traditional image of Him as a wise old patriarch kept imposing itself.'

Despite her amusement, Taygret felt frustrated. Touching on spiritual matters had awoken a yearning in her.

'Do you have a muse? Some source of inspiration?' she asked.

'Well, I can see you are determined to be profound. But no, not really. I merely look and try to reproduce the beauty in what I perceive. I'm sorry if that sounds rather dull.'

'But you just said you tried to paint The Divine. What made you want to do that? It must have been some sort of inspiration.'

Niklay considered for a few moments.

'That was really only for some diversion. A friend, who is religious after a fashion, claims that The Divine is present in nature and that by painting natural scenes, I was, in truth, painting The Divine Himself. So I tried to create a picture of how The Divine may actually look. But as I said, it wasn't very successful.'

'Is your friend a member of the clergy?'

'Oh no. The clergy certainly doesn't approve of his ideas,' Niklay replied. 'He's too much of an original thinker.'

'Would it be possible for me to meet him?'

'Yes, if you don't mind visiting him in prison. He got rather too drunk and voluble at a tavern one night and started claiming The Divine was in him and everyone else. The Faith is still trying to get him to sign a repudiation. I've heard rumours the new government may eventually get around to clamping down on such practices but until then… Well, he's too stubborn for his own good, in my opinion.'

Taygret recalled Mistress Hettrig's warning not to tell anyone about the mardene. The story of Niklay's friend showed just how real the danger was. Her concern was genuine when she said, 'I'm sorry to hear that.'

When Fredrik returned to Niklay's house around midday, Taygret was sitting at a small desk in their room, pen in hand.

'Are you writing a letter?' he asked.

'No. I find writing things down helps me put my thoughts in order.'

'Ah, yes. I suppose you have a lot to think about with everything that's happened to you.'

'Yes. A lot has happened. It will take some time to write it all down.'

'Shall I leave you in peace for a while then? I can tell you my findings later if you like.'

'No, no. This can wait. I want to know what you found out.'

She cleaned her pen and replaced the cork on the inkwell. Then she sprinkled a fine powder across the page she had been writing on. When she was satisfied the ink was dry, she got up and shook the powder off into their little fireplace. She then folded the paper and tucked it into one of her pockets. She did not want anyone else reading it. Sitting down again, she gave Fredrik her full attention. He rather awkwardly drew up the only other chair in the room.

'I hope you haven't been drinking wine all morning,' Taygret said.

'No, but I've had rather a lot of strong coffee. My hands are shaking. Anyway, I learned that finding a ship's captain willing to smuggle you aboard his vessel will not be difficult. But their price is high. I got as far as asking two men how much, and one said thirty aurum, the other forty. I tried to haggle a little, but they were much better at it than me and wouldn't go any lower.'

'That is a lot. I suppose most people wanting to get out of the country are rich and desperate.'

'Yes. Royalists are usually wealthy. But something else I discovered was that there may be openings for stevedores at the docks. I could work here for a while and make you some extra money if need be.'

'I can't ask you to do that. What about your job at the inn in Peridere?'

'I'll write to Master Jaurey. I'm sure he'll understand.'

'No. I won't hear of it. I should have expected the smugglers to charge exorbitant fees. I will have to pay them and be satisfied that I can get across to Rarland at all.' Taygret stared at the disappointment on Fredrik's face. She sighed. 'But thank you. I know you are keen to help me as much as you can. I do appreciate it. It is very gallant of you.'

She leaned forward and took his rough hands in hers and squeezed. In response, he gave her a rueful smile and nodded.

'The man who asked the lower price said if I decided to buy passage, I should return tonight with the money.'

'All right then. Let's go and explore the town this afternoon,' Taygret said, trying to brighten the mood. 'I could do with some relaxation, and we are supposed to be on holiday after all. This evening we'll see if I can't barter with these greedy pirates.'

They spent a pleasant enough time wandering the back streets as they meandered along the hillside rising up from the harbour. The quaint little houses were painted in cheerful colours that shone in the sun. They sat in a quiet square under the shade of a large oak tree and watched some old men playing a game of bowls, tossing little black balls at an even smaller white one nestling in the sand. After a while, the men invited Fredrik to join them.

He got up, muttering, 'I've never played this game. It might be embarrassing.'

Taygret called encouragement whenever he threw his ball and laughed when he got nowhere near the target.

When the game was over, Fredrik thanked the men for asking him to play and for affording his wife such rich entertainment. He returned to her, smiling ruefully and shaking his head.

'I never was any good at sports.'

'It was a nice bit of fun,' Taygret said happily. 'Well, for me, at least.'

He extended his hand to help her up. 'That makes it all worthwhile.'

'I hear you have been asking about a job at the docks, Fredrik,' Niklay said. 'A curious thing to do on holiday.'

They sat round the table in the artist's dining room, eating a hearty supper. Taygret had been enjoying her first taste of haddock until that moment. She and Fredrik exchanged glances, then she put down her knife and fork.

'We're not really on holiday, Niklay,' she said. 'Nor is Fredrik my husband. I'm sorry for the deception. He is kindly helping me to find a crossing to Rarland, where I intend to find the man I truly love, who is Rarlish and has been deported. The ship's captains are asking more than I expected, so Fredrik thought to earn some extra money, but I won't allow him to.'

Niklay gave her a sympathetic smile. 'My dear, this is not Amdris. Tidings reach many ears in this town, especially regarding strangers. I also heard you were enquiring into ships to Rarland,' he said, looking at Fredrik. 'You should have been more careful. The police have informers hanging around the taverns from time to time listening out for just such talk.'

'I was careful to say I was enquiring on behalf of a Rarlish friend,' the ostler said. But he glanced about the room as if he feared a constable might suddenly emerge from behind an item of furniture.

'Very well,' Niklay said. 'In any case, I think if the police had taken notice of you, they would have paid us a visit by now.' Turning to Taygret, he went on. 'As it happens, I may be able to help you. I know someone who owns a ship that carries goods over to Rarland. I can take you to meet him if you like. We could probably negotiate a price you can afford.'

During the next morning's portrait session, the servant interrupted them with the news that Niklay's ship-owning acquaintance would be at home to receive them that afternoon. Taygret wondered what she ought to call herself now she was no longer married to Fredrik Draillis. Should she claim to be married to Eldam and become Linna Medloe? This could get more than a little confusing.

'What did you tell this friend of yours my name was?' she asked.

'I didn't,' came the answer from behind the canvas. 'I just said a young lady required passage. It's more discreet that way. He doesn't really need to know your name.'

That settles that, then, she thought. *Now I don't have a name at all.*

After lunch, Niklay took Taygret to meet the shipowner. As they walked along the quay, she watched a team of men unloading cargo from a large three-masted vessel. She was glad that Fredrik was not among them; it looked like back-breaking work.

They turned into a street that led up from the dock. The houses here were grander than in the district she had toured the day before. Niklay opened a gate, and they crossed a well-tended garden. As they approached the front door,

Taygret noticed the curtains were closed which seemed odd given the time of day.

Also closed were several doors that the maid led them past. Taygret heard a burst of high-spirited female laughter from behind one of them. As they entered a parlour at the back of the house, a man rose to greet them. He was not young but cut something of an imposing figure, tall and broad-shouldered. His tawny hair was swept back from his high forehead.

'Ah, Niklay, and this must be the young lady your note referred to. I am Helton Robikoy, and this is my wife, Flora.' He said, indicating a woman sitting in one of the purple armchairs. 'We are pleased to meet you, my dear.'

Mistress Robikoy smiled and nodded at the newcomers. A frilly white bonnet encircled her round face. Taygret thought the red colouring the woman had applied to her lips and cheeks was rather overdone. When her husband invited his guests to sit, Flora poured cordial for them from a glass decanter. The couple seemed gracious enough; the room was comfortable and well-furnished, so Taygret was uncertain where her uneasiness came from. Something prickled along the edges of her mind. A warning, but of what?

When they were all settled, Master Robikoy said in a kindly tone, 'Niklay tells us you want to sail over to Rarland.'

'Yes. My friend, Fredrik, was making enquiries for me, but Niklay heard about it and said you might be able to help,' Taygret said.

'I think that may well be possible. My ship is due to go across in a few days.'

'That will give us more time to work on your portrait,' Niklay said with a broad smile.

'Indeed,' said Mistress Robikoy. Taygret saw the lady was scrutinising her rather closely. It added to her discomfort.

'I also have a proposal for you,' Flora went on. 'I run a little escort service for the better-off gentlemen of the county. Lonely old widowers, on the whole, who simply wish for some delightful female company. Something you are well suited to provide. If you were to agree to do this on, say, three or four occasions while you wait for my husband's ship to sail, he would allow you to cross the bay free of charge.'

'Oh… I'm not sure,' Taygret stammered. 'I've done nothing like that before.'

'No, I don't suppose you have. But you would merely be giving them the pleasure of your society. Accompanying them when they went out to dine or to the theatre. We do have a theatre in Gennlar, you know. Of course, if you were to come to some private arrangement for something more intimate, I would have no objection. Although I would insist on a percentage.'

'Mistress, please, I…'

Flora Robikoy laughed. 'Forgive me, my dear. As Niklay will tell you, I have a wicked sense of humour. The look on your face. I wish Niklay would paint that.'

Taygret's face burned. She realised why she had felt so apprehensive. The closed curtains and doors, the saucy laughter. She was in a bawdy house.

Seventeen

Abren and Jessel

As Abren related his tale, Madame Esprit seemed to withdraw into her trance-like demeanour again. After a while, he stopped, wondering if she was still listening to him.

'Please continue,' she murmured.

When he had finished, she remained with her eyes closed. Abren held his breath. When she eventually looked at him, she had a slight frown on her face.

'Spirits are our departed ancestors,' she told him. 'They sometimes return if they have something important to tell us. But only if we have the sight. From what you have said, it would seem that you do. Your visitor may well be a forebear of yours. But Elias, my late grandfather, tells me this matter is clouded. The nature and intentions of the spirit attending you are unclear to him. This is rather unusual and a little troubling. They may be perfectly benign. They seem to punish the wicked, after all. But the fact they do not reveal themselves to Elias, who is perfectly good, I assure you, may mean they have become impure, corrupted, their purpose not altogether wholesome. Spirits do not always remain as they were in life. We will not be certain until they tell you what task they want you to perform. Return to me when you know more. I will help you if I can. But it would be wise not to speak to anyone else about this. Most people would not understand.'

She even declared that, in the circumstances, it would be improper to charge him for her services and gave him back his silver.

On his return journey to Faren, Abren decided to walk, leading the donkey along. Partly to lighten the burden for the old beast but mostly to give himself time to reflect on what Madame Esprit had told him. He wished now he had asked her what kind of help she could offer him if the spectre turned out to be evil. He wondered which of his ancestors it might be and why it had not told him.

Then he thought of something else. The clairvoyant could apparently commune with her deceased grandfather whenever she chose. Would it be possible for him to call upon his own forebear somehow, to initiate contact, instead of having to wait for them to appear? Would they respond as Elias seemed to? There was still much he needed to learn about this 'sight' as Madame Esprit called it. But at least he had found an ally with knowledge and experience of such things, and his conversation with her had gone a long way to convince him his visions were not the product of insane imaginings.

He began the repairs as soon as he returned to the tavern. He used a lean-to at the back of the building as his workshop and constructed a makeshift bench from some boards and empty barrels he nailed together. Initially, he had to fight to maintain his concentration. His mind still kept slipping back to the conversation in the clairvoyant's sitting room. But eventually he got into the swing of his work and made good progress. Planing and shaping the pieces of wood, glueing them together and clamping them in place.

By the following afternoon, he was bringing the first items of restored furniture back into the tavern's public room. The children got used to him being around. Judi overcame her bashfulness and stood curiously watching him work from time to time, asking him questions about what he was doing. Tam kept a sullen distance but seemed resigned to tolerating his presence.

That evening Abren sat in the tavern's saloon enjoying a glass of porter and, inspired by Madame Esprit's example, was writing a notice advertising his availability for carpentry work. If the prediction of the patron Abren had met when he first arrived proved to be correct, word would soon get around the little town about him and job offers might start coming his way.

He paused for a moment and sat gazing absently across the room, wondering if he should try to draw a hammer or saw for those not well versed in their letters.

A man in a well-tailored woollen coat and shiny black shoes entered the saloon and crossed to the counter. He seemed better dressed than the tavern's usual customers. Distracted from his deliberations, Abren watched as the newcomer spoke to Martia who was serving behind the bar, then stiffened when she pointed in his direction. The man strolled over to Abren's table.

'Mister Medloe? The carpenter?'

'That's right,' Abren replied, cautiously.

'Good evening. I'm Felix Mennan, a local historian. May I join you?'

'Of course,' Abren said, relieved that the man was not an officer of the law.

'Thank you.'

Felix pulled out a chair but instead of sitting down he inspected it with interest.

'I see this is newly repaired. Is it an example of your work, perchance?'

'Yes it is, actually.'

'Very good.' The historian finally seated himself and smiled. 'The fact is, I need someone to build a bookcase for me. I heard about you from a friend who comes for a drink here from time to time and I thought, "How fortuitous". I know there are one or two others in the town who may be coming to offer you work, my friend is such a gossip, you know. So I thought I'd come over this evening and speak to you before they do.'

The man was quite fidgety, he kept smoothing his black moustache and adjusting his round spectacles. 'I'm in desperate need of another bookcase, I've got piles of books everywhere. I thought of buying one but it must fit into an alcove next to the fireplace in my sitting room and I can't find one of the right size. You understand my plight, Mister Medloe?'

'I do, certainly. I'd be happy to come over to your house and measure the alcove. Then we can discuss the job in more detail. I should finish my work here tomorrow, so I could call on you late tomorrow afternoon.'

'That would be splendid. Thank you so much. Please take this card, it has my address on it. Until tomorrow then.'

They both got up and shook hands. Once the historian had taken his leave, Abren sat back down and smiled to himself, things here were not turning out so badly after all.

Martia came over and wiped the top of his table with a yellow cloth. 'He's quite well off is our Mister Mennan,' she whispered with a wink. 'Make sure you charge him full rates.'

The next day Abren did indeed complete his task and drinkers at the tavern had a full complement of tables and chairs to choose from once again. Ross said he was happy to continue the provision of board and lodging for a reasonable rent now that Abren was beginning to get more work. The arrangements suited everyone.

Abren visited Felix Mennan's house in the afternoon and set off to Marfryd early the next morning to get the timber needed to construct the bookcase. It was now Harninsday. Tomorrow would be Lordsday. He was now sure he wanted to go to Bornell, even if he had to walk there. He had little doubt Jessel would say the peace officers were still actively looking for him, but that would not be his real reason for meeting her. It was strange, he realised, not so long ago, he had not known of Jessel's existence. Now there was a gap in his life where she should be.

Jessel stared at the portrait on the poster. It was a fair likeness she had to admit, but the vicious scowl that marred Abren's features was not something she recognised as being part of his nature. She had never lingered in front of a peace station before. Although she was barely a mile from her home patch, she felt like she was in enemy territory and that a trap might close in about her at any moment.

'Can I help you, Miss? Do you know this man?'

Jessel started and spun around.

'Oh, no. I thought it was my cousin for a moment,' she said and forced a laugh. 'But it isn't, of course.'

'Well, you'd best keep an eye out for this one,' said the peace officer, nodding towards the poster. 'A right nutter by all accounts. You wouldn't want to come across him in some dark alley.'

Jessel did not like the shape of his grin as he peered into her face. When his gaze slid down to her chest, she drew her shawl more tightly around her.

'I shall, don't worry,' she replied. She moved to hurry away, but the peace officer stepped into her path.

'You've got a stall over on the high street, haven't you?'

'Yeah. So what?'

'You must see a lot of people going past. You could be our lookout.'

'I don't have time to gawk idly at passers-by, thank you. I've got a business to run.'

Her escape was as dignified as she could manage.

Walking briskly back to the high street, Jessel reflected on the poster she had seen. Her mother had taught her to read the few words she knew, including 'danger,' so she would be wary whenever she saw it written on a sign. She could guess what 'peace officer' meant from the large letters above the door of the 'peace station'. And her father had shown her how to write numbers so she could put prices on the goods she sold. From this and what Abren had told her she deduced the poster proclaimed he had attacked a peace officer, was considered dangerous, and that there was a reward of ten somethings for anyone helping to catch him. She knew it was not coppers or silvers, it must be gold. They were taking it that seriously.

Lying to the peaceys had been part of her upbringing, so she had no compunction at denying she recognised Abren's face, and the poster had given her the information she wanted. It seemed he might not be able to return for some time, if ever. But then, why should he come back to the neighbourhood? He had left his job and his lodgings. He had nothing to return to. Except her, maybe. Was she beginning to doubt the strength of his feelings for her? The notion raised a little hollow sensation within her that she carried back towards the stall.

She supposed it was possible he would not risk going to Bornell this Lordsday, but she wanted to be there just in case. She realised in his present predicament, she might be his only friend. Had he found a bed to sleep in? Work? Could he buy food?

As she approached the stall, all these questions suddenly evaporated from her mind like idle daydreams. Fran was talking to a peacey.

Sitting in the interrogation room in the peace station, Jessel felt a trap had truly ensnared her. The bare, brown walls seemed to stifle the very idea of freedom.

Of course Father Laniolus would have remembered eventually that she was a friend of Abren's. It had only been a matter of time before the peaceys came to ask her if she knew of his whereabouts. And now they knew she had lied about recognising him on the poster. The peace officer standing behind her now was the very one who had confronted her outside the station little more than an hour earlier.

When the sergeant returned, he had an indulgent smile on his hairy face.

'Now then, Miss Weglin, I hope you've had time to think about what's best,' he said as he sat in the chair opposite her again and folded his arms across his barrel chest.

'Lying to a peace officer is a very serious offence. You may think you are protecting your friend, but we know from Father Laniolus's testimony that he needs to be in a place of safety. For his own sake and that of the public. Now, I'd be willing to overlook your moment of dishonesty if you agree to help us. And there's the reward to consider. Ten gold would be a handsome sum to a young lady such as yourself, I'm sure. Much better than a few months in jail. So I'll ask you one more time. Do you know where Abren Medloe is hiding?'

Jessel sighed. She had looked defiantly into the sergeant's eyes while he spoke. Now she turned her head to one side. The thought of prison frightened her, but she was determined not to let that show. She had her hands clasped together in her lap, and she tightened their grip on each other as she said, 'No… But perhaps I could find out.'

It was the sergeant's turn to sigh.

'Well then,' he said. 'Am I supposed to just let you go in the hope you come back with the information?'

'I'm not going to run away. Where would I go?'

'There're plenty of places. Same place as Medloe, for one.'

'I promise I'll come back when I know, all right? He's not that much of a friend. I only met him a few days ago.'

'Hmm. I don't know if I can trust you. Maybe we should lock up your sister to make sure you come back.'

'No! She's done nothing wrong. You can't just lock up innocent people.'

He sat regarding her for a while with an expression of amused scrutiny. Jessel could see he was actually enjoying himself; it disgusted her.

'All right then.' It was a hard stare he gave her now. 'I'll give you twenty-four hours. Report back here by this time tomorrow, or I'll put you on the wanted list along with your friend.'

Jessel calculated. Tomorrow was Lordsday. She should just have enough time to meet Abren in Bornell and make it back to the peace station before the time was up.

If he's there, we can talk about what's best to do. Lord, I hope he comes.

She nodded. 'I'll find out what I can. I promise.'

'You'd better. I'd really hate to see you in jail. You're too sweet a girl to be in a place like that.'

Eighteen

Eldam

Eldam stared at Portius Lytham, wondering what on earth his brother had done to warrant the attention of such a high-ranking politician. Jessel had told him that Abren had evaded capture but not what his original crime had been.

The Director of the Interior Department returned his gaze and rubbed the side of his prominent nose. 'You see, we have reason to believe your brother may be a spiriter.'

Eldam was shocked. He had heard this word before. 'A kidnapper?' he asked, his voice shrill with disbelief.

'No, no. One who can talk to spirits.'

'Spirits?' He was hardly less incredulous at this accusation.

'Yes. He went to see a priest at his local faith house and claimed he saw an angel and that this angel spoke to him. The priest was quite alarmed, thinking Abren might be insane or even a heretic, which would be worse from his point of view. So he called a peace officer, but your brother proved too agile for him and escaped. The thing is, if he really spoke with some spiritual entity, he may be of great use to us.'

'I'm sorry, I don't follow. Abren said he saw an angel, and the priest thought him a heretic?'

'Well, it seems from how Abren described the encounter the priest believed it could not be an angel, unlikely as that would be in any case. But… have you heard of the Mardene Heresy?'

'No, never.'

'Several centuries ago, a woman called Elonir Mardene wrote a book entitled *Spirits Bright and Turbulent* in which she related her experiences in communing with these entities. She insisted they are an order of being existing in a realm separate from ours but that they can cross over, so to speak, and contact those of us who are receptive to them. The Faith declared such beliefs to be a heresy because in her book Mardene claimed that angels, devils, even The Lord Himself are all just spirits speaking to the chosen few. In the past, they confiscated and burned any copies of the book they got their hands on. There are probably very few left in existence. Anyone espousing its doctrine tended to disappear.'

Eldam shuddered. 'The Faith has obviously done a good job in suppressing the heresy.'

'Indeed. In fact, it remains a criminal offence to preach it openly, although, thankfully, no one has been charged with it for over fifty years. The Faith is, of course, still quite influential in Rarland, but the government, whilst not wanting to offend them, is keen to present itself as promoting rational, scientific progress rather than prosecuting suspected heretics.'

'But you just said that if my brother can commune with these spirits, he might be of use to you.'

'There is often, you understand, Mister Medloe, a need for pragmatism. At the very least, your brother struck a peace officer and resisted arrest. Whilst these are serious offences, they are trifling in comparison with what Abren may be able to do in service to the kingdom.'

Lytham glanced across the desk at Gleagan. The Foreign Director gave Eldam a searching look, then nodded. 'We think there might be something in this matter of communing with spirits that is worth exploring,' he said. 'But no word of this exploration must be uttered beyond the three of us and your brother.'

'We would be willing to overlook Abren's offences if he agreed to help us,' said Lytham. 'Now, at present, we cannot be certain that he has this talent. It is very rare, apparently. But if he has, then there is an area in which we may exploit it.' He sat back in his chair and stared at his hands as if composing himself before elaborating on this idea.

Eldam waited.

'As you know, there has been a revolution in Mellia, and they have deposed their king and declared a republic. The reaction in Rarland has been mostly one of outrage, but there are certain elements within our society that welcome it and even seek to bring about a similar revolt here. We know there are Mellian operatives in Damlon trying to foment such a revolt.'

'Mellia is isolated,' Gleagan told Eldam. 'That letter you brought me is evidence that their situation is perhaps becoming critical. Their new government cut off all diplomatic ties with us, something they are now regretting, I should think. But it's no doubt why they sent the letter via such unconventional means. What I didn't tell you is that they say they are prepared to cede the Kimmikk Islands to us if we help them.'

'Are they indeed?' said Lytham. 'They must be desperate.'

'But why send a message asking for aid on the one hand and at the same time have agents here trying to turn Rarland into another republic?' Eldam said.

Gleagan shrugged. 'It's pure hypocrisy, of course. No doubt, if we caught any of these agitators, the Mellians would deny responsibility for them. They would have the agents themselves trained to say they were acting without their government's knowledge. But obviously, their navy is not up to the task of defending their own coastline, and they need our help.'

'It is this business of catching Mellian operatives that we think your brother may be able to help with,' Lytham said. 'They have proved rather elusive.'

'You think Abren might ask his spirits to track down Mellian secret agents? So much for promoting rational, scientific progress.' Eldam immediately regretted his derision as both men scowled in irritation.

'It may sound like fantasy to you, Mister Medloe, but I assure you we would not be pursuing this course without good reasons to think it may enjoy some success.' Gleagan was drumming his fingers on his desk. 'I will not go into those reasons at present, but it could indeed prove to be a pragmatic approach.'

Eldam shook his head. 'Be that as it may, you are aware my brother is, at present, in hiding, and I don't know where he is.'

'He has a lady friend. A Miss Jessel Weglin,' Lytham said. 'She runs a market stall over in Ellford, on the high street. She probably knows his whereabouts. Peace officers will interrogate her today. I doubt if she will tell them anything useful, but you, on the other hand…'

'I've already met her.' Eldam felt a little thrill of satisfaction at being one step ahead of the authorities. 'She told me she doesn't know where Abren is either, and I believe her. I'm sure my brother would want to protect her.'

Lytham gave his hands another prolonged examination. 'Very well then, this is what I'll do. I will instruct my secretary to write an official pardon for your brother, which I will sign and attach my seal of office. If he comes here, I will give it to him if he agrees to help us. You may be correct regarding Miss Weglin, but I have a feeling that between the two of you, you might locate this slippery brother of yours.'

'All right, I'll see what can be done. Now, gentlemen, I find myself embarrassingly short of funds.'

As he walked back to the house used by The Rarland Defence League, Eldam kept his hand on the purse in the pocket of his coat. The Interior Director had been quite generous. There was also the promise of more to come if he persuaded his brother to meet with Portius Lytham. At least, he could now offer some payment for the board and lodging the Rardles were giving him.

His feet still hurt, but being rid of the Mellian missive had lifted the fear of being accosted to some extent, and he tried to think of what he should say to his hosts when he returned.

When he arrived at the grimy door in the narrow, dingy alley, he gave the knock he had been told. Lon opened the door. To his credit, the little man allowed Eldam to take off his coat and seat himself at the kitchen table before asking any questions. Polly was busy at the stove, and a delicious smell of cooked meat hung in the air. The dog, whose name they had informed him was Howler, was already eating greedily from a bowl on the floor.

'What took you so long?' Lon said. 'I thought you were only delivering a letter.'

'The director interviewed me himself. He wanted to know where I had got the letter, but he wouldn't tell me what was in it. I told him I was followed, and he said he knew there were Mellian agents in the city.'

'So what's he doing about it?' Polly asked as she put two plates of food down in front of the men.

'He wouldn't tell me that either. I suppose it's a state secret or something like that.' Eldam was uncomfortable lying to these people who were being so helpful to him, but he had been told to be discreet, and he did not want to jeopardise Abren's amnesty.

'Ha! That means he's doing nothing,' Polly said. Then she went over to the door and yelled, 'Yag. Dinner's on the table.'

Eldam told the others everything he thought he could about what had happened at the government office. Then the four of them gave their attention to the meal, and they ate in silence for a while. Eldam enjoyed the sensation of the boiled mutton, potatoes and greens filling his belly.

Then Yagbert said, 'What were you studying in Amdris?'

'Chemistry and medicine mostly.'

'Chemistry?'

Eldam became aware that the room had gone quite still. The others had stopped eating. He looked up to find they were all looking at him.

'What of it?' he said.

'Could you make gunpowder?' Yagbert asked.

Nineteen

Abren and Jessel

'So, you have been to see a so-called clairvoyant.'

Abren glared at the spectre. Another nocturnal visitation was disturbing his sleep.

'You really have no need of her assistance. You have nothing to fear from me as long as you do as I ask.'

'Why won't you tell me what that is?' He understood the threat it was making.

It must be impure, after all. A thing of wickedness.

The silence that followed went on for some time. So long in fact that Abren was about to repeat his question when the spectre finally spoke.

'There is a man, an evangelist. Brother Eusebius, he calls himself. He has been preaching to the working people in the east of this country. His religious zeal has beguiled many into an unquestioning faith. Now he is coming to the capital to work his corruption among the poor there. I want you to stop him.'

'Stop him, how?' The tension in Abren's belly tightened. He did not think he really wanted to know the answer to that question.

'You must put an end to him. Once you have done that, I will, of course, look after you, as I promised.'

'Why can't you put an end to him? You seem fully capable of doing people harm.' Abren had to think his way out of this nightmare. He had to rid himself of this malignant being somehow, even if it was an ancestor of his. But he did not think he could just tell it to go away and leave him alone. He knew how vindictive the spectre could be.

'Another spirit has chosen to watch over Eusebius and would defend him from me. But I will engage with this spirit and keep it occupied while you rid the world of this preacher and his vile teachings.'

'But if he is a preacher, then surely he is a good man. Killing him would be doubly sinful.'

'He is not a good man. He preaches a base falsehood convincing the poor that his divinity has dictated their subservience and wretched existence. He would condemn them to a life of grinding hardship with no hope of relief except in some illusory next world and only then by mindless devotion to his faith.'

Abren grimaced in confusion. He had heard some priests teach such things. He had never accepted their creed. Did the spectre truly want to rescue people from poverty?

'I don't understand. Has The Lord sent you to get me to kill someone who is preaching a false doctrine? And what are you exactly? Some long-dead member of my family?'

'Oh, Abren, your notions are so naïve. You are not a religious man, I know, but religion has tainted your views. One almighty Lord, saints and angels, phantoms from the afterlife. But the reality differs greatly from what you imagine. Those of us who take an interest in your world seek to influence your affairs as we see fit, sometimes with the aid of one chosen receptive soul. Yes, some masquerade as angelic beings or the ghosts of the dead. Others seek only to do mischief, but in truth, spirits are as varied and changeable as humans.'

'Are you saying there's no Lord?' Although he did not indeed think of himself as religious, Abren found the idea of there being no Lord profoundly shocking.

'Some spirits, alas, have allowed people to believe they have infinite powers, but it is no more than an artful conceit.'

Abren sank down onto his bed. His body could no longer support his shattering bewilderment.

'You're lying,' he managed to mutter.

'I realise you may find this overwhelming. I will leave you to think over what I have told you and what I am asking of you. I will return before long.'

Abren put his head in his hands. So the spectre, whatever it was, wanted him to commit murder. His worst fears had come true. What was he to do? He thought he ought to consult with Madame Esprit as soon as possible, but he found himself aching to see Jessel. Now he was even more determined to go to the graveyard in Bornell tomorrow afternoon. He only hoped she would be there as well.

They practically flew into each other's arms. It had seemed entirely natural, but as they finally pulled apart after the long embrace, Abren felt something new and momentous had happened. He was going to kiss her when he saw a look in her eyes that told him he was not the only one with distressing news.

'What is it?' he asked, frowning his concern at her.

'Let's walk,' said Jessel.

They followed a path through the tombs. She put an arm around his and kept close to his side.

'The peaceys took me to the station and questioned me about you. Father Laniolus told them I knew you.' There was a new tone in her voice, Abren heard the fear in it. He halted, and she turned to face him. 'They said that if I don't tell them where you are by this afternoon they'll lock me up.'

Abren clutched her shoulders. His hands were shaking. 'But why? How can they? You've not broken the law. Not by just knowing me.'

'I… A peacey caught me looking at a poster about you. There's a poster up outside the station.' She put a hand over her eyes. 'Oh, this isn't how I wanted to tell you about it.'

He took her in his arms again, and she put her head against his chest. After a while, she was able to continue.

'There's a reward. Ten gold. It had a picture of you.'

'What did the peacey say?' He was holding her as tight as he dared.

She lifted her head and looked up into his eyes. Her breath brushed his lips as she said, 'He asked me if I knew you and without thinking, I said, "no". But they knew I did because of the priest, and now I'll go to prison if I don't tell them where you are.'

He pulled away, taking her hands in his.

'Turn me in.'

'No.'

'Lead them to me. Get the reward.'

'No!'

'I will not see you go to jail because of me. You took a risk hiding me because you did not want me to go to jail. Now I feel the same about you. Ten gold is a lot of money.'

'Stop talking that way. I wouldn't rat on you for a thousand gold.'

For a few moments, they stood staring at each other. Abren felt an exultant anger run through him. She really cared for him that much. Damn her.

By some unspoken understanding, they continued their walk, Jessel again clinging to his arm. They passed an older woman in a black dress arranging some flowers on one of the graves.

'What are you going to do then?' Abren asked, a fierce frustration in his voice. 'What are we going to do?'

'I don't know,' she replied. 'I could hide with you, I suppose, but that would only leave Fran in the same scrape I'm in now.'

Ahead of them, Abren saw they were approaching an ancient-looking stone wall. The path led to an opening where an old wooden door stood open. Jessel stopped.

'There's a main street on the other side of that wall,' she told him. 'Let's go back.'

Abren had been keen to tell Jessel about what the spirit had said to him, but he thought they should try to deal with her predicament first.

'What did you say when they asked you where I was?'

'I said I didn't know, but I would find out.'

'Then say you weren't able to find out. Say you need more time.'

'I'm not sure they'd like that. They… What's the matter?'

Abren had stopped abruptly and was staring past Jessel, his face taut.

The woman who had been placing the flowers walked by them.

'Good afternoon,' she said solemnly. They both ignored her.

'Abren, what is it?' Jessel said.

'There, under that tree,' he said. 'Can you see anything?'

She shook her head, 'No. Well…'

'Wait here.' He strode off towards the large yew tree and entered the dense shade under its spreading branches.

'What are you doing here?' he demanded.

The spectre seemed to shiver as if unsettled by what little daylight penetrated beneath the tree's thick canopy.

'Inform your lady friend that she no longer needs to be concerned about being detained by the peace officers. I have taken care of it.'

'What do you mean?'

But the apparition was already fading. Abren groaned and threw his arms up in frustration.

'Damned thing,' he spat when he had returned to the fretful-looking Jessel.

'Did you see your angel?'

'It's no angel. I don't know what it is. Did you see it?'

'No. It looked to me like you were talking to the tree. But there was something though, some peculiar little lights in the air.'

Abren nodded, then shook his head.

'It had a message for you.'

'For me?' She glanced towards the tree again. 'What did it say?'

'That you needn't worry about the peaceys. That it had taken care of it.'

She snorted. 'Well, that's very nice of it,' she said, her voice steeped in incredulity.

They resumed their walk in tense silence.

When they reached the front of the faith house, Jessel said, 'Your brother came to the stall the day before yesterday. He asked after you.'

'Eldam? But I thought he was in Amdris.'

'Not any more. They kicked him out.'

'What did you tell him?'

'I said the peaceys wanted you, but I didn't say why. I thought you'd better explain that bit. I didn't tell him I might meet you today either. I wanted to talk to you first. He's going to come back to the stall tomorrow or the day after to see if I've heard anything.'

'How did he look?'

'Well enough, I guess. Concerned after what I told him about you, of course. And tired. He had to walk from Magshead because he's short of money.'

'Where's he going to stay?'

'I don't know. Some poorhouse, I suppose, until he can get your dah to send him something.'

'Yeah, my father will do that.'

Jessel must have heard the resentment in his voice. 'Do you get on with your brother, Abe?'

Abren smiled despite everything. It was the first time she had used his nickname.

'Yeah, Jess, I do. It's just that dah always favoured him, and after the incident with the horse, dah won't give me anything. But that isn't Eldam's fault.'

Jessel returned a rueful smile. 'What do you want me to tell him?'

'I think you're right. It's best I tell him about the… spirit thing if and when I see him. Say I'm all right and not to worry. I haven't done anything serious, and it will all blow over soon.'

'I bloody well hope so. Look, I need to get back. I left Fran trying to talk our aunt out of going to Altakere. They're probably having a right old row. I haven't told either of them everything the peaceys said yet.'

'Altakere?' Abren said. 'It gets pretty cold up there.'

'Yeah, exactly. We have an uncle who went there. Our aunt's brother. Fran's convinced cousin Stina doesn't really want to go… Anyway, I'll do what you said. I'll make up some story that I can find out where you are, but I need more time. If they're that keen on catching you, they'll give it me.'

'But what then? Even if they give you more time, you will need to do something. Maybe we should go to Altakere with your aunt.' He did not know how he felt about this idea, but it was no more daunting than the other that was in his mind. He was certain that if Jessel was arrested, he would hand himself in.

'I don't want to do that,' she replied. 'I'll think of something.' If she had intended to reassure him, it did not work.

'I've got a job I need to finish, then I'll come to see you the day after tomorrow and make sure you're all right. I'll come after dark and creep up to your rooms.'

'Oh, Abe, do be careful. Morriline locks the door after dark. Toss a stone up at our window. I'll come down and let you in... or Fran will.' Then she frowned. 'How are you getting about?'

'I've got the use of a horse. A customer loaned her to me. Which is why I have to finish this job.'

She nodded. 'You've got work then.'

'Yeah, plenty.' There seemed to be an understanding between them that he should not tell her where he was living.

'Good.' She gave him a quick kiss. 'I'll see you the day after tomorrow, then.'

She walked towards the gate, when she reached it, she stopped and looked back. She waved briefly then turned and strode away.

Abren stood for several minutes, alone amongst the buried dead of Bornell. He had not even told her he was expected to commit a murder.

On their walk home from their aunt's house, Fran asked about Abren. Jessel had told her sister the peace officers wanted her to find out where he was, but she omitted her lie and its potential consequences.

'He's got some paid work and somewhere to live but I didn't ask where.'

'So, he's all right then?'

'Seems to be.' Jessel knew that beneath the brusque exterior, her sister's heart was as soft as her own.

'What are you going to say to the peaceys?'

'Still haven't found out anything, I suppose.'

'They know you won't help them. I don't know why they bothered asking.'

Jessel merely shrugged and turned the topic onto their aunt and Altakere.

As she approached the peace station, Jessel was aware that her body was sending her alarm signals. From the trembling in her legs to the queasiness in her belly, her anatomy told her she should not be heading in this direction.

Then she stopped. It was such an extraordinary sight. Seven or eight peace officers came bounding out of the station door and rushed towards her, a phalanx of tight blue tunics and brass buttons. She thought for one mortifying moment they were about to seize her and drag her into custody. But as she shrank back against a wall, they raced past her and stampeded off down the street.

The peace officer on the desk looked up at her irritably. His tiny, dark eyes seemed to want to repel her from their sight. He offered her no greeting, merely returning his gaze to the papers before him. Jessel cleared her throat.

'I've come to see Sergeant Millins,' she announced. 'He's expecting me.'

'Oh, no, he ain't,' returned the peacey without looking up. 'He was shot dead this morning in a raid. We've every man out hunting his killer. So unless your business is very important, Miss, I suggest you come back another time.'

'No… no, it's not important.'

And then she was back out on the street. She was not in the dismal interrogation room or behind bars. Her feet were free to take her wherever she wanted to go.

It had taken care of it. Was it possible?

Twenty

Taygret

'Why didn't you tell me we were going to a brothel?' Taygret's annoyance was amplified by apprehension. She had agreed to act as a companion for three or four of Mistress Robikoy's clients. And having done so, she had to give her a name. On the spur of the moment, she thought she should not, under the circumstances, claim to be a married woman. So she had now become Miss Linna Draillis.

'I didn't know Robikoy's wife would involve herself in the conversation. Besides, I was afraid you might not come if you knew. But her offer is fair, don't you think?' Niklay sounded a little breathless. He was struggling to match her pace as she strode back along the quayside and to make himself heard above the cries of the fish sellers and the shrieks of the gulls.

Taygret did not answer and kept her thoughts to herself until they were back in Niklay's house. After the servant had taken their coats and hats and they were seated in the parlour with Fredrik, she said, 'I did not like that woman, but it's a generous enough offer.'

She had calmed a little. Perhaps she could forgive Niklay for being less than completely open with her. She had not been entirely honest with him at first, after all.

'What offer?' Fredrik said.

Taygret told him of her interview with the Robikoys.

'Are you sure you want to do that? If you are seen in town with older widowers, people will know what you're doing.'

'I need hardly be concerned about my reputation here. I will be gone in a few days. And I think it is far preferable to you working as a stevedore.'

'But, I…'

'No, Fredrik. You should get back to Peridere and return the horses to their owner. I have imposed upon you and Master Jaurey long enough.' She was aware of the harshness in her voice. Was she trying to overcome her own doubts?

'I'll look after her, Fredrik. I know how precious she is, and I want to finish her portrait,' Niklay said with a smile. 'You may not approve of Mistress Robikoy's line of business, but she and her husband are honourable people.'

The next morning Taygret bid farewell to Fredrik. 'I shall never forget your kindness,' Taygret said as she hugged him.

'And I shall never forget you. Safe journey, Tay… Err, Linna. I hope you find Eldam soon, and I hope he knows how fortunate he is.'

She watched as he rode off, leading the other horse. He turned when he reached the end of the street and waved. She felt her eyes overflowing as she waved back.

During the painting session, word came from Mistress Robikoy that Taygret's first assignment was to be with a retired pastor. She was to call at his house after lunch and accompany the cleric on his daily walk.

'I don't think I know him,' Niklay said when Taygret told him the pastor's name. 'He must have retired some time ago. It will probably be only a short stroll.'

Taygret had not expected that her first experience as a hired companion was to be with a member of the clergy. Niklay told her how to get to his address, and she found Pastor Mavier's house easily enough on the outskirts of the town. It was smaller than she expected, with a thatched roof and a neat little garden. She was further surprised when the man who opened the door was the cleric himself.

'Yes, yes, that's me,' he said, smiling broadly. 'And you must be Miss Draillis. Delighted to meet you. I'll just get my coat and hat, and we'll set off, shall we?'

Before she could answer, he had taken down the garments from their pegs in the hallway and, putting them on, stepped briskly out to join her. He was slender and half a head shorter than Taygret, but his movements were quick and energetic.

'I thought we might have a nice little hike up to the cliffs,' he told her. 'Just for an hour or so. Then we can come back and refresh ourselves with some tea or mulled wine if you prefer.'

'That would be lovely,' Taygret said, smiling and wondering if she would be able to keep up with him.

He led her along a path that wound around the back of his house, and soon they were climbing a steep grassy slope.

'Mistress Robikoy tells me you are newly arrived in our town,' Pastor Mavier said, striding effortlessly up the hill.

'Yes, that's correct. I'm still getting to know the place. I thought being a companion for a while would be a good way for me to meet people.'

'What a fine idea. Watch out for your hat. It can be quite windy up here,' the wiry, old cleric said as they neared the top of the ridge. 'Wonderful view, though.'

When they reached the summit, Taygret's breath was swept away as both predictions proved accurate. White clouds sailed in a pale blue sky above a vast expanse of shining, green water. The stiff breeze made her decide to take off the little straw bonnet she had borrowed from Niklay's maid, and, feeling the exhilaration in the wind, pulled loose the restraining ribbons and let her long dark hair stream out behind her.

She stood gazing out into the distance. She thought she could just make out the coast of Rarland across the wide bay. Eldam was over there somewhere, and the sight made her feel just a little bit closer to him.

Mavier grinned as he clasped his tricorne to his head.

'The Divine's creation in all its glory,' he declared.

Taygret looked at the pastor. She was smiling too.

'Do you feel The Divine's presence here?' she said.

'I feel The Divine's presence everywhere, my dear. It is His world, after all. This is just a particularly magnificent aspect of His works.'

'But what about the ugly things or the things we call ugly, like mud or weeds? Do you think The Divine made them as well?'

'Of course. Just because we mere mortals decide we don't like the look of something doesn't mean The Divine's hand did not create them.'

As she pondered the implications of his remarks, the pastor turned his attention back to the vista before them.

'These scurrying clouds always remind me of the story of Saint Jostal and the angels,' he said.

'Oh really. I don't think I've heard that story.'

'Haven't you read *The Labours of the Great Saints*?'

'Err… no, I'm afraid not.' Taygret was a little daunted by the reproach in his voice.

'Well, I'll lend you my copy when we get back then,' he said, smiling again. 'Anyway, Jostal was walking on some cliffs much like these when he saw a host of angels flying along over the sea. He was so awestruck, he prostrated himself and decided, there and then, to dedicate his life to serving The Divine.'

'Did the angels speak to him?'

'Oh no. I don't think they even noticed him. But he heard them singing, and it filled his heart with joy.'

'People don't seem to see them anymore. It's a pity.'

'We may not see them, but they are still there.'

Taygret had to bite her lip to stop herself from telling Pastor Mavier about the mardene. What if she said she had heard of the heresy and asked his views on the matter? He seemed benign enough, but then…

They will have anyone professing such beliefs placed under arrest. Some who have refused to recant have never been released.

Mistress Hettier's strong words checked her again and the thought of Niklay's poor incarcerated friend.

Invigorating as the walk and conversation had been, Taygret was glad to return to Mavier's snug house and the promise of tea. The old man had tired her out.

After they had taken off their coats and gone into the parlour, the cleric said, 'I'll put the kettle on. Hildred, my housekeeper, died a couple of weeks ago, and I have yet to find her replacement. Please make yourself at home.'

'Oh, I'm sorry to hear that.'

'Thank you. It was very sad. She had been with me for nearly fifteen years. I don't suppose… No, let's have tea first.'

He began to head for the kitchen, and Taygret was about to sit down when he stopped suddenly.

'Oh, before I forget, I'll find you that book.'

He began looking through the many volumes on the shelves along the parlour's back wall. Taygret was curious to know what type of reading would interest an older cleric and peered at the titles over Mavier's shoulder. She spotted the name just as the pastor said, 'Ah, here it is,' so he did not hear her gasp. He turned and handed her his copy of *The Labours of the Great Saints*.

'Err… thank you,' she managed to say, her mind reeling.

'Not at all. Keep it as long as you like. Now I'll go and make us a nice pot of tea.'

When he had gone out, Taygret put the book down on a small table and reached for another. She reread the title and author etched on the light brown leather spine to make sure she had not imagined it. No, it was there, clear enough. *Spirits Bright and Turbulent* by Elonir Mardene.

With trembling fingers, she opened the book, reading short passages as quickly as she could.

The spirit came to me in glory and magnificence, its body a matter of fire. It spake in my own tongue and did charm me with words courteous and affable. It sought my allegiance most avidly…

Be it but one in a hundred thousand that can see, that can hear, that are blessed, that are accursed…

Accursed? she repeated to herself, staring at the word. She shook her head and read on, hoping to find something that elaborated on this alarming statement.

They do quarrel and cause strife among themselves and even amongst the people. In many guises, they come and beguile. Some sincere, some treacherous, some virtuous, some malign…

She heard the rattle of crockery and hastily returned the book to its place. Then, flopping into an armchair, she took up *The Labours of the Great Saints*.

Mavier put down a small tray with two cups and a little jar of honey.

'The kettle will soon boil. I cannot carry all the things at once, I'm afraid. My arms are not as strong as my legs.'

'Oh, I'm so sorry, Pastor,' Taygret said, closing the book. 'I'll fetch the tea.'

'Thank you, my dear. The kitchen is at the back of the house. I've already put the leaves in the pot.'

A cloud of steam was filling the little kitchen as Taygret entered. She lifted the kettle off the stove and poured the boiling water into the pot. The hot handle re-awoke the stinging in her hands. When she had finished, she stood looking out the kitchen window at the garden and hill beyond, breathing in the tea's earthy aroma.

Why would a cleric have a heretical text in his house? Were pastors allowed to have it so they could learn about the heresy, the better to detect and combat it?

She was again tempted to broach the topic with him, but it still felt the risk was too great.

When she returned to the parlour, Pastor Mavier had *The Labours of the Great Saints* open in his lap.

'I've found the incident of Jostal and the angels for you,' he said, placing a piece of card between the pages and putting the book on the table. 'A truly uplifting tale.'

As she poured the tea, it reminded her of all the occasions she had performed this simple task in the presence of her beloved uncle. The recollection brought a feeling of tender melancholy with it.

'Now, my dear, I expect you already know what I'm going to ask you next,' the little cleric said, looking at her with a serious expression.

Oh, my Divine. Does he somehow know I've looked at Mardene's book?

She could not stop herself from glancing up to see if she had pushed the volume back into its place properly.

'Would you consider becoming my housekeeper?'

Taygret sighed and smiled and said, 'Oh, actually, I didn't expect you to ask me that.'

In other circumstances, she might have welcomed the offer. It would presumably give her more opportunities to read *Spirits Bright and Turbulent*.

'I have little experience to speak of,' she continued. 'You haven't tasted my cooking for one thing.'

'Having spent much of my life listening to people, counselling them, hearing their confessions, I think I'm a pretty good judge of character. Experience isn't as important as being a worthy person. As for cooking, I enjoy that myself. We could make our meals together.'

'I'm flattered, Pastor, thank you. I will think about it, I promise.'

'Good. There's no hurry. Take as much time as you like.'

As she walked back towards Niklay's house with Pastor Mavier's book under her arm, Taygret felt sad. Such a good-natured, sprightly man who must have befriended so many people in this town, seemed largely forgotten and now needed to hire companionship. She supposed many of his former congregation must have died, like his housekeeper, or at least be unable to accompany him on his walks.

A message awaited her when she returned. She was to meet her next client that evening. Mistress Robikoy certainly meant to keep her busy.

Taygret watched as the shiny, deep blue carriage drew up outside the house at quarter to eight, and a man in a sombre, grey suit stepped carefully out. Master Boannix was obviously not as agile as Pastor Mavier. She went out to greet him. His face was heavily lined, and the top of his head was bald, but his white beard and moustache had been neatly trimmed. His career had been in politics, according to Niklay, and he had served as the mayor of Gennlar for a time. He bowed stiffly as Taygret advanced towards him, and when he had straightened again as best he could, he kissed her outstretched hand. No one had ever done this before, and she simpered a little.

'Good evening, Miss Draillis. Very pleased to make your acquaintance. I am Lannal Boannix, at your service.'

'Charmed,' was all she could say because she was.

'I have a table reserved for us at the Golden Gannet. If you would be so good as to step into my conveyance.'

He handed her up into the carriage. When he joined her, he tapped on the roof with a black cane, and the coachman urged the horse forward.

As they rode, Master Boannix confided in her that he had bought two of Niklay's paintings.

'He has a modest talent. But to be honest, I purchased them mainly to support and encourage him. But do not tell him I said so, I beg you,' he said with a wink and a grin.

When they arrived at the Golden Gannet, a doorman came forward and opened the carriage door. After tipping the man, Boannix crooked his arm, and Taygret took it. As they entered the glittering restaurant, she almost felt like a proper lady. She recalled the night she and Fredrik had spent in the barn. Was that really only five nights ago?

A waiter showed them to their table and told them what was on the menu. Boannix recommended the dressed crab which Taygret agreed to try.

'They used to do a wonderful wild boar casserole,' he told her once the server had gone. 'The meat came all the way from the Craggiston Hills, but the conflict in the area has sadly made it unavailable. So we must make do with more local produce for the time being.'

'I do hope that will all be over soon,' Taygret said.

'Well, our brave troops are certainly holding their own at the moment. They are dug in around Vorskran, and the Pragnars cannot dislodge them. But I'm sure you don't want to dwell on such frightful things. Tell me, where are you from, my dear?'

'Amdris. I left when my uncle died. He was my last remaining relative in the city, so I thought I would come and live by the coast.'

'What did your uncle do in Amdris?'

'He was a professor at the university.'

'Oh, I heard of a university professor who had been killed there recently. They think it was probably murder. A most horrible acid attack, apparently. That wasn't your uncle, was it?' He peered into her face with pained concern.

How had the conversation got to this point? Why must he be so well informed? She was trembling. So Master Rassish had died. She looked down at the silver cutlery and felt quite sick.

'An acid attack?' she murmured.

At that moment, the waiter brought their wine. Taygret wanted to take a drink but her hands were shaking too much.

'I'm sorry,' Boannix said. 'I have upset you with my insensitive prattle. Let's talk of more pleasant things.'

'But… the professor who was killed must have been a colleague of my uncle's. Do you know any more about it?'

'Not much, I'm afraid. But I understand from my acquaintances in the police that they are expecting some notices of a woman who is a suspect in the case. They should arrive any day now. I'm sure they will receive more details then. I will inform you of anything else I hear if you really wish to know.'

Taygret rallied a little as she picked at her food. She reminded herself that she was entertaining a paying client. She had to put aside the surging dismay and smile and be congenial. It was as well that Master Boannix seemed to put her discomfiture down to feminine sensibilities.

He invited her to call him Lannal, and she felt obliged to allow him to use her assumed first name. She was thankful for Mistress Hettrig's advice not to use her real name, but she had become complacent, thinking the police would have more pressing matters than pursuing her. If these notices had a good likeness of her, though, she was bound to be identified. She was aware she turned heads even in Amdris, let alone here.

Twenty-one

Eldam

'They're posing as a royalist Mellian family who have fled their country in order to avoid persecution,' Yagbert told Eldam. 'But we've seen foreign types with satchels going in and out, sometimes at night. We think they're carrying secret messages. The house must be the headquarters of a Mellian spy network.'

'You're not seriously proposing to blow up their house?' Eldam said as he regarded the fervent gaze of the Rardles' leader.

'We don't intend to destroy the entire building, my dear fellow. Just do a bit of damage to the kitchen. We'll send them a note saying we know what they're about and the blast will augment the warning. No one will be hurt. Everyone sleeps on the upper floors.'

'It'll be a glorious act of patriotism,' said Lon, leaning as far across the table as his diminutive frame allowed. 'The king'll be right proud of us. While his cowardly government refuses to act, the Melons plot to overthrow him under their very noses.'

Eldam rubbed his chin. 'This is rather more than just keeping a lookout for Mellian provocateurs.'

'We haven't had anyone with your expertise before,' Yagbert told him. 'With your help, we can seize the initiative. Put a stop to their nefarious activities and hopefully persuade them to bugger off back to Mellia.'

'Hmm, well, in order to make gunpowder, I would have to do a little research. I know the ingredients but not the proportions needed to do a job like that. I'll have to go to the library and look it up.'

Yagbert grunted, but Eldam wasn't sure if it was in agreement or frustration.

As it happened, the next day was Lordsday, and the public libraries were closed, so in the morning, he let Yagbert take him to view the house in question. It was in one of Damlon's more affluent districts. They strolled along a lane at the back of the premises. Eldam could just see over a wall built between the lane and a small garden.

Yagbert paused and bent to brush at a leg of his pantaloons. 'The door across the garden leads into the kitchen,' he said. 'It will be locked, of course, but Lon can pick it easy enough.'

As Eldam gazed up at the three storeys of white stuccoed elegance, it seemed to him like a smaller version of the Foreign Department. He thought of the patriotic mission given to him in that other building. The idea of getting mysterious spirits to catch foreign revolutionaries made blowing up their kitchen seem rather more sensible.

But Eldam shook his head. 'I don't like it. Peace officers would make frequent patrols in an area like this.'

Yagbert walked on down the lane. 'Best not to linger too long,' he said when Eldam caught up. 'We can come to an accommodation with the peaceys. Some feel the same way we do. Once you tell Lon what you need to make the powder, his contacts can procure it for you. Will you come back to the house? Polly is cooking chops for lunch.'

'No. I'll walk for a bit. It's been a while since I saw the sights of Damlon.'

'I'm glad your feet have improved.'

'Yes, that salty soak last night helped a lot.'

'Good. Well, I'll see you when you return then.'

Eldam wandered the length of a couple of streets, each lined with respectable-looking houses much like the one he and Yagbert had reconnoitred. He wanted to think about what he should do regarding the Rardles and Abren, but the one person who came to his mind was Taygret. He decided to buy a newspaper and find out what was happening in her embattled country. Hopefully, the Mellian army could prevent their enemies from reaching Amdris somehow and that Taygret and her uncle would be safe.

He found a newsstand at the entrance to a park and looked for a bench where he might sit and read. The park was busy with Lordsday leisure seekers. Couples strolled along the broad pathways while children and dogs capered on the grass. A band played rousing music from a raised, circular platform. He came to a lake with families in boats and a great number of ducks, coots and swans. War seemed as remote as rain from the bright spring sky.

He eventually found a vacant seat and sat down. He had to turn several pages before he came to the foreign news. As Mister Gleagan had told him, Rarland kept aloof from the troubles of other countries. The reports were good on the whole. The Pragnar army was held up trying to take a Mellian town far to the west of Amdris and were apparently suffering heavy losses. Dysentery had broken out amongst Skiglander troops in the north, halting their advance.

Eldam gazed out over the lake. He imagined being in a boat with Taygret, him rowing, her wearing a beautiful white dress, trailing her hand in the water.

He shook himself out of his fantasy. First, he had to dissociate himself from the Rardles. The more he learnt about them, the more fanatical they appeared. The plot to cause an explosion in someone's kitchen was not something he wanted to be involved in. An act of patriotism or not, he was sure the authorities would not take kindly to it. Which meant he had to collect his bag, leave their house and find some other temporary accommodation. He could simply tell Yagbert that he thought their idea was reckless and walk out. But that risked the Rardles concluding that he was a traitor, however he tried to reassure them otherwise. He knew of their plans, and their zeal made them dangerous. He did not want to find himself at the wrong end of Lon's dagger.

They had accepted that he needed to go to a library tomorrow. Might that be his opportunity? Taking all his belongings with him would no doubt raise their suspicions, though. Or he could sneak out tonight and hope that if he disappeared amongst Damlon's multitude, they would not try to find him. There were enough suspect foreigners to keep them occupied. He decided upon the latter option. He had some experience of slipping out of a building at night, after all.

Then there was contacting Abren. His only lead was Jessel. He would have to go to her stall tomorrow, tell her of his brother's pardon and hope she has more information about him.

He spent a few hours walking, thinking, eating at a lakeside coffee shop and reading the rest of his newspaper, basking in the holiday mood of the park. When he returned in the late afternoon, the gloomy, squalid condition of the Rardles' neighbourhood was all the more oppressive in comparison. When he knocked, no one answered. He knocked again. Still no response. He tried the door. It was locked.

They must all be out. Walking their damn dog, probably.

They had not given him a key, Yagbert said they did not have a spare one, but if he could just get in, he could collect his bag and be off without any fuss. He knew the house backed onto an alley even narrower than this one. He retraced his steps onto the street. There were a few people about, mostly gathered on their doorsteps, talking to neighbours, children playing in the gutter. He passed an old man sitting huddled in a tattered, grey blanket. Eldam stopped, pulled a copper coin from his purse and pressed it into the man's outstretched hand.

'The Lord bless you, sir,' the man muttered.

Eldam hoped his benevolence would indeed bring a blessing upon his mission.

The back alley was dark and stank of urine. All manner of rubbish had been left strewn about. Picking his way through the detritus and peering into dirty windows, he soon recognised the Rardles' kitchen, but they had locked its door as well. He looked up and saw that he had left the window of his bedroom slightly open.

The house opposite was clearly abandoned, the door hung half off its hinges. The alley was so narrow that if he could get to the upstairs window, he might be able to jump across. Entering, he stood a while until his eyes could make out the shapes around him. The smell of mould hung in the air. A few pieces of dusty, broken furniture lay scattered about on the bare floorboards. He wondered why no homeless person had claimed the place.

When he found the stairs, he saw the bannister had fallen away and that the steps looked rotten. Keeping close to the wall, he walked gingerly up. The further he went, the louder the creaking became. Halfway up, he paused. He detected another odour, one of decay. He had smelt it before in gruesome anatomy classes at the university as Master Rassish blithely dissected a diseased cadaver for the students' edification. As he resumed his assent, the stench grew stronger.

When he got to the landing, he realised that the window opposite his own was in the room where the body must be. Covering his mouth and nose with his sleeve, he opened the door and gagged. It was an emaciated old woman laying on her side, a rat nibbling her ear. Big, black flies covered the open sores on her hands and ankles. This must be why the house was unoccupied, and even the impoverished shunned it, fearful of the dead.

He shooed the predators away, then went to the window. With some difficulty, he pulled it up. The frame was rotten and small pieces of white-painted wood broke away, adding to the debris littering the floor. He leant out and drew in a lungful of air. When the nausea subsided, he looked back at the corpse. She made a pitiful sight.

Hot anger burned in his watering eyes. While the well-to-do strolled in the park and government officials took jolly rides on steam engines, the destitute starved to death alone in derelict houses. How would building railways improve the life of poor souls like this woman? He began to understand what Abren meant when he wrote of the blight of poverty his brother saw every day since coming to live in Damlon.

He would need to inform the peace officers of his discovery after he retrieved his bag. He looked at the window opposite and saw it would not be as simple as he imagined. Leaping across would not be so difficult, but the ledge he needed to land on was narrow, and there was nothing he could grasp onto. He had left a gap of three or four inches at the bottom of his window, but it would be extremely precarious trying to balance on the ledge while he reached down to pull up the lower sash.

He would have to attempt his escape tonight, after all. Of course, the Rardles would make sure their house was locked up fast when they went to bed. Then there was the wretched dog. If he woke it up in the middle of the night, it would no doubt yap its stupid head off. He considered dropping from his room into the alley, but the clutter below made it hazardous.

It'd be just my luck to break an ankle.

Then an idea struck him. He could take the route he had been planning in the opposite direction tonight. If he left a gap at the top of this window, he could jump over from his room and grab it.

'Peace be with you, Mother,' he murmured to the old woman's remains. 'Your struggles are over now.'

He left the run-down dwelling and went out onto the nearby street. The beggar was still at his post, and he willingly directed Eldam towards the local peace office at the presentation of two more coppers. As he approached the building, he was surprised to see a familiar figure come out of it.

'Jessel,' he called.

She turned and smiled uncertainly at him. She seemed a little nervous.

'What were you doing in the peace office?' he asked, thinking it must have something to do with Abren.

'It's a bit of a long story,' she said. 'I'll tell you about it but not here. Will you walk with me for a while?'

'I have to go in and report a dead body I found.'

'Oh Lord. Where was that?'

'In an abandoned house near where I'm staying.'

'Well, they're pretty busy at the moment. They just sent me away. But I suppose you'd better tell them about that. Be careful though, they might take you for Abren. You'll see his wanted poster up outside.'

'Oh right. I hadn't thought of that.'

'I'll wait for you on the next corner.'

As Jessel walked away, Eldam turned towards the peace station. He glanced at Abren's likeness displayed on the wall beside the door. Even though Jessel had warned him, it was still something of a shock seeing it there. And she was right, he had to be wary, their resemblance was so striking. He hesitated. Should he risk going in? Then he thought of the old woman laying abandoned amongst the dust and the vermin. He entered the building rubbing at his forehead to hide his face, but the peacey on desk duty was so patently absorbed in the paperwork before him he only raised his head enough to see the approaching feet meant another interruption.

'What?' he snapped.

After hastily taking down the details of the body and its location, he asked, 'And your name and address, sir?'

'Oh, Eldam… Egring. I haven't got an address yet. I've only just arrived in Damlon.'

The peace officer sighed in frustration but still did not look up. 'Just give me somewhere local where we can contact you. An inn or something.'

'The Dog and Duck.'

'Right then. Thank you for the information. Good day to you, sir.'

'I saw Abren earlier,' Jessel said as they walked. 'He told me to tell you he's all right and not to worry about him.'

'I know why he's wanted by the peaceys.'

Jessel stopped and turned to him. 'Oh yeah? What do you know?'

There was a hard ferocity in her voice. Eldam liked it. He glanced behind him.

'I know he can talk to spirits,' he whispered. 'He spoke to a priest about it, and the priest reported him to the peaceys.'

'And who told you that?' She fixed him with an icy glare. He liked that too.

He thought he ought to start from the beginning if she was to believe him. He patted his chin and resumed walking.

'I acquired a letter while I was in Mellia addressed to the Foreign Department here in Damlon. When I went to deliver this letter, they asked my name and somehow knew I was related to Abren. They want to talk to him about his… ability. They said they would give him a pardon.'

He looked at her. Jessel's hostile expression had changed to one of suspicious confusion.

'Why are they interested in him talking to spirits? The peaceys think he's a dangerous lunatic.'

Eldam smelt foetid mud. They must be nearing the river. He surveyed the street. No one seemed to be taking any notice of them, but he still did not like the idea of saying what he needed to in such a public place.

'Well?' Jessel demanded.

'Do you fancy a boat ride?' he asked her.

Jessel finally let go of the little boat's gunwales. She had been clinging on as if she expected them to capsize at any moment. It had not helped when a large sailing vessel passed them, causing the boat Eldam had hired to rock vigorously. He rowed the craft steadily upstream, waiting for her response. He had told her everything that had transpired at the government office.

'You can appreciate the need to ensure our conversation is strictly private,' he said as Jessel remained in silent reflection.

She nodded. He was not sure if her scowl was because of her digesting the information he had given her or her obvious discomfort at being on the water.

'He said he would come to Ellford the day after tomorrow,' she said at last. 'At night. In secret. To see me. They threatened me with imprisonment if I didn't find out where he's hiding, and he's coming to see if I'm all right.'

'So that's why you were at the peace station.'

'Yeah, but this pardon changes things.' She managed a small smile. 'Can we go back now? Please.'

He grinned and began turning the boat.

That evening Jagbert, Polly and Lon recounted a thrilling tale of how they had pursued one of their unfortunate 'foreign types' through the backstreets of a nearby district.

'We got this tip off, see,' said Lon. 'These two fellas were at the Dog and Duck. They were sitting in a corner, muttering secretively to each other, but Denry's got good ears and he overheard them say something about a mass rally. Old Den could tell they weren't Rarlish, even though they were talking in our language.'

'He sent his lad round to warn us,' Polly said. 'But by the time we got there, one of them had gone, So we waited for the other one to leave and we collared him outside. Should have seen the look on his face.'

Jagbert took up the narrative. 'I told him we don't tolerate agitators in this country. He just stood there with his mouth open, white as a sheet. But when Howler barked at him, he pushed me aside and bolted. Well, we gave chase of course.'

'Pol got left behind,' Lon said, his eyes bright with excitement. 'And Jag slipped over but me and Howler nearly had him. But then he tossed something behind him and Howler went for it. I tripped over the dozy dog and the man got away.'

'Turns out it was his purse he chucked,' Polly said. 'He must have thought we were out to rob him, so he threw us his money to save his skin.'

Eldam shook his head as if in commiseration of their failed heroics, but really he was trying not to smile.

So that was why there was no one in this afternoon.

'It was a shame you lost him, but at least you got some money out of it,' he said. 'Speaking of which, I should repay you for your hospitality.'

'Oh no, my dear fellow,' replied Jagbert. 'We could not accept anything from you. You are one of us now. An honorary Rardle.'

Thinking of what he planned to do that night, Eldam could not help feeling like a rotten traitor.

He waited until he thought everyone in the house must be asleep, then he dropped his bag out of his bedroom window. It landed in the alley with a dull thud. He tensed, listening for a few seconds, but there were no other sounds.

He could just see the outline of the window opposite.

It's not far, he told himself.

It did not look as if the peace officers had closed it when they removed the old woman's body. Clambering out onto the narrow ledge, he took a deep breath. Suddenly this seemed like an absolutely mad idea.

Damn it, Quist. If you're looking down on this, I hope you're enjoying the spectacle.

He leapt across.

For one heart-stopping second, his hands could not find the gap at the top of the window. He swayed backwards. Then his desperately scrabbling fingers got a hold. The frame creaked and cracked as he clutched it one-handed. He quickly reached down and pulled the bottom sash up as far as it would go. When he scrambled, panting, into the room, he knew at once that the peaceys had not come for the corpse. The stink was every bit as bad. He hurried down the dilapidated staircase and out into the alley. He retrieved his bag and strode off into the dark, urban world.

Twenty-two

Taygret

The morning after her troubling conversation with Lannal Boannix at the Golden Gannet, Taygret received another note and a package.

Dear Miss Draillis. Your third and last assignment will be this evening with Master Vostermein. He wishes to take you to the theatre, I believe. He will call for you at seven-thirty. I say it is to be your last as my husband begs me to inform you that you are to be ready to sail with the morning tide tomorrow at seven. A cart will come to take you and your effects to the harbour at six. Have on the clothes sent herewith and tie back your hair. Wear no ornamentation of any kind. Sweet and tender regards to you, and safe travels. Mistress Flora Robikoy.

At the bottom, written in large letters, she saw, *BURN THIS NOW.*

She was sitting with Niklay having breakfast in the bay window overlooking the street. A thrill of excitement rose inside her as she handed him the note and began unwrapping the package. So she was to depart in less than twenty-four hours. Surely before any notices arrived from Amdris declaring her a murder suspect. Once she had pulled off the string and begun unfolding the brown wax paper, the contents of the parcel were revealed to be rather dirty and a little smelly.

'Oh, I'm so sorry,' she said, grimacing. 'I should look at these upstairs.'

'Not at all,' said the artist as he crumpled the note and tossed it into the fire. 'I'd like to see what they want you to wear. I'll open a window.'

She stood and held up a pair of ragged, baggy and very stained, dark blue pantaloons. When Niklay turned from the window, she looked at him, and they both burst out laughing.

All that day, Niklay worked feverishly at her portrait, trying to bring it to a point where he could finish it once she had left the country. She reflected what a bitter irony it would be if he proceeded with his project of painting multiple copies of her likeness to sell to admiring patrons only to find her image displayed on walls around the town associated with a heinous crime. Although she felt sad and guilty at the thought, she could do nothing about it. She could hardly warn him.

In the late afternoon, he declared he was satisfied. Taygret shook her head as she looked at herself, smiling a little coquettishly back, but she was not displeased.

'Not bad,' she said. 'You've made me into a paragon, and I can hardly complain about that.'

Niklay simply bowed, and she left his studio for the last time. She charged him with returning *The Labours of the Great Saints* to Pastor Mavier and informing that warmhearted gentleman that, regrettably, she would not be taking up his offer of becoming his housekeeper. Then she began preparing for her final evening in Mellia.

Master Vostermein's carriage was even grander than that of Lannal Boannix, needing two horses to pull it. Inside, the seats were covered with dark green velvet and even the walls were lined with it. Vostermein described himself as an investor and speculator and spent the ride to the theatre explaining what he invested and speculated in, mostly land and property. Taygret was grateful they were going to see a play and that she would not have to listen to his self-satisfied boasting all evening. He was a deal younger than her other clients. His hair, bushy moustache and eyebrows were a rich ginger, and he spoke with an easy languor as he regarded her from beneath his long eyelashes.

When they drew up in front of the theatre, Taygret saw a large group of people had gathered around the main doors, clamouring for admittance. But after they descended from the coach, Vostermein led her towards a smaller entrance a few yards to the right where several couples were filing in. The men in their dark, sleek suits made the ladies' colourful silks and feathers all the more dazzling. Taygret had on the best dress she still possessed, but she thought she must look almost dowdy in comparison.

When it was their turn, Vostermein presented two tickets, and an usher led them up some narrow red-carpeted stairs to a little box containing just two seats. Taygret realised they would have a good view of the performance whilst the audience crowding onto the floor below and in the other gilded boxes opposite would have a good view of them. A chandelier holding numerous candles hung from the ceiling, illuminating the auditorium and the small stage. Taygret had been to theatres in Amdris with her uncle and once with Eldam. She thought they made this one look almost cramped in comparison.

No, don't be so snobbish, she chided herself. *Not cramped, intimate.*

The play was a satire, lampooning the erstwhile royal family, with many bawdy jests about the old king's alleged promiscuity. This delighted the spectators standing in the pit, who hooted and jeered raucously. Vostermein also seemed to enjoy it, his broad shoulders shaking as he snickered at the lewd japes.

In the interval they went down to the foyer where drinks were being served. Vostermein bought Taygret a glass of red wine, and they mingled with some of the more wealthy members of the audience. She was annoyed when he jokingly introduced her as his 'new consort', especially as the men grinned and winked, apparently interpreting this as meaning his latest conquest.

The conversation largely revolved around the effect the war was having on the price of imported goods. The men grumbling about how it made commerce less profitable, and the women complaining of the increase in their household expenditure. None of this was of much interest to Taygret and she spent the time observing how the undercurrent of social competitiveness played out, whose business was the most flourishing or which family was the more prominent.

During the second half of the comedy, Vostermein seemed to lose interest in the performance. He kept leaning in close as he spoke into Taygret's ear, making unflattering observations about the people with whom he had been conversing cordially just a short while ago. But then his remarks found another topic.

'You really are a most splendid jewel, Miss Draillis, far more fascinating than this shabby show.'

She smiled. 'You are very kind to say so, Master Vostermein.'

She knew at once it was a mistake to acknowledge the compliment so frankly. She was trying to play the gracious companion, but Vostermein took encouragement from it.

'I hope we may become good friends, you and I,' he said.

'Please, sir. I'll thank you not to take liberties with me,' she replied as she pushed his hand from her knee.

'Forgive me, Miss. I have allowed my captivation to make me forget myself.'

They watched the rest of the play in silence.

There were a few carriages awaiting their owners under the twinkling lamps outside the theatre. As Taygret and Vostermein walked down the line towards his vehicle, he said,

'What did you think of the play, Miss Draillis?'

'It was rather vulgar for my taste.'

'Yes, I was afraid you might say that. I apologise. Both for my choice of entertainment and for my deplorable conduct towards you earlier.'

Knowing she would sail out of Gennlar on the morning tide, she felt secure enough to say, 'You are forgiven, Master Vostermein. But I hope you will be more gentlemanly in your behaviour towards ladies in future.'

'Of course. I… Oh, look, that man is about to post something on the wall there. Notice of a new play, I expect. Perhaps it will be something more to your liking.'

She watched with mounting horror as the man in question began unrolling the notice, Vostermein looking eagerly on.

'Oh, Well, I, err…' A numbing wave of panic was rising up inside her. 'Would you like a little kiss?'

'I beg your pardon.' Vostermein's attention wheeled back to her.

'As a reward for regretting and amending your behaviour. I'll allow you just one quick, little kiss. But not here. Perhaps on the quay… in the moonlight?'

'Very well,' he said with a bemused smile. 'Kimson, bring the carriage round to the quay and meet us in fifteen minutes.'

Taygret was sorely tempted to glance back at the notice as they walked away, but she did not want to break the spell she had her companion under.

When they came out onto the waterfront, the moon did indeed shine down gently upon them, contrasting with the bright, little pools of yellow light cast by the lanterns hung at intervals from wooden posts along the quayside. Taygret stopped under one of them. She could hear the water lapping gently against the jetty. A few of the other theatregoers had also chosen to stroll here. It might have been a rather romantic spot if not for the pungent smell of fish. She turned to face Master Vostermein. Her heart was racing. She was afraid he would try to take advantage of her generosity and thought of how the magistrate in Peridere had clutched at her. But his civility held, and when she stretched up and met his mouth with hers, he only put his hands lightly on her arms.

'Thank you, Miss Draillis. I hope I may be able to meet with you again.'

'Perhaps. But you will need to apply to Mistress Robikoy.'

As the carriage made its way through Gennlar's darkened streets to Niklay's house, it was Taygret who did most of the talking, telling Vostermein of the plays she had seen in Amdris. They alighted outside the artist's door and bid each other a courteous good night.

The servant let her in and informed her Niklay had already retired to his bed. It was not until she reached the sanctuary of her room that she began shaking. The candle she was carrying almost toppled from its holder. She put it down and hugged herself as she paced the floor. The notices were already going up. In the morning, everyone in the town would know.

She sat on the bed, her feet tapping on the floor in restless agitation. Bending forward, she put her face in her hands and moaned softly in desolate anguish. When the mardene appeared, she felt such a surge of gratitude that she wanted to embrace it, but she guessed its apparent insubstantiality would make that impossible.

'What am I to do?' she asked, her voice as unsteady as her insides. 'Do I really deserve to be hanged?'

'I do not believe so, dear Taygret,' the spirit replied in its soft, high voice. 'But many of your people no doubt will. As to what you should do, you need only proceed with the course set in motion. You have nothing to fear. Those sheets you saw do not concern you.'

'Oh, thank The Divine. Thank you, sweet… angel.' She was smiling through her tears of relief.

'It was not of my doing, but of course I am glad. I want to see you safely to your destination.'

'I read a little from a book about you, your kind, I mean. It said some of you are mean and that you sometimes quarrel.'

'Yes, alas, that is true. It is because of this that I will need your help.'

'What can I do?'

The light that seemed to be the substance of the spirit's body quivered slightly like an unsteady flame.

'When you were in the old woman's cottage, did you discern anything unusual?'

'Yes, and I feel it again now. I'm sure it has something to do with you mardenes.'

'But no spirits were manifest at that time. You see, if two of your ability meet, it is really rather exceptional, and things that you would consider extraordinary may sometimes occur. This is how you may be able to assist me when you reach the city where your lover has gone. A troublesome spirit has beset his brother there, and great misfortune may come of it. Your intervention may be crucial. I will guide you as best I can. I hope you will trust me in this.'

'Yes, I do trust you. You have proven yourself a friend to me.'

'That is good. Farewell then. We will meet again before long.'

Once more alone, she began to remove her clothes. As she was untying the pockets from around her waist, she remembered the piece of paper she had been writing on earlier, before Fredrik interrupted her. She took it out and reread it, then shook her head. So foolish to carry around something so incriminating. She thought of what Mistress Robikoy had put at the end of her last note, *BURN THIS NOW*. She held the page above the candle until it was alight and dropped it in the fireplace.

When she had finished undressing, she snuffed out the candle, and lay down, but she could not find sleep. Her dread of capture and prosecution had been replaced by something else.

Troublesome spirit. Crucial intervention.

A sense of foreboding twisted inside her.

Your lover.

Taygret felt a longing like never before.

Twenty-three

Eldam

Eldam Medloe,
Room 13,
Chennswell House,
Bradderbridge,
Damlon.

Esteemed Father,

It is with the deepest regret that I write to inform you that, due to the upheavals in Mellia, as referred to in my previous letters, I have been obliged to leave that country and return to Rarland. You will, I am sure, appreciate the magnitude of my frustration at having my studies disrupted in this way. I will, of course, apply to the university here in Damlon at the earliest opportunity.

I know you will be disappointed at my having to attend what you believe to be an inferior institution, especially after the expense you and Sir Nortach went to in order to place me at such a prestigious university as Amdris, but the authorities in that city left me no choice. Indeed, I count myself fortunate that I was not put in custody, such is the mistrust that has fallen upon foreign nationals there.

I have taken up temporary lodgings at the above address and I would be extremely grateful if you would kindly redirect

your generous allowance to the Damlon offices of Cinder's
Bank. The bursar at Amdris University assured me that
an appropriate portion of this year's fee will be refunded to
you. I will inform you of the particulars regarding the fees to
Damlon University as soon as I have them.

I would also like to take this opportunity to urge you
to consider a reconciliation with Abren. On arriving here I
found that his employment at the city docks has unfortunately
been terminated through no fault of his own and he now finds
himself in rather straightened circumstances.

Eldam stopped writing, gave a deep sigh and looked up at
the ceiling. Then he crumpled the sheet of paper on the
table in front of him in a tight fist. He shook his head. He
was sending his father bad news about himself and begging
a favour from him. Much as he wanted to see the breach
between him and Abren healed, it would not be wise to
broach the subject in this letter. Their sire was by nature
stubborn and unforgiving. He had best wait until he could
arrange a visit to the irascible old gentleman and try to
muster the courage to persuade him then, face to face.

Once his father's money arrived, he would help Abren as
best he could until his brother got his life back onto an even
keel. He smoothed the paper out, drew a fresh sheet in front
of him and began copying the first part of the rejected letter.

When he had finished, Eldam took the short walk to
the General Post Office. After handing his letter to the clerk
and paying the postage fee, he asked for directions to the
university. He thought he could at least make enquiries
about when he might present his credentials and have an

interview, although he knew he would be at the back of the queue of those students returning from Mellia after the inopportune delay in Frenbar.

Wending his way through the bustling streets, he reflected on his father's derogatory remarks about the university in Damlon.

You'd be lucky if you got more than two lectures a week and even they won't teach you anything useful. Most of what the students there manage to learn is self-taught. All the damned professors are idlers, more interested in drinking, feasting and gambling.

Eldam was not sure what his father had based this assessment on, not having attended a university himself. He thought it was probably a gross exaggeration, he certainly hoped so now.

He emerged onto a wide street with a line of birch trees down the centre. Walking past the bookshops, tailors and coffeehouses, he noticed there were fewer people about here, which he thought was rather strange. Even the shops and eateries seemed curiously empty.

Ahead he saw the street led into what appeared to be a large square and as he approached, he heard shouting. Emerging into the plaza, the sight before him revealed why the surrounding area was so unpopulated. A sizable crowd of people had gathered, filling nearly half the square. They were all facing a substantial, grey stone building which, if Eldam judged correctly, was the administrative offices of the university. A young man was standing on a cart in front of this edifice. He had a wild mane of long blond hair which tossed about as he shook his fist and shouted.

'Every man with any sort of power in this country is appointed by the king. Every law passed in this country must have his approval. Our lives, the lives of millions, are in his hands alone, subject to his whims. Is it any wonder that he sits on a golden throne in a vast palace while we and our children go hungry?'

Several people in the crowd responded to this question. There were cries of 'no' and 'shame', 'down with the king' and 'The Lord bless HIs Majesty'. Whatever the response of the individuals, the passions of the people were clearly being excited by the young man.

This must be the rally those men in the Dog and Duck were talking about. The ones Jagbert and his cronies had tried to intimidate.

Eldam looked around. Some peace officers were grouped on the fringes of the throng, watching as the drama unfolded. There were too few of them to wade into the mob and arrest the speaker, as they no doubt wanted to do. Perhaps they were waiting for reinforcements. Several of the officers had drawn their clubs ready for any opportunity to intervene. The sight suddenly brought a chilling recollection to Eldam's mind. How Lon had pulled a similar weapon from his coat outside the ministry buildings when he saw their little group was being pursued. Eldam frantically searched the mass of people before him. This was indeed just the sort of event the Rardles feared. It would not surprise him to see one or all of them here somewhere.

The crowd was becoming restive and one or two scuffles were breaking out. He hastily retreated into the boulevard. He would have to forget about visiting the university today.

Twenty-four

Abren

Madame Esprit's worried frown gazed at the curtains that covered her window onto Upper Field Street.

'If it wants you to kill someone, it is an evil spirit indeed. Even if it says it wants to help the poor, that doesn't justify murder.'

'I'm not convinced its motives are philanthropic at all. But what am I to do? Can I get rid of it somehow? Protect myself against it?'

Abren was no longer curious about being able to summon the spectre, he wanted nothing more to do with it. He was almost whispering, hoping that keeping his voice down would prevent it from overhearing him. It was the day after his meeting with Jessel, and he had spent the daylight hours building the bookcase for Faren's local historian, Felix Mennan. Then, as dusk was descending onto the country roads, made a brisk march to Marfryd.

'There are amulets, certain stones that help ward off evil influences. Prayers…'

'It claimed there's no Lord, no angels or ghosts, only spirits… beings like it is.'

'Did it, though? It would seem to be deceitful as well in that case. That is only to be expected, I suppose. All good spirits acknowledge the one true source of all things.'

She got up and turned towards the mantelpiece, where she took down a wooden jewellery box. Shadows shifted as she moved about the candlelit room.

'I can give you a small schorl crystal,' she continued, opening the box. 'It may help to repel the spirit.'

She handed him what appeared to Abren to be a tiny piece of coal.

'Keep it on you at all times. But be careful; it is not a hard stone. Wrap it in some cloth.'

She then went to a sideboard and, from a drawer, produced a card that she also gave to him.

'You might find this prayer helpful. I suggest you say it out loud, first thing in the morning and before you go to bed at night.'

Abren saw that on one side of the card was a picture of a man with a long, grey beard dressed in white robes, a golden halo around his head. Turning it over, he read *Saint Pieton's Shield* above the words of the prayer.

'Thank you,' he said. 'I feel I should give you something.'

'Not at all,' replied the clairvoyant. 'I only hope these things may be of some use to you.'

Walking back to Faren, Abren kept his mind on finding his way in the almost total darkness, trying not to think about what might happen if the spirit confronted him in the lonely, rural lanes. Nevertheless, he felt relief when he saw the lights from the tavern windows ahead of him. As he went in by the side entrance, he glanced through the open door to the bar. There were still a few drinkers keeping Ross and Martia busy. He realised it was exactly a week ago that the altercation took place and the furniture got broken. The last seven days had flown by.

He had not knelt by his bed since he was a boy, nor anywhere else for that matter. He had said his prayers mainly to please his mother. When she died, he had concluded prayers were useless.

'Lord be always with me, protect me with your love. Always walk beside me, behind me and above.' He felt self-conscious, ludicrous even. 'Lord be always with me, in waking or asleep. Surround me with your goodness, and in your care me keep.'

The card was lying on his bed, barely illuminated by a candle on the window ledge. He clutched the black crystal in his right hand.

'Lord be always with me, hold me close, I pray…'

Then the light from the candle was overwhelmed by an altogether greater radiance.

'The Lord will not aid you, Abren. Only I can truly be of help to you. But now it is time for you to help me.'

Abren bowed his head so that it almost touched his blanket. He let the disappointment and frustration wash over him, then, sending out an exasperated puff of air from his lungs, he stood and faced the spectre. He waited for it to continue.

'Brother Eusebius has come to the capital. You must now do as I have asked. Seek him out. Say you have heard of his teachings and wish to confess your vain and rebellious nature. He loves to have people humble themselves before him. Conceal your sharpest tool about you. When you are alone with him, deliver it into his heart, and you will have done an immense service to the poor folk of your city.'

'And if I refuse?'

'As I told you, I have seen to it that your lady friend is safe. I could just as easily do the opposite. I do not enjoy making threats, but this mission is more important than you might understand. I will be watching.'

Abren clenched his teeth and bit down on his fury. 'You… you don't really care about the plight of the poor, do you? You only spout that stuff to try and manipulate me. Why do you really want me to kill this man?'

Again he had to wait for a response.

'I told you that another of my kind protects this Eusebius. That spirit chooses to be meddlesome in the affairs of your people. It is true I care little for the doings of this world, but those of this other spirit are a different matter. We are… at odds. I will say no more of this. Do as I tell you, and all will be well, but if you disappoint me, you will not be the only one to regret it.'

With that, it vanished, leaving Abren shocked and numb by the spectre's implication. Devious, malignant thing that it was, it knew a threat against Jessel had more power over him than one against himself.

The next morning Abren put the finishing touches to the bookcase and was gratified to find Felix, so pleased with it he gave him an extra five silvers above what he had asked as well as a further loan of his horse. Before he handed his bag of tools to Ross for safekeeping, he slipped a slender chisel into a pocket of his coat. Then, shortly before noon, he mounted the mare and took the now familiar towpath towards Damlon. This time instead of turning onto the road to Bornell, he continued on, following the part of the canal he had walked a week previously. He pushed the horse into a trot from time to time, anxious to discover if the spectre had indeed protected Jessel from the peace officers.

After leaving the canal, he braved the streets of Ellford, even paying the copper toll for his mount at the turnpike gate on Radial Road. He knew he was succumbing to recklessness, but it had been a long couple of days since the tryst in Saint Harnin's graveyard.

At a cabstand, he gave a waterman six coppers to tend the horse. Then, picking his way through the waiting cabs, horses and mounds of manure, he headed towards the high street and the fruit stall where he prayed he would find Jessel. He had let his whiskers grow during his sojourn in Faren in the faint hope that he would be less recognisable, but Jessel had not even commented on his burgeoning beard when they met, so he put little faith in the disguise. His cap would need to hide his features.

Approaching the stall, he saw only Fran serving a well-heeled-looking man with a shiny top hat. His heart was a thundering panic inside of him. As he reached the stall, the top hat moved on, and Jessel popped up from behind the piles of produce. A surge of relief brought a broad grin to his face, but she stared back at him in wide-eyed astonishment.

'I thought you were going to come tonight,' she said.

'I had to see if you were all right. I finished the job and came straight away. What happened with the peaceys?'

She grimaced then gestured for him to go with her. She retreated a little way into the perpetual shadows of the nearby alley. Once they were cosseted in this relatively secluded spot, Jessel folded her arms.

'Well, you wouldn't believe it, but the sergeant who was on to me was killed, shot by some crook.' She hesitated. 'Do you think your angel might've had something to do with it?'

'Yes, I do. It's ruthless. Evil.' He was speaking in whispers again now. He paused before he said, 'It wants me to kill someone.'

'What! You're joking. Tell me you're joking.'

'No, it's no joke, I assure you.'

'But why? Who? And why does it have to be you?'

'It's someone called Brother Eusebius.'

'The preacher?'

'Yeah. Have you heard of him?'

'Yeah. Our landlady mentioned him. All the faith house crowd are talking about him, apparently, and she's really keen to hear him. Wanted me to go. He's at Saint Raul's hall tonight. You're not seriously going to try and kill him.'

'No, of course not. I need to warn him, though. The spirit wants him dead, and if I don't do it, it might get him some other way.' In truth, he was not as resolved as he was trying to sound. He decided not to mention the spectre's threat to her. 'Shall we go tonight? I'll try to see him in private.'

Jessel sighed. 'Someday, you and I will walk out together like normal people do.'

Abren could only wish it were true.

'I saw Eldam again,' she continued. 'I told him you were coming back tonight. He has something important to tell you. But after what you've just told me about your angel… He knows about it. Oh, it's best if he explains it all to you. Lord, my life was really simple before I met you.'

'I'm sorry. If you'd rather I…'

'No. I didn't mean that. I guess I think you're worth all the craziness.' She smiled ruefully then kissed him, long and exciting.

When she finally broke away, Abren did not have the breath to say anything.

'Ooh, well,' Jessel gasped. 'The meeting's at seven. If Eldam hasn't shown up by then, Fran can tell him where we've gone.' She rubbed her chin. 'I don't suppose you could have a shave.'

'I'm trying to look different. I'm still a wanted man, remember?' Abren said. 'Speaking of which, I'll need somewhere to lie low until this evening. Would it be all right to use your place again for a few hours?'

'No, Morri is about most of the day, in and out. I don't know what she gets up to, to be honest. I dunno though, the peaceys are still busy looking for the fella who shot the sergeant and Eldam said you could get a pardon from the government.'

'A pardon?'

'Yeah, but it's complicated. Like I said, it's better if he tells you about it tonight. Anyway, maybe you're right and you should still stay hid for now. You can't use our place, but there's our lock-up. It's not what you'd call comfy, but it might do for a little while.'

'That's a good idea, Jess. I'm sure it'll do fine.'

'Right, well, it's on Gild's Hill, on the left as you go down. The door's got our name on it, Weglin. It's got two padlocks.' She pulled a bunch of keys from under her apron. 'Those two. We'll be down to get Tinker and the cart in a couple of hours. I'll bring you something to eat. Then we'll haul our stuff down and once it's all stowed we can set off for the hall. We should just be able to make it in time for the meeting.'

She handed him the keys, gave him another quick kiss and headed back to the stall. He waited several minutes, watching people walk past the end of the alley, clutching the keys so hard they dug into his palm.

A pardon? How? Why? What's Eldam gone and done?

As soon as they set out for Saint Raul's hall, it became clear it would not be a straightforward trip. Peace officers were in the streets. They were knocking on doors, talking to the inhabitants, stopping people passing by, asking questions. Abren supposed Jessel was right, they were putting all their efforts into tracking down their colleague's killer. Nevertheless, they could not risk being intercepted. Fortunately, Jessel knew some roundabout routes, but it meant they were late, and by the time they pushed open the front doors of the hall the meeting had already begun.

The place was almost full. Mostly people from Saint Raul's congregation, Abren suspected. Ellford was not generally renowned for religious zeal. He and Jessel lowered themselves onto a bench in the back row. A tall man in a black robe stood on a dais at the far end of the hall below a large sign that read, *Praise the Everlasting Maker.*

The man had his arms outstretched, and Abren immediately found the figure captivating. Some sort of benign ardour radiated from him that was palpable even at this distance. It reminded Abren of the times when the spectre had beguiled him with its own warm radiance. He seemed to have been speaking for a while and was working up to his finale.

'Friends, the scriptures tell us that The Lord made heaven and earth and all that they contain.' The man paused for a moment to survey his hushed, rapt audience, then he continued. 'All things! Whether visible or invisible. All Have been created by Him.'

Another pause, and the man, Brother Eusebius as Abren took him to be, bestowed a magnificent white-toothed smile upon his listeners.

'In this world, created by our loving Lord, all things have their rightful place from mighty rulers down to the humblest of The Great Maker's children such as yourselves. Scripture says that you should keep not only the precepts of The Lord but also obey your earthly masters in everything. Know and accept your place in the world, for the compassionate Creator has so ordained it. Of this you may be certain. Heed my words well, for this is how you will please our Heavenly Father and earn for yourselves the wondrous reward of eternal peace. Now let us pray.'

Abren found himself on his knees again, unable to resist the general motion to prayer. Brother Eusebius's deep, rich voice resonated through the hall.

'Dear friends, here in the presence of The Almighty Lord, let us kneel in humility and, with contrite and obedient hearts, repent our sins.'

As the preacher's words rumbled over him, Abren felt their seduction.

'Marvellous and most merciful Maker, we have erred and strayed from thy righteous path like little lost lambs.'

Who would not want to believe in an all-powerful, loving being? Abren thought.

'Give us the strength to amend our ways, that we may warrant Your goodness and consolation and let Your gracious spirit move among us.'

The word 'spirit' jolted Abren out of his reverence. He slipped his hand into his pocket and ran his fingers down the chisel's wooden handle. The congregation rose, and Brother Eusebius began singing a familiar hymn.

The congregation joined in, including Jessel. She sounded sweet and beautiful. Abren released his grip on the chisel and reached for her hand. She let him take it, and he stood there listening to her. Then he heard a male voice start to sing on his other side—badly. He felt a surge of irritation until he realised the voice was familiar.

'Eldam!' Abren put his free arm around his brother.

When the hymn was over, he let go of Jessel's hand, and the brothers embraced fully.

'Hell, it's good to see you,' Abren said as they sat down.

'You too, Abe.'

They sat grinning at each other, and Abren was just dimly aware that Brother Eusebius was making some sort of announcement. He pulled his mind back to his mission.

'What did he say?' he asked Jessel.

'He said he would give his blessing to anyone who wanted it.'

Abren saw that most of the people were moving into the central aisle and lining up before the preacher.

'What are you going to do?' asked Jessel.

'Let's join the back of the queue. I'll ask to make a confession.' To Eldam, he said, 'I have to speak to this man. It's very important. I'll explain later.'

'I'll wait here then,' Eldam said. 'I don't want a blessing.'

Abren and Jessel got up and slowly shuffled forward behind the others. Would he really kill this man to protect her? She would surely want nothing to do with him if he were a murderer, even if the spectre kept him from hanging. But at least she would be safe from its retribution.

A woman came up to them after being blessed, her face a beaming glow.

'Such a wonderful man, isn't he?' she gushed. 'And I'm so pleased to see you here, Jessel. You must start coming to the devotions again on Lordsdays.'

'Hello, Morriline. I'm glad you enjoyed the meeting.'

The landlady had no time to chat further, however, as there was a press of people behind her wanting to leave. 'I'll talk to you later, my dear,' she said as she continued towards the exit.

Jessel received her benediction, and finally, it was Abren's turn. He knelt before the man who laid a firm hand upon his head and said simply, 'Bless you, my son. May The Lord be with you always.'

Another curious swirl of reverence came over him. Empowered by this, he rose and said, 'Please, sir, would you hear my confession?'

After a slight hesitation, Eusebius said, 'Yes, of course. There is a small room at the back where I may hear you.'

Abren glanced at Jessel.

'I'll wait with Eldam,' she said, wringing her hands.

The preacher led the way through a door, and Abren found himself in a short corridor that ran across the width of the building. There were three further doors in the back wall. Eusebius opened the nearest one and invited Abren to go in ahead of him. It was a simply furnished room with a dressing table, a large mirror and two chairs. A metal rail ran along one wall, and an assortment of colourful clothes hung from it.

'Please, make yourself comfortable.' Eusebius indicated a chair, then sat down in the other one. The preacher folded his hands in his lap and looked at Abren expectantly.

'I'm sorry,' Abren said. 'I don't really want to make a confession.'

He reached into his coat pocket again and gripped the handle of the chisel. He thought of Jessel, smiling. Looking at the man in front of him, into his cool blue eyes, Abren felt his potent benevolence directed solely at him.

'Oh? Is there something else I can help you with?'

'I… I want to help you. I came here to warn you. There may be someone who wishes to hurt you… stop you doing what you're doing…'

Abren halted and swallowed. It was like his mind was being enveloped in some sort of debilitating fog. Words could no longer find their way out of his mouth.

'My dear man, are you quite well?'

The preacher's voice seemed to sink into the same miasma. Then he thought he heard someone shout, 'Fire!'

Twenty-five

Taygret

Despite the roiling emotions of the evening before, Taygret was asleep when a knock at her door came and the servant's voice announced that it was five o'clock. When she went down for breakfast, she had on the scruffy mariner's garments Mistress Robikoy had sent her.

'Don't laugh,' she said. 'Don't you dare laugh.'

Niklay smirked, went a little red in the face and snorted, clearly struggling to comply with her warning.

'When you've quite recovered yourself, perhaps you would be so kind as to tell me if I'll pass for a sailor in this awful costume.'

The artist coughed, his expression barely controlled.

'You're the most fetching sailor I've ever seen,' he said. 'Perhaps I should have painted you like that.'

'You're not being very helpful. If I'm caught, I'll go to prison.'

'Hmm, yes. I'm sorry,' he said, frowning. 'It's your hair. Didn't Mistress Robikoy send you a hat of some sort?'

'Well, yes, she did, but it itches. It feels like I've got something crawling on my scalp.'

Taygret pulled a red woollen cap from one of her large pockets. When she put it on, it fitted tightly around her head.

'That's better,' Niklay observed. 'Turn round… Yes, I think your hair needs to be more restrained at the back. Into a pigtail, I think they call it. I'll get Tendrie to do it for you.'

'Thank you. I wish I'd had time to wash these clothes, but I suppose their distastefulness is part of the guise.'

When the cart pulled up outside the house, she bid Niklay a fond farewell and promised to write to him as soon as she was able. She went out and threw her bags into the back of the wagon with as much manly swagger as she could summon. It helped that she had discarded some more of her belongings. Then she climbed up beside the driver. He merely nodded to her and said nothing as they drove away. She was glad of his taciturn nature and the inscrutability of his weather-beaten features. She was not sure if he knew who or what she really was and did not want to engage in any conversation with him.

The cart jolted through the busy market square, then into a street that led down to the port. Ahead Taygret saw a notice on a brick wall. Curious to see what it was about, she kept looking at it as they approached. When she could make out the larger words, she froze in shock. They stood out bold and stark.

Foul Murder

She covered her mouth to muffle a sob of dismay. The mardene had been wrong. It was about her. As they got nearer, she saw a drawing of some sort. It appeared to show a woman with her hand raised and a man falling backwards away from her. The figures were too small to convey any accurate likenesses, but there was sure to be a description of her. She leaned forward so she could read the smaller lettering. Then she finally made it out.

The Gennlar Players are proud to present

Foul Murder

A dramatic and exciting new production
from the pen of the renowned playwright
Jenolyn Coltrikk

Taygret could not help letting out a giggle of relief. The cart driver looked at her in surprise, then glanced at the notice.

'Don't know why you find it so funny, lad. Don't look like it's a comedy,' he said.

Taygret managed to regain her composure. 'No, it doesn't, does it?'

When they reached the ship, she jumped down and retrieved her bags. The quay, so peaceful the evening before, was bustling with activity. Mostly stevedores engaged in loading cargo using the ship's hoist. She saw a couple of men counting barrels. Customs officers, she presumed. One glanced up as she approached the gangplank but showed no particular interest in her and quickly returned to his task. Up on the deck, she stopped and looked around, wondering where she should go. There was a large open hatch in front of her, and she saw that the hold was almost full.

'Don't stand there 'less you want to get hit by the crane,' shouted a swarthy man dressed not unlike herself. 'You the new boy? Captain wants to see you. Stern cabin, through there.' He pointed to an opening beneath a raised part of the deck. 'Why've you got saddle bags? Never mind, just get out the way.'

Taygret hurried down the passage and knocked on the door at the end. When called, she went in and found herself in a little compartment with hardly enough room for the large table and two chairs that furnished it. A man with a broad, tanned face and straw-coloured beard looked up from the papers he had been studying.

'Ah, you must be Miss Draillis,' he said. 'I'm Jod Ameron, Captain of the Elizabelle. Welcome aboard. Please, take a seat.'

When she had settled herself, he went on.

'We have a favourable wind this morning, so we should make the crossing in under five hours and dock at Polleton around midday. Is someone going to meet you there?'

'No. The only person I know in Rarland has gone to Damlon, and he doesn't know when to expect me.'

'Is he Rarlish, though?'

'Yes, he is.'

'Do you have his address?'

Taygret shook her head. 'I've been travelling for a while, so I couldn't receive any letters from him.'

Captain Ameron scratched at his bushy beard. 'Then you'll have two options. Either way, there's a risk, I'm afraid. The authorities are getting more and more nervous about Mellians in Rarland. You could apply for a passport at the customs house, giving your friend as someone who will vouch for you. But if you don't have an address for him, they may well detain you until he can be found, which might take a long time. Or you could try travelling without a passport. Some do, I've heard. But if you get caught, the police may assume you are a spy or a courier of some sort and arrest you. Can you speak any Rarlish?'

Taygret rubbed her hands on the coarse fabric of her corduroy pantaloons and cleared her throat. 'How far is it to Damlon, fella? I think I've got a bit lost.'

The captain rocked back in his chair, laughing. 'The Divine's breath, you should be an actress on the stage. You sound just like the lads who hang around Polleton harbour.'

'My Rarlish friend used to lodge with us in Amdris,' she said, smiling. 'We often spoke in his language, and I would mimic his voice, just for fun.'

'All right then. I suggest you keep up your masquerade while you're in Polleton. You'll pass for a member of my crew. No one will give you a second glance. There's a trader who buys a lot of my goods. A wine merchant. He'll take the brandy to Eastill, which is a town inland from Polleton, on the way to Damlon. You can travel with him. I'll say you're having some shore leave. In Eastill, you can change back into a woman. You should have no trouble in finding a coach to Damlon from there.' He grinned. 'I take it you've got at least one dress in those bags of yours.'

Taygret stood at the rail of the Elizabelle and looked out at the Rarlish coast as the ship rocked ever closer. She had left her homeland, probably for good, beyond the reach of

Mellian justice that would have been no justice in her case. Rassish had deserved his fate, of that she was certain. She felt no guilt. He would have gotten away with killing her uncle. No one would have believed her.

She was glad Master Robikoy had told his captain that she was not really a young man joining his crew. She had not relished the idea of working amongst the other sailors. Word had obviously got round the ship about her and, while she got some amused stares, no one bothered her. She thought perhaps she was not the first illegal migrant to sail aboard the Elizabelle.

Being up on deck made her feel less queasy. She knew the voyage across the mouth of Kimmikk Bay was shorter than further north, where the gulf widened out, but it was also rougher. The wounds from the broken glass she had used to burst her uncle's gas balloon had healed, and Captain Ameron jokingly told her that the scars would help her disguise. Any lad dressed as she was would not have soft hands.

As she watched the rolling hills of Rarland grow before her, she prayed she could find Eldam quickly. All she had to go on was that he had a brother who worked in the Damlon docks. What was his name? Abren? Then she thought of the mardene. Was that where her prayers really went? There was still much about the spirit she did not understand. What had it meant by extraordinary things happening when two of her abilities meet? It must have been referring to her and Abren. Could they do something about this vexatious spirit together? It did not seem very good at explaining things.

She had said she trusted the mardene. She hoped that trust was not misplaced.

Captain Ameron's confidence that she would be taken for a young Rarlish sailor made her decide not to get a passport, but she was still apprehensive when he took her to a money changer in Polleton. The man behind the counter made the transaction with no apparent concern, however, so Taygret supposed she had passed the test. She only exchanged a little of her funds, no more than a common seafarer might be expected to have. Outside, Ameron discreetly explained to her the Rarlish coins and their worth.

When the captain introduced her to the wine merchant, the trader looked her up and down, suspicion in his narrow eyes. He was a short, chubby man with a florid complexion and a haughty manner.

'Very well,' he said at length. 'But you'll need to ride in the back of a wagon. You don't look as if you can lift a barrel, so just stay out of the way while we load up.'

Taygret was surprised to see that the little convoy of three wagons had an armed escort. A man rode beside each one, pistols and short swords hung from their belts. She supposed the goods must be valuable. She had not seen how much the merchant had paid Captain Ameron.

She sat huddled with her bags into a narrow space between the barrels and the boards at the side of the rear wagon. The Rarlish customs officers had subjected the goods to a hurried, clumsy inspection, and a strong smell of alcohol still lingered on the casks.

As the wagon bumped along, the day grew warmer. Sunlight spilt down through the branches overhanging the road. Taygret felt herself slipping into drowsiness despite the discomfort of her billet.

Suddenly there was a loud bang, and a grunt, and Taygret jolted into alertness. More bangs, shouts, horses screaming. They were under attack. She shrank down, her body shaking. The driver of her wagon howled and slumped backwards above her. She heard his pistol clatter onto one of the barrels. A shot hit the board beside her, and she convulsed in shock. She continued to cower as chaos seethed around her. Surely the guards would see off the ambush. They had looked quite formidable to her.

Taygret instinctively hunched over into a rigid ball of terror, trying to make herself as small as possible. Waiting in tense anxiety for the fighting to end, it seemed an age before a relative calm eventually descended.

'Right then. Paik, Tanner, tend the wounded. The rest of you round up those horses. Now let's see what we got.' The voice was loud, harsh and excited.

Incredibly, the bandits must have won.

Taygret slowly looked up. A man's head appeared at the back of the wagon. His eyes widened when he saw her, timorous and trembling amongst his booty. He lowered the backboard and glared at her from between his black slouch hat and the red kerchief that covered the bottom half of his face.

'Well, what have we here then?' he said. 'Aren't you a pretty boy?'

Another man appeared beside the first, taller and similarly disguised. 'What are we going to do with him?' he asked.

The first man did not answer but merely gazed blankly at Taygret as if deep in thought. She remembered the driver's pistol. It must be lying nearby. Could she jump up and make a grab for it?

'Let's take him back to Sonnet,' the second man said, then gave a bark of crude laughter. 'She likes pretty boys. Best tie him up, though. I'll get some rope.'

'No,' the first man said abstractedly.

'What?' The other brigand looked at his companion in obvious confusion.

'Let him go.' He seemed to have shaken off his reverie. 'If we take him back with us, we'll have to keep him prisoner, keep a constant eye on him. If he got away, he'd know where we are. You know what old Sonnet's like. Drunk half the time.'

'Shoot him then and be done with it.'

'No. Shooting armed guards and traders is one thing. Killing an unarmed boy is something else. Come here, lad.'

Taygret scrambled to her feet and picked up her bags. She needed to lean awkwardly on the boards and barrels to support her quaking legs. She dropped unsteadily to the ground beside the masked men.

'Them's saddle bags you got there. Does that mean you can ride?' the shorter man asked her.

'Yeah, I can,' she replied as gruffly as her fear allowed her.

'You're giving him a horse?' the taller man said.

'Shut up, Badger. We've got a dozen horses out of this. I think we can spare one.' Seizing Taygret by the arm, he led her to the nearest animal. It nosed at a body lying lifeless on the road. *Its former rider*, she supposed.

'Take this one. It didn't bolt like most of the others.'

'Thank you, sir.' She slung her bags over the horse and went to mount, but the robber gripped her arm again.

'Don't tell anyone what happened here, understand? If you do, we'll find you, and I'll let Badger have his way.'

'I won't tell a soul, I promise. I'm indebted to you.'

He nodded, then released her.

Her mind was still stunned in the aftermath of the battle, but once she was up on the horse, her body knew what to do. She rode carefully past the bloody corpses, the guards on the ground, the wagoners and the wine merchant sprawled on their seats. Once clear of the massacre, she urged the horse into a trot. She did not look back.

She took the road in the direction the wagons had been travelling as it cut its way through the forest. After a mile or so, she stopped, dismounted and brought up the meagre contents of her stomach under a beech tree. She was shaking in every limb and had to lean against the tree's smooth trunk. The horse stood watching her, and when she was able, she went and stroked its head.

'Good girl. Brave Girl. Well done,' she said, choosing to believe it was a mare. The horse snorted in response.

Taygret listened for any sounds of pursuit. There were none. She took in some deep breaths and tried to make some sense of what had happened.

The man who had let her go must have been the leader. His benevolence had been so unexpected. The band were obviously ruthless outlaws. They had killed everyone else in the convoy, perhaps even some who had tried to surrender. Why had he been so lenient to her? Was it the mardene's doing?

She looked around. Trees stretched away on either side of the road. She mounted again and walked the horse on, looking back over her shoulder from time to time. After a while, she came to a village. In the square at the centre of the settlement, there was a tavern with a stone water trough outside. She let the horse drink before tying the reins to a hitching post. Then she went into a store beside the tavern and bought some bread and cheese for herself and a couple of apples for the horse.

'How far is it to Eastill?' she asked the storekeeper.

'You riding or walking?' asked the woman in return.

'Riding.'

'About two hours then. Just watch out for robbers. The woods are full of them these days.'

There was a little column with a clock in the square which told her it was just after three.

'We'll be in a big town in time for supper,' she told the horse as she fed her the apples. 'You can have a proper meal then.'

She ate a little of the bread and cheese and drank some water from a fountain below the clock. She did not want to linger here in case the bandits came into the village to celebrate their heist. Things might go differently if she encountered them a second time.

In Eastill, Taygret reconsidered her plan. She had originally thought to follow Captain Ameron's advice and change back into a female here, then take a coach on to Damlon. But now she had a horse. In the bustling streets of the town, she saw women riding in skirts, sitting sideways. It looked odd to her. In Mellia women wore breeches on horseback and straddled their mounts like men.

They must have a special saddle to stop them sliding off. That would be costly, I expect.

Although her uncle had left her a good bit of money, she did not want to go to any unnecessary expense. She did not know how long it would need to last. So she put off her transformation until she got to Rarland's capital. She now regretted leaving her own riding breeches in Gennlar. She would have to wear the shoddy sailor's outfit for a while yet.

She found an inn with a stable where they could both eat and drink and where she could rub down the horse.

'I don't know your name, but I'm going to call you Fearless,' she told the steed. 'Because you didn't bolt when they shot your rider.'

She was tempted to stay the night in the town, but she estimated there were still a couple more hours of daylight, so she mounted again and took the road towards Damlon, eager to get there as soon as possible. She passed through another village, but it did not have an inn. Recalling how she and Fredrik had spent a night in an isolated barn, as the sky grew dark, she found another.

It was a relief to undo her hair and shake it loose. There was a blanket strapped behind the horse's saddle, she unrolled it. She hoped the cold of the night would not keep her awake. She needed a good sleep. But her preparations for repose were interrupted.

'I am sorry you were involved in that horrible incident. I could do nothing to prevent it.' The mardene did not seem as dazzling as on its previous appearances, as if regret had somehow dimmed it.

'But they let me go. Did you have anything to do with that?'

'Yes. When the dreadful skirmish was over, I was able to put an inclination towards mercy in the bandit chief's mind once he had calmed a little.'

'Well, thank you for that. I don't want to think about what might have happened to me otherwise.'

'You should reach the capital of this land on the morrow. Seek out your lover's brother first of all. The sooner you are united, the better.'

'Are we to fight this wicked spirit you spoke of?'

'I hope that will not be necessary, but we shall see what can be done. Remain steadfast, dear Taygret.'

Twenty-six

Abren

The door of the small dressing room burst open, and Jessel rushed in.

'The hall's on fire,' she hollered. 'Oh my Lord, Abe, what's wrong?'

Abren tried to focus his attention on her, but everything was a blur.

'We need to get out,' Jessel said as she hurried to his side.

Brother Eusebius leapt up and helped Jessel pull the distressed carpenter to his feet.

'There's a side exit,' Eldam called from the corridor. 'Hurry.'

With difficulty, they manoeuvred Abren out of the room. He staggered and leant heavily on them. Eldam had already reached the door at the end of the passage.

'It's locked,' he called back to them in dismay.

'What! It wasn't earlier,' said the preacher.

'Don't you have the key?' Jessel demanded.

'No. The caretaker was to come and lock up when I left.'

'We'll have to go through the hall,' she said. But although Eldam had thought to shut the door to the hall, smoke was already curling up from beneath it.

'We wouldn't stand a chance,' Eldam said. 'The fire caught so quickly. Are there no windows back here?'

'No,' said Jessel. 'There's a factory right behind this building.'

'What are we to do then?' gasped Eusebius. 'We're trapped.'

'We have to risk the hall,' Jessel told them. 'There's no other way.'

'Wait.' Abren broke free of them and lurched groggily towards the side door. He stopped himself from crashing into it by putting out his left hand, and with his right, he drew out the chisel. From somewhere, he found the strength to drive the sharp edge between the metal lock and the wood of the door. By sheer force of will, he rammed the tool down twice more with gathering might. After the third blow, he wrenched the chisel back. Eldam added his own desperate strength, and the lock fell, clattering onto the floor. They pulled the door open.

The four of them scampered into the alley outside. Abren filled his lungs with cool air and, looking up, saw dancing red patterns behind the high windows of the hall, blazing in the twilight. Without a word, the fugitives made for the street. On the other side, a large group of people had assembled to watch the fire's ghastly spectacle.

'Hell, I hope everyone got out safely,' Abren muttered.

Brother Eusebius hurried across the street. Abren took Jessel's hand and started after him. He had not gone more than a couple of steps when Jessel cried a warning and pulled him back. Two crazed horses careered out of the swirling smoke pulling a helpless carriage behind them. It barely missed him. Then the air itself seemed to close in around him with ominous menace like the coming of a storm.

'It's the spirit,' he grasped. 'It's angry with me.'

'Let's get to the faith house. It might give us sanctuary.' Jessel said as she gripped his arm. Eldam took the other as they ran together towards that uncertain refuge.

Saint Raul's faith house was not far, but Abren had not wholly shaken off the enervating hex that had assailed him earlier. He tried to draw fortitude from his determination to defy the spectre's malice and from Jessel and Eldam's close support. At last, they stumbled up the steps and crashed through the doors of the faith house into the vestibule.

A savage, howling wind struck at them, and they staggered into the main chamber. Jessel threw her arms around Abren in a despairing embrace. She pulled him to a smooth, white column, and they clung on. Eldam lurched towards one of the benches.

Amidst the tumult, Abren felt an assault of a different kind strike at him. His mind was filled with a wrath not his own, and he was berated by a wordless furore of betrayal and vengeance even more terrifying than the storm.

As he struggled to combat this new threat, he heard Jessel begin to pray, tremulous and frantic. 'Oh Lord in heaven be our strength.'

The tempest tore at them with frenzied fingers as if trying to wrench them apart. About them, benches were being overturned and scattered. Eldam was thrown down with them.

'Let Thy will rule on earth. Walk among us, we pray…'

Abren felt she was trying to push all the might she could muster into her shrill voice. She screamed as the shrieking blast ripped into them with greater ferocity. His hold on the column began to slip. At any second, he thought he and Jessel would be flung helplessly across the floor of the faith house.

She lifted her head as if to summon one last, defiant cry. Filling her lungs, she bellowed, '... and keep us from evil.'

Abren became aware that the vehemence invading his mind was being further poisoned by a dire frustration, as if the spirit was being made to exert more power to enforce its will.

At that moment, in what little light still filtered in from outside, he saw a dark, feral-looking figure come flying through the door. It landed in front of him and rolled onto all fours, staring wildly about. His beleaguered senses tried to comprehend what was before him. Was this some baleful emissary of the spectre taking humanoid form? Long, tangled hair writhed around its head. It looked at Eldam, who let out a startled cry. Then it saw Abren and began scrabbling towards him. It bared its teeth as the gale raged about it. Piercing dark eyes glared fixedly at him.

'Get away,' Jessel yelled, and Abren felt her try to tighten her hold on him.

But the figure continued to crawl, fingers clawing at the tiled floor. Abren was transfixed as the outlandish creature approached. He was speechless, but Jessel shouted again,

'Get away from us.' She tried to aim a kick at it, but it did not flinch.

It reached an arm up towards him.

'Take my hand.' A fierce, screeching voice.

Abren just stared at it, confused by fear, fascination and the irate onslaught filling his head.

'Just take my hand.' It was imperious and strangely alluring.

Abren crouched and began putting out his arm.

'No!' Jessel tried to yank him back.

From the corner of his eye, Abren saw Eldam had managed to scramble closer as if he, too, wanted to intervene.

He heard his brother say something. Just one querulous, bewildered word.

'Taygret?'

Then Abren touched the outstretched fingers. The figure cried out something he did not understand, and a sudden, intense spasm ran through his body, both thrilling and alarming. The hurricane ceased, and a vast, still silence filled the faith house. He gaped at the freakish form before him. Then it seemed as if all the air around him turned white, and the pale, quiet world began slipping away.

As his awareness returned, Abren heard Jessel's voice. She sounded anxious. He could not imagine why. He felt so peaceful, so calm, blissful even. Perhaps he had died, and Jessel was an angel after all. Or had she died too? The thought roused him a little from his tranquillity. He opened his eyes. Jessel's face was hovering before his. She looked so worried. He tried to smile at her, reassure her.

'Are you all right?' he heard her say.

He did not want to speak just yet; it was too soon, so he merely nodded. It was then he realised that there was something hard behind his head. He was lying on the floor. It seemed such a funny thing to be doing that he let out a little laugh. This brought a smile to Jessel's lips. Such a lovely smile she had. He reached up and touched her cheek. She brushed the hair from his forehead. He felt he could just stay here with her forever. That idea made a question form in his mind.

'Where are we?' he murmured.

'Still in the faith house,' she said.

The faith house. Memories began to come.

'That… creature. Was it an evil spirit?'

'No, she's Eldam's sweetheart.'

'Eldam's sweetheart?'

'Yeah. She passed out as well when you touched her hand, but she came round a little while ago.' Jessel looked away. 'They're sitting over there.'

Abren turned his head. Someone had lit some candles. His brother sat on a bench alongside the woman. She still looked odd in her tattered, grimy garb, but she did not seem so savage now. In fact, she looked pale and in need of the comforting arm Eldam had around her.

As he sat up, the couple noticed.

'How are you feeling?' Eldam said.

Abren rubbed his face and arched his back. 'Like I've been to paradise but have had to come back to earth with a bump.'

'Yes,' said the woman. 'I feel a bit like that too.'

'This is Taygret,' Eldam told him. 'We met in Amdris.'

'Pleased to meet you, I'm sure,' Abren said as Jessel helped him to stand.

Eldam got up, and he and Jessel pulled another bench upright. Abren seated himself on it, and Jessel joined him. Eldam sat back down beside Taygret.

Abren stared at the wreckage in the shadows surrounding them, the scattered benches and candelabra, the torn-down sacred paintings and tapestries. Then he looked from one to the other of his three companions. 'What happened?' he asked.

'A mardene visited me,' Taygret said. 'She told me you were in danger from one of her kind. That you had the gift, but the spirit that came to you was bad. I somehow knew that if I could just touch you, our… prowess together might banish it because we were both desperate to be rid of it. The mardene must have put the idea in my head. I still don't fully understand them.'

'You call it a mardene?' Abren asked.

'Yes. I met a woman in Mellia who said that's what they're called.'

'And you said "she". Are they female then?'

'No. I just thought it was disrespectful to keep calling her "it" and I didn't want her to be he because… I was afraid Eldam would get jealous.' She giggled, and they all laughed.

Abren sensed some of the dazed tension of the group relax a little.

'I remember you shouting something, but I couldn't make it out. Was it in Mellian?' Jessel asked Taygret.

'Oh, no. I didn't understand it either. It just came to me at that moment. Perhaps it's the language the mardenes speak.'

They all sat in perplexed silence for a few moments.

'I'm sorry I tried to kick you,' Jessel said at last.

'Don't be sorry,' Taygret said, smiling. 'I must have looked quite frightful. I don't normally dress like this.'

'How did you find us?' Eldam asked. 'Did the mardene guide you?'

'I don't think so. I went to the docks looking for Abren. The gates were closed for the night, but a guard said he didn't work there anymore. I didn't know what to do, so I just started riding around the streets. Then I felt the anger in the air, and it led me here.'

'Well, we clearly have a lot to tell each other,' Eldam said. 'But may I make a suggestion?'

Twenty-seven

Jessel

Initially, Fearless was a bit hesitant about being accommodated in the little stable alongside Tinker but soon settled when she saw the abundance of fruit available. Jessel then took Taygret home so she could wash and change into something more feminine.

Eldam insisted on paying for a cab to take the four of them to a nice, comfortable inn for the night, in another part of the city.

'Somewhere they won't know us,' he said. 'It's all on the Interior Department… or Foreign Department, I forget which. We deserve it, and we can talk more over a good supper.'

Jessel had never been anywhere so opulent. There were upholstered seats, white linen cloths on the tables and smartly dressed servers ready to bring them their food. When the waiter told them what was available that night, most of the meals were unfamiliar to her. So in the end, she settled for something she knew, fried cod and boiled potatoes, even though the fish had some funny sauce on it. To her surprise, Taygret ordered the same.

'Hmm, potatoes,' she said. 'I like potatoes.'

Jessel listened to the tales the other three had to tell. They were all incredible, scary and tragic. Eldam was stunned when Taygret spoke of her uncle's death and how it came about.

'He was such a kind, brilliant man,' was all he could say as he gripped Taygret's hand.

'But now I have you back,' she said, smiling at him.

Jessel felt there was something Taygret had not told them. Something big and important. But she could see the love flow between her and Eldam, and she instinctively reached out and caught hold of Abren's hand.

Let her have her secret. I'm sure she'll tell Eldam when she's ready.

Towards the end of the meal, talk turned to the present.

'I need to tell you about the government's proposal,' Eldam said to his brother. 'But perhaps we should go somewhere more private.'

'I'm not going on another bloody boat,' Jessel said.

'I was thinking of one of our rooms.' Eldam grinned at her.

Abren looked at the other diners sitting at the tables dotted around the inn's plush saloon. 'We'll be safe enough here,' he said. 'No one's paying any attention to us. Besides, I haven't finished my ale.'

After Eldam had outlined what he had been told by the government officials, Abren laughed.

'I don't think my spirit friend, mardene or whatever, would have agreed to chase down Mellian agents,' he said.

'It didn't really care about our affairs. It only wanted me to kill the preacher because some other spirit was protecting him. I think they've got some kind of feud going on. In fact, I suspect a lot of that mayhem at the hall and faith house was caused by them fighting each other.'

'Yes, well, you don't need to tell the government any of that.' Eldam replied. 'Just acknowledge you have the gift and say you'll try and help them. The main thing is that you get your pardon.'

'I suppose.' Abren nodded thoughtfully.

'Speaking of Mellian agents…' Taygret said.

'You don't need to worry,' Eldam reassured her. 'I can vouch for you. We're married, by the way. I told the innkeeper.'

As Taygret stared at Eldam open-mouthed, Abren raised his glass. 'Congratulations,' he declared.

'It should be a double celebration,' Eldam said. 'I told him you two were married as well. He seemed quite taken by having two mister and missus Medloes staying at his inn.'

When Jessel awoke, Abren's arm was across her belly. He was still sound asleep. They were in a strange bed, in a strange room. She felt grateful for what Eldam had done. He and the foreign girl, Taygret, were in a room nearby. Jessel wondered if their night had been as glorious as hers. Probably, if the stories about Mellians were true.

She went over the events of the evening. The hall, the fire, the storm. Running to the faith house and then Taygret appearing like some bizarre apparition. She still found it hard to believe that the man lying next to her had some sort of magical power. He could talk to unearthly spirits, for Lord's sake. Or did The Lord even exist? It would take a long time for it all to make sense, if it ever did.

She knew she should get up and wake Abren. He needed to go to the Interior Department and get his pardon. She thought of Fran. It was hard work setting up the stall on your own. But as she looked at Abren's slumbering face, she could not quite make the effort to drag herself out of bed.